THE
DISTANCE
BEACONS

The Last P.I. Series

Book Two

Richard Bowker

Book design by eBook Prep
www.ebookprep.com

Cover Design by Jim McManus
Complexstories.com

October, 2017
ISBN: 978-1-947833-14-2

ePublishing Works!
www.epublishingworks.com

Not in vain the distance beacons. Forward, forward let us range,
Let the great world spin for ever down the ringing grooves of change.
—*Alfred Tennyson*

CHAPTER 1

It was one of those May days that make you wonder what's so bad about being alive. Sun shining, birds singing, flowers blooming—the Earth seemed to have shrugged off the awful things we had done to her, and she was offering the same old beauty and warmth and hope that had always been her gift to us, It was the kind of day that could make you half-believe that nothing awful had happened. It was the kind of day you had to take advantage of, in case the Earth changed her mind.

So why, I wondered, was I sitting in a dingy office on lower Washington Street, staring out into the sunshine and feeling sorry for myself?

Here are the answers I came up with:

~Because I am a responsible professional, and anyone responding to my ad in the *Globe* would expect to find me here.

~Because I don't have an answering machine to take a message, should anyone try to call. Don't have a telephone either, for that matter, so calling would not be easy.

~Because I am a dreamer, still trying to live my dream.

~Because I'm a fool.

That seemed to about cover it.

This is the life of the private eye, I told myself—the long stretches of boredom punctuated by the occasional burst of excitement. But this particular stretch was beginning to seem like a life sentence. I had arrived back in Boston from England in early January, having muddled through my first case, and there was nothing to do but set up shop once again. So I put a log in the wood stove and picked out a book from one of the many tottering stacks that littered the office. Then I said a prayer to the poster of Humphrey Bogart, my patron saint, who smiled a crooked but encouraging smile at me from the opposite wall, and I waited for the sound of footsteps on the dim staircase, the tentative rapping on the frosted glass door of my office.

And I waited. I ran out of books. I used the wood stove less and less as the weather grudgingly improved. I went home every night and faced the uncomfortable silences as my friends tried not to ask me why I was wasting my life. And now a beautiful spring day was drifting away from me and my money was all but gone, but still I sat in my office, and stared out my window, and hoped.

And eventually something happened.

It wasn't exactly what I was hoping for, of course: the mysterious blonde, dressed in black, desperate for my help; the dying man with a priceless figurine he could entrust to no one but me; the eccentric millionaire whose strange predicament only I could solve. Not this time, anyway. This time it was two young soldiers driving up in an ancient jeep. They parked and looked dubiously up at the building I occupied. I pulled back from the window. Wouldn't do to appear too eager. I hurriedly tossed aside the book I was rereading and spread some papers on my desk in what I hoped was impressive-looking disarray.

It occurred to me as they clomped up the stairs that these guys probably weren't interested in my professional services. Why would soldiers need a private eye? I tried to think if I had broken any laws lately that would merit an official visit. I was hardly a model citizen, but surely the government had more important things to do than bother with an insignificant private eye. Besides, the local police, not Federal troops, would be the ones to arrest the likes of me. But you never can tell.

They rapped on the frosted glass door.

"Come in," I said in a busy but welcoming tone.

The door opened, and the two soldiers entered. The first one in was short and had a spray of acne on his face. The other was lantern-jawed and hung back a little, as if loath to deal with the strange creature sitting behind the desk. Both had the requisite army haircut, so short they might just as well have been bald.

"Good afternoon," the short one said. "Walter Sands?"

"That's me. Have a seat."

"No thank you, sir," he replied. He had a flat Midwestern accent. He used the official tone of a soldier who is carrying out his orders and is therefore not required to think. "Mr. Sands, we'd like you to come with us, sir."

"Am I being arrested?"

"No, sir."

"Then what's up?"

"There is someone who wants to see you."

"Who?"

"We're not at liberty to say, sir."

"What about?"

"Don't know, sir."

I could have continued the interrogation indefinitely, but it would have been pointless. I had been a soldier once, not so very long ago, and I knew the situation he was in. He was supposed to be as polite as possible but say nothing. And he was to come back with me. No excuses accepted.

I decided to ask one more question. "What's your name?" I asked.

The question caused a flicker of indecision to cross the short soldier's face. He hadn't received orders about this. "Smith, sir," he said finally. "Private Daniel Smith."

I smiled. "Hi, Danny. And you?" I asked the lantern-jawed fellow.

His comrade's response had given him courage. "P-p-private Gus Ziegler, sir."

I kept smiling. "Pleased to meet you." They didn't smile back, but I think maybe they wanted to. It never hurts to be friendly. I stood up. "Shall we go, then?"

"Yes, sir," Danny replied.

I winked at Saint Humphrey as I followed the soldiers out the door.

I was a little excited as I got into the jeep. Anyone who could send troops to fetch me had to be a big shot. A government big shot, to be sure, but even dealing with the Feds was better than staring out the window.

We headed up Washington Street, with Gus doing the driving. Except for another government jeep or two, and a couple of cop cars, we were in the only motor vehicle to be seen. Not that we had the streets to ourselves. Gus had to bully his way past the pedestrians and the cyclists and the horses and even a few pigs; traffic was actually pretty thick around Downtown Crossing and the Salvage Market. No one seemed particularly interested in getting out of our way; there were the usual sullen stares, and the occasional utterly hostile ones. But still we made progress.

VOTE YES, the red, white, and blue posters urged us from the otherwise useless telephone poles and mailboxes.

I did my best to ignore the posters. "Where are you guys from?" I asked.

"Out of state, sir," Danny replied.

"Ah." That was hardly news. The Feds don't let their troops serve in their native states; they also don't like for them to fraternize with the locals. If there's an uprising of some sort, they don't want a soldier facing friends and relatives at the other end of his rifle. Much easier to kill a stranger. "You like it here?"

"It's fine."

They hated it. They were scared and lonely and not used to being around people who didn't like or trust them. They couldn't figure out why they were being forced to do this, and they just wanted to get it over with and go home. At least, if they were anything like me when I was a soldier, that's the way they felt. "Write letters," I suggested.

"Huh?"

"Write long letters home. Describe everything you see and do. Even if it's all so boring you can't stand it. Even if you never send the letters. That's what I did. It helped."

Danny stared at me, then nodded silently. It occurred to me that he might not know how to write.

Gus took us to Government Center, on the far side of Beacon Hill. I wasn't surprised. We stopped in front of the John Fitzgerald Kennedy Federal Building, and the two soldiers escorted me inside. There were more VOTE YES signs in the lobby. Seemed like a waste of time to me: preaching to the converted.

The lobby was air-conditioned; soft fluorescent lights shone down on us; the elevator that we waited for actually worked. Sometimes I've thought that it would have been better if all the elevators had stopped working forever after the War, if there were no more touch-tone telephones and laptop computers and stick-shift sedans and CAT scans. If all of that stuff was just a temporary aberration of a society that didn't quite work out, then we could maybe shrug our shoulders and go back to living the way human beings had lived for thousands of years before such wonders existed. But the wonders still existed, damn them. You could get almost anything you wanted (short of a nuclear reactor, maybe) if you had enough money or ingenuity or luck; I had certainly proved that, when I jetted over to England for my first case, then jetted back in triumph (more or less). And that meant we had to live with these constant reminders of what had been lost, of what was once so common and now shimmered just out of our reach, and it was almost impossible to go through life without a daily dose of self-pity.

Dealing with the Feds was a sure way to keep the dose high; they treated themselves pretty well, and were not inclined to hide it. To keep us all striving to regain what had been lost, their supporters might explain. Because they have the power and use it for their own benefit, their opponents would retort.

Whatever the explanation, the elevator arrived and smoothly lifted us ten stories into the building. The doors opened onto a corridor. On the opposite side of the corridor, a soldier stood guard in front of a glass door. The sign on the door said:

Francis Bolton

Governor of the Commonwealth

My, my, I thought. A big shot indeed.

The guard gave a nod to my two pals. He frisked me, but I was clean—I had left my revolver back at the office. "You can go inside now, Mr. Sands," Danny said when the frisking had been completed.

"Thank you. And thanks for the ride." I smiled.

Danny looked uncomfortable for a moment, and then said, "Good luck." Then he and Gus walked off down the corridor.

Why did I need luck? I wondered. I went inside.

I was in a large reception area: potted plants, framed paintings, air conditioning, and a view of the city that you just don't get one story up on lower Washington Street. There was also the unavoidable VOTE YES poster. I walked over to a woman seated behind a large oak desk. "Hi," I said. "My name is Sands. I was summoned."

"Yes," she agreed. "Please have a seat."

She was a pleasant-looking blond, maybe a bit old for my taste, and maybe with a bit too much makeup on—nobody wore makeup anymore. But she had the kind of figure you can only get when you you're allowed to shop at the Feds' own grocery store. I smiled at her. "What's your name?" I asked.

She stared at me as if I were a particularly disgusting mutant.

Friendliness doesn't always work. I let the smile fade, and I wandered over to a leather couch, where I parked myself while the secretary ignored me and I awaited the governor's pleasure.

I tried to imagine what he wanted with me. Something to do with the VOTE YES posters? Security at the polls, maybe. I'd rather be staring out my office window, I thought. But surely Governor Bolton didn't bother himself with details like who to hire for security. Maybe he had a priceless figurine....

Whatever he wanted, I knew that this was going to be an interview. So I tried to prepare. I considered Governor Bolton.

He had been around for a long time now—about eight years, I figured. The Feds had appointed him governor of the New England region shortly after their troops came up from Atlanta and put a stop to the anarchy that had been plaguing us for years. And in the time since then he had become the symbol of the Federal presence here: tough, distant, and a little bit mysterious—at least to me, who didn't spend a great deal of time thinking about such things. What did the Feds want from us? What was in the occupation for them? The taxes they managed to collect didn't pay their expenses; the men and women they drafted (like me) didn't make up for the number of troops they had to commit to the region. So why bother?

In a way, the most mysterious thing about Bolton was that he was a local. Somebody—probably my buddy Stretch—had told me that Bolton had sold real estate before the War. Not a lot of call for real estate salesmen in this new world, where mansions were free—all you had to do was be able to defend them. But somehow he had landed on his feet. And somehow he had made the Feds trust him enough to put him in charge of the region where he had grown up. And somehow it didn't bother him that many— perhaps most—of his fellow locals thought of him as a semi-traitor, zealously carrying out the edicts of the well-fed rulers from down south.

Or maybe it did bother him. How would I know? To me, he was just a photo in the *Globe* and a bunch of rumors.

After a while I began to wonder if he would ever be anything more. Men wearing suits and ties came and went. The blond secretary had a smile for most of them. No one paid any attention to me, except perhaps to glance at my Salvage-Market jersey and jeans and wonder how I had gotten past the guard. This was not much better than being in my office. I didn't even have a book to read.

Finally the summons came. "The governor will see you now," the secretary said.

I got up and smiled at her. "Thanks a lot," I said.

She pointed silently to a door. I walked over to it and knocked. "Come in," a loud voice responded. I went in.

Governor Bolton was sitting behind a huge mahogany desk, flanked by the American flag and some other flag with what looked like a Native American on it. It took me a second to retrieve the flag's identification from my freakishly complete memory. It was the Massachusetts state flag. This struck me as somewhat incongruous, since Massachusetts didn't really exist as a separate political entity in the Feds' scheme of things.

There were no VOTE YES posters.

Bolton was scribbling on a piece of paper—or maybe, I thought, he was pretending to scribble, so I could see he was a busy man and a great deal more important than me. I was willing to concede the point. "Have a seat," he said, continuing to scribble. I sat. The chair was a little too low; I found myself staring up at the governor. He had gray hair, cut short, and a long scar next to his right eye. I hadn't noticed the scar in the photos I had seen of him; it made him look even tougher than my image of him—he was a man who took risks, the scar said, a man who understood physical danger. He was wearing a white shirt. His tie was loose; his shirtsleeves were rolled up. He was ready for action.

After an appropriate interval he put his pen down and looked at me. "Walter Sands," he said. His voice was deep and powerful. It sounded out of place in a private conversation; it should have been addressing a political rally.

"Pleased to meet you," I said. I smiled.

The governor didn't smile back. "Did my bodyguards treat you well?" he asked.

"They were perfect gentlemen. They both deserve promotions."

He nodded, although I got the impression he hadn't heard my answer. "I talked to Charles Moseby about you," he went on. "Mr. Moseby recommends you quite highly."

I nodded in turn. Mr. Moseby is my pal Stretch, and I would have killed him if he hadn't recommended me quite highly. "How did you get my name?" I asked.

"From that article in the *Globe* a few weeks back. Interesting business over there in England. Although why anyone would want to be a private detective nowadays is beyond me."

"Uh-huh." The article in the *Globe* had been written by another friend, named Gwen Phillips. I have a lot of friends. Gwen and Stretch are the ones I live with.

"Still, there might be circumstances where a person with your skills and contacts might be useful." He was dithering, I could tell. A common problem with clients, my extensive reading of private eye novels had told me. It's tough to tell someone you've got a problem. Maybe his wife is cheating on him, I thought. But no—I'd heard he was a widower.

"Perhaps you could tell me what your particular circumstances are," I said in that smooth professional tone I had mastered over the course of my single case, "and then we can decide if I'm the man for the job."

Bolton gazed at me. "Tell me," he said, still dithering, "what's your position on the referendum?"

My heart sank. He *did* want me to guard some damn voting booth. The referendum was the latest development in the Federal government's relationship with its fractious stepchild. It was a simple enough question that the Feds wanted us New Englanders to answer: "Do you support the government of the United States of America?" But the ramifications of their asking the question, and our answering it, had kept a lot of people in a tizzy all spring.

I knew what Bolton wanted me to say: *I'm proud to be an American. I'm going to VOTE YES, and I don't care who knows it.* But I figured we would both be better off if I didn't try to mislead him. "I haven't given it a great deal of thought," I said. "I'm an apolitical kind of guy."

"Now is no time to be apolitical!" Bolton thundered.

It seemed to me to be as good a time as any to be apolitical. "Why not?" I asked.

Bolton gave me a disgusted look. "At least you're not one of those sniveling isolationist types who prefer savagery to civilization—are you?"

Well, when you put it like that...I shook my head. "No sir, I'm not one of those."

"And you have no objection to working for the Federal government?"

That was a little trickier. "Um, perhaps if you could give me a few more details..."

Bolton tapped the fingers of his right hand on his desk. The dithering was about to come to an end, I figured. Either he'd give me the case, or he'd throw me out of the office. "Mr. Sands," he intoned, "the president of the United States of America is corning to Boston."

He sounded as if he was expecting a round of applause from his audience. "That's great," I said.

"It's the first time since before—" He waved his hand. I knew what the wave of the hand meant. People still had difficulty mentioning the War. Maybe if we were all very quiet about it, it would retroactively go away.

"She's coming here to get us to vote for the referendum?" I guessed.

"Precisely." Bolton stood up and stared out his window. He was shorter than I expected. Maybe that's why my chair was so low. All of a sudden he looked a little silly to me as he stood next to the American flag—as if he were playing at being governor. And I wondered just how tough he really was. Maybe he still thought of himself as a real estate agent, and couldn't really believe where life had brought him. I wondered if, in his heart of hearts, he thanked God for the War and the opportunity it had granted him. There had to be a few people around who thought like that.

My mind was wandering. It returned when Bolton started to speak. "This referendum is important, Sands," he said. "New England is part of America. People have to understand this—they have to *believe* this. They complain about the emigration controls and the out-of-state troops and the privileges for government workers, but they forget about what the government saved them from—and they forget about their *heritage*. We can't just let our heritage slip away from us.

"So that's why President Kramer proposed the referendum. She believes that, if people can be made to focus on the positives, they will understand what we're trying to do, and they will support us. And once she has New England's support, she can lead America back to the forefront of the world's nations once again. So she is coming to Boston to give a speech a few days before the voting—a speech that will make people realize just what is at stake here, that will convince them to give her the vote of confidence she needs."

Bolton sounded as if he were giving a speech himself. But his delivery was curiously rushed, as if this was a speech he was rehearsing for a different audience. I didn't mind, but I was still trying to figure out what all this had to do with me. "You want me to protect the president while she's here?" I guessed.

"Not quite." He returned to his desk. He took a piece of paper out of the top drawer and handed it to me. I read the message typed on it.

We know Kramer plans to come.

Boston is ours. If she comes, she faces our wrath.

THE FEDS MUST GO!

The Second American Revolution

The Second American Revolution: TSAR. I didn't like the sound of that acronym. I studied the message, and then returned the sheet of paper to Bolton.

"Have you heard of this group?" he asked.

I shook my head.

"Neither have I. This sheet appeared on the outer door to my office this morning. I need to know who's behind it."

"And that's my job?"

Bolton nodded. "We have to find The Second American Revolution and prevent them from doing anything to President Kramer."

I thought about it. "Why me?" I asked finally. "You've got your troops, you've got the local police—and the president has her own security people, I imagine. Can't they take care of this?"

"Maybe. They'll be on the case too. But I thought a local might bring something to it that they can't. You know what I'm talking about, Sands. Contacts. Sources of information. No one around here talks to the Feds; that's part of our problem. But they'll talk to someone like you."

Quite true. But...Bolton studied me as I tried to think it through. People weren't standing in line to obtain my services. Maybe they never would be. But I didn't like this case. Didn't like the way I got it, didn't like what I'd have to do to solve it. "I'm sorry," I said finally. "I don't think I'm right for this."

"Why not?" Bolton demanded. "We'll pay you your usual rate. Moseby told me you're not working on anything else at the moment."

Thanks, Stretch. I tried to explain. "If I work for you, I become just like the troops and the police." *And just like you,* I managed to avoid saying. "People may talk to me now because I'm a local, but then they won't be sure in the future whether or not I'm one of you. And then they'll stop talking."

"Doesn't the safety of the president of the United States matter to you, Sands?"

I wasn't sure it mattered to me more than the safety of any other poor soul in this godforsaken world, but I guessed that wasn't worth getting into. "Of course," I replied. "But I've got my career to think of."

Bolton gave me a look that told me what he thought of my career.

"Why not just have her stay in Atlanta?" I suggested. "That's the best way to keep her safe. And I doubt her speech is going to make much difference to the referendum, one way or the other."

"And give in to the terrorists' demands? That's precisely what we can't do. So are you with us, Sands?"

I took a deep breath and shook my head.

Bolton picked up his phone. "Lisa, get me General Cowens," he said, and he replaced the receiver.

Lisa, I thought. The blond secretary, presumably. Nice name. And then I thought: I'm not sure I like having General Cowens in on this.

The phone rang almost immediately, and Bolton picked it up again. "Bob, this is Frank," he said. "That private detective I was telling you about is here. He needs some persuasion. Can you come? Thanks."

The governor hung up and glared at me some more. "This is serious business, Sands," he said, "and you are a part of it, whether you want to be or not."

The governor's scar seemed to throb. He looked much more impressive sitting down; he looked like the kind of man who could make threats and carry them out. I decided it was time to start worrying.

CHAPTER 2

There was an uncomfortable silence while we waited for General Cowens to arrive. Bolton started scribbling again. I started thinking about General Cowens.

He was the commander of all Federal troops in New England. That was impressive enough, I suppose, but there was more—stories about him that had transformed him into a legend, at least among the veteran soldiers I had talked to while serving my time in the army. Cowens, they said, had been there at the beginning—in Atlanta during the days after the War, with Washington obliterated and the nation stumbling toward extinction. He was the one who rounded up all the civilian leaders he could find and brought them to Atlanta; he was the one who used the forces under his command to protect the leaders while they thrashed out the terrible issues that had to be faced in the new world; he was the one who, more than anybody else, was responsible for the continued existence of the United States of America. The rules of government had been changed, of course— how could they not have been? But we were still a nation, and many people would say we had Cowens to thank for that.

Of course, there were many others who would say that resentment or outrage were more appropriate responses than gratitude. Those were the people who were not going to VOTE YES.

So why had Cowens ended up in New England? That wasn't clear to me. But I think it was for the same reason that President Kramer was foisting the referendum on us. Because New England mattered. The rest of the country was either uninhabitable or more or less meekly back in the fold. But we New Englanders seemed to be a problem; we just didn't want to make it easy on the Feds. Our stubborn Yankee heritage perhaps: we have revolution in our genes. So maybe this was the last great challenge for Cowens: to whip us into shape and make the Union whole once again.

I found it interesting that Cowens, for all his status as a living legend, was deferring to the ex-real estate salesman. It was the general who returned Bolton's phone call; it was the general who was making his way to the governor's office. I found this refreshing in a world where having the weapons could so easily translate into having the power. Maybe the Feds weren't as bad as a lot of people thought.

There was a knock on the door. "Come in," Bolton called out.

The door opened, and General Cowens entered the room.

He had the presence of a legend; there was no doubt about it. I instinctively found myself standing as he approached (although at least I managed to keep from coming to attention). He projected an intense aura of authority that seemed dissociated from his rather fragile physical appearance, and even from the gray-green uniform he wore. He had a lined face topped by a sparse fringe of white hair. His blue eyes were watery and tired. His posture was stiff-backed and military, but he walked with care, as if, having made it this far through the minefield of life, he didn't want to make any missteps.

Governor Bolton stayed seated. Maybe he didn't feel what I felt in the general's presence because he dealt with the man every day; or maybe he consciously repressed his reactions in order to maintain the dignity of his office.

"Thanks for corning up, Bob," Bolton said. "This is Walter Sands."

Cowens looked at me, and once again I was a private instead of a private eye, and I was quaking before an officer's cold-eyed stare. He sat down without shaking hands or speaking to me. I sat down too. "I don't see why we need an outsider," Cowens said. His voice was soft— far softer than Bolton's—but you paid attention to it, precisely because of its softness. "We can protect the president, if we're allowed to do our job."

"We've been through this, Bob," Bolton replied.

"Surely there can't be anything wrong with using every resource available to us?"

The general flicked his gaze toward me. *Some resource,* his blue eyes seemed to say. "Outsiders are disruptive," he said. "They don't follow the lines of authority."

"But Sands can find things out precisely *because* he won't follow the lines of authority."

Cowens gave a hint of a shrug. "If you insist," he said.

Bolton nodded. He insisted. "But as I mentioned, he needs to be convinced."

Cowens turned slowly in his seat to face me. His hands were folded in his lap, I noticed. I found it difficult to meet his gaze. "Mr. Sands," he murmured, "you were recently in the armed forces of the United States of America?"

"Yes, sir," I replied.

"Do you recall signing anything upon your discharge?"

Oh, shit. "Uh-huh."

Cowens glared at me. He hadn't liked that *uh-huh.* "The paper you signed provided for your re-induction into the armed forces in the event of certain contingencies," he explained unnecessarily. "One of those contingencies was an emergency declared by the president or by the military commander of the region in which you reside. I am the military commander of this region. You have two choices, Mr. Sands. You can take on this assignment as a civilian, or you can take it on as a private in the United States Army, pursuant to a military emergency that I will be happy to declare right now. Which do you choose, Mr. Sands?"

My momentary admiration for the Feds had disappeared. This was what people didn't like about them, after all: the arbitrary imposition of their will on the hapless guy just trying to make it through life. What was I supposed to do? Take them to court? That might have worked in the old days, but not anymore. You don't win cases against the Feds anymore. No, you basically have to do what they tell you to do, and hope that their incompetence will keep them from bothering you too much. Right now, unfortunately, they were being pretty competent.

"I get two new dollars a day, plus expenses," I said. "Ten dollars in advance."

General Cowens turned away. Bolton smiled and picked up the phone. "Lisa, would you bring me ten dollars from petty cash?"

Ten dollars was not petty cash to me. Lisa hurried in with the money. I didn't feel like smiling at her. She wouldn't have noticed anyway; she was too busy being efficient in front of her boss and the general. I signed a receipt and put the money in my pocket. Back in business again.

"Well, I'm glad that was settled so amicably," Bolton said when Lisa had left. "Now, how can we assist your investigation?"

I tried to think like a private eye. "When is the president arriving?" I asked.

"Soon," Bolton replied.

"I don't recall seeing anything about this in the paper. Has it been made public yet?"

"Government employees were told this morning. The public announcement will be made later this afternoon."

I thought. Bolton waited. Cowens looked bored. "Have you considered the possibility that this is an inside job?" I asked.

"What do you mean, 'an inside job'?" Bolton replied.

"Someone from the government trying to stop the president's visit." I summarized the theory I had just come up with. "None of us have heard of this Second American Revolution, right? Doesn't prove anything, but it's suggestive. And the president's visit isn't common knowledge, but obviously people within the government had to know. Also, there's the message itself. On white bond paper, and typed—looks like with an electric typewriter. How many radical groups have access to that kind of paper and that kind of typewriter? And there's the way the message was delivered. I don't imagine it's that easy to get into this building and up to your office—your guard looked pretty alert out there."

Bolton shook his head. "I don't think so, Sands. First of all, you might not have known about the president's visit, but I'm well aware that there have been rumors about it for some time now. As for the paper and the typing—well, there's nothing particularly conclusive about that. Not all the typewriters in existence are owned by the government. And the outer door to my office is guarded only when I'm here. I don't see much of a problem for someone to come up in the early morning or after work without being noticed. And anyway, why would someone from the government want to stop President Kramer's visit?"

"All you need is one secret radical sympathizer," I suggested.

Bolton didn't look convinced. I wasn't especially convinced myself.

General Cowens broke the awkward silence. "All of this," he murmured, "ignores the fact that TSAR does in fact exist."

Swell, I thought. Five minutes on the case and already I'm making a fool of myself.

"Have you learned something, Bob?" Bolton asked. "When we talked earlier you said you hadn't heard of them."

"I can't personally keep track of every anti-government group that comes and goes around here," Cowens replied. "That's why we maintain files. I went and checked the files we keep in the basement on these sorts of organizations, and there they were."

"But wait a minute, I checked those files too—right after I received the message. I didn't see anything for The Second American Revolution."

"Where did you look?" Cowens asked.

Bolton considered. "Well, I looked under 'Second.' And also under 'TS,' for 'TSAR.'"

Cowens nodded. "It was filed under 'The.'" He didn't look especially impressed by Bolton's investigative prowess. Bolton's scar throbbed again.

"What was in the file?" I asked.

Cowens stared at me as if I were being impertinent. Finally he deigned to answer. "It was empty," he said.

"Empty? Did someone remove whatever was in there? Who has access to these files?"

The general's stare turned colder, if that was possible. "You insist on assuming that someone in the government is involved in threatening the president," he said. "This seems to me to be utterly absurd. In fact, there is no reason to assume that anything was ever in there in the first place."

"Then why was a file started?"

"Someone hears a name or a rumor and decides to start a file. If no more information is forthcoming, nothing gets placed in the file."

"Do you have a record of who started the file, or when, or why?" I asked.

Cowens shook his head.

"This doesn't seem like a particularly efficient system, Bob," Bolton said. He seemed glad to have the attention shifted from his own mistake.

The general's stare was approaching absolute zero. For all his deference to Bolton, it didn't look as if he was particularly fond of the governor. "There are limitations on manpower and other resources," he said in his softest, frostiest voice. "We do the best we can with what is available to us."

"I'd like to take a look at your files," I said.

Cowens glanced at me. Another impertinence from the local. "Out of the question," he replied.

"Show him the files, Bob," Bolton said. "Show him whatever he wants to see."

"Those files are highly confidential," Cowens pointed out. "This man is—"

"This man has been hired to help us. And it looks to me like we need help. Understood?"

Cowens assumed the blank expression of a military man following orders. "Yes, sir."

Suddenly I was impressed with Bolton. He certainly didn't seem to have any problem handling the legend sitting across from him. Bolton stood up. "Good. Thank you both for coming, then. Sands, I expect a report before the president arrives—or as soon as you find out anything. If you have any problems getting people to cooperate, just let me know."

I stood up too. "Yes, sir."

General Cowens got slowly to his feet. He headed out of Bolton's office without glancing at either of us. I followed him, assuming he was going to carry out Bolton's order. I smiled at Lisa as we walked through the reception area; she ignored me. The guard at the door saluted as Cowens passed by.

We waited silently for the elevator to come. Cowens wasn't the sort of guy I felt like starting a casual conversation with. When the elevator arrived, he pressed B, and we headed down to the basement. Cowens then led the way down a long, gray-tiled corridor. At the end of the corridor was a barred door; beyond the door a uniformed man sat at a desk reading a newspaper. Above the door was a hand-lettered sign that said "Records."

The soldier jumped to his feet when he saw Cowens approaching. He unlocked the door and let us in.

We stood in a large open area half-filled with battered green file cabinets. There were no windows, and the electric lighting was poor; the place felt damp and musty, like some abandoned cellars where I have spent the night in my time.

"Sergeant Hennessey," Cowens said. "Governor Bolton has given this man permission to study the files related to dissident organizations and individuals. He is not, however, to remove anything. Understood?"

"Yes, sir," Sergeant Hennessey said. He was a tall, hairless man with a cleft palate.

Cowens turned to me. "And you are not to divulge the contents of these files to anyone else. If I find that you have, I'll throw you back into the army so fast you'll think you never took the uniform off. Understood?"

"Uh-huh."

Cowens stared at me. "You weren't a very good soldier, were you, Sands?" he said after a moment.

I considered. "I was a terrible soldier," I replied. He nodded, his insight confirmed, and then he walked stiffly out the door. Sergeant Hennessey locked it behind him, then turned to me. "It's all yours," he said, and he went back to reading his newspaper.

I wandered through the rows of file cabinets, looking for the 'T's. Finally I found a cabinet labeled "Tabard to Timothy" in pencil. I slid open the bottom drawer. It was crammed full of manila folders. I thumbed through them until I found the T's, and the folder for The Second American Revolution. As Cowens had said, it was empty. So now what?

Just for fun, I looked through the S's. Did the government snoops have a file on one Walter Sands? Why, yes they did. I took it out and opened it up, eager to see what they had on me.

There was nothing in it but the article my friend Gwen had written for the *Globe* about my adventure in England. I didn't know whether to feel annoyed or relieved. On the one hand, my pride was hurt. Hadn't I done lots of other things worth their attention? Did it take Gwen's article to make them notice me? On the other hand, surely it was a good thing not to be noticed. There was no telling when they'd decide to stick you back in the army.

As I looked at my folder, something struck me. My name had been written in pencil, and the black letters were already smudged and faded with handling, even though Gwen's article was only a few weeks old. The tab on which my name appeared was soft and wrinkled. I got out TSAR's folder again. No smudges; no fading; no wrinkles. A nice, fresh, new folder.

I closed the drawers and returned to Sergeant Hennessey, who looked up from his paper. "Through?" he asked.

"Well, no, I've got a couple of questions I'd like to ask you, actually."

"General Cowens didn't say anything about answering questions," the soldier pointed out.

I raised an eyebrow. "All right, let's get him back down here and straighten this out," I said in my too-busy-to-put-up-with-this-nonsense voice.

Hennessey shrugged. "Ask your questions. If I don't like them, you can go get him."

Your typical helpful Fed. "Do many people come down here to look at these files?"

Hennessey considered. "Enough," he replied helpfully.

"Do you keep a log of the people who look at the files?"

He shook his head.

"Is there a list of people who are allowed in here?" Another helpful shake of the head.

"Then how do you know who's authorized to look at the files?"

"I know," he said.

"Is anyone allowed to add a new folder to the files?"

"If you're allowed in here, you can add folders."

I pondered. "Well, thanks a lot," I said finally. Sergeant Hennessey went back to reading his paper. I thought about going upstairs to Bolton and getting him to make this guy cooperate, but I decided I didn't have things clear enough in my mind just yet. Instead I returned to the files.

I couldn't think of any other angles to check here on the case, so I looked up what the Feds had on my friends. Nothing much. Gwen had some of her articles clipped out; the *Globe* was more or less anti-government, so I wasn't surprised that the Feds would keep track of its reporters. And there were a couple of items about a guy I knew named Linc, who had hated the government and had been more than willing to say so.

But Linc was dead. I wondered if anyone was responsible for removing folders for dead people from the file cabinets. Not enough manpower, I supposed; not enough resources. It was more important to add empty new folders.

"Quitting time," Hennessey called to me after a while. I shut the drawer and returned to the desk. Hennessey had the door open for me. "Someday," he said, "we'll get one of them big old computers running, and we'll really be back in business again."

"I can hardly wait."

Hennessey grinned. I headed back to the elevator while behind me he turned out the lights.

CHAPTER 3

It was a little early to go home, so I headed over to the waterfront. In the old days, apparently, the waterfront had been valued chiefly because the harbor was considered picturesque, and condos and hotels and restaurants jostled each other in the effort to get the best view. Now the condos and the hotels and the restaurants are all abandoned. People don't care about the view anymore; they care about the fish, and the wharfs are filled with the boats that go out and get the fish.

Today I was interested in neither the fish nor the view. I knew that my housemate Stretch liked to run along the waterfront after work when the weather was good, and I figured I'd meet up with him there.

Stretch's love of exercise struck me as being insane. Life is hard enough, it seemed to me, without making it any harder for yourself. But I didn't voice my opinion to him. Stretch is a man of firm beliefs, and nothing is to be gained by taking issue with them. So I sat on a bench near the ruins of the aquarium and waited for a dwarf in his underwear to come jogging by.

"Are you expecting a commission?" I asked when he finally appeared.

He stopped and smiled. "Hello, Walter." He wiped the sweat from his tiny features. "Isn't it exciting?"

"That I finally got another case?"

"Well, yes, that too. But I mean, aren't you excited about the president corning to Boston?"

"Oh. Sure. Is she going to bring a new sewer system with her?"

Stretch is assistant director of sewers for the city. In a sense, this made him a Fed like Bolton and all the others; the city administration was separate from, but subordinate to, the Fed's regional bureaucracy. But in any case no one seemed to hold this against Stretch. No one dislikes sewers, and no one dislikes Stretch. "Of course not, Walter," Stretch replied. "But things are changing—can't you feel it? And they're changing because of her."

We headed over to where Stretch had hidden his clothes and briefcase in a pile of rubble. Stretch trusted his fellow man, but not enough to leave his clothes out in the open. I started thinking about President Kramer. She was less clear to me than Bolton and Cowens, just as the goings-on in Atlanta were somehow less real than what happened here in Boston. I decided to risk a lecture. "Why is President Kramer so important, Stretch?"

Stretch brightened as he pulled on his pants. It wasn't often that I expressed any interest in such matters. "President Kramer represents the new generation, Walter—our generation. The generation that's going to change the world." I imagine Stretch saw my eyes start to glaze, because he quickly started giving me some facts. "I mean, she's older than us—she was born before the War—but she's more a part of this world than the old world. You know what I mean?"

I knew. "The other presidents have all been from the old world, right?"

Stretch nodded. He was buttoning his shirt now. "They were good men, and they worked hard, and we owe them a tremendous debt of gratitude, but there's a difference. They were just trying to keep America alive. Oh, they had policies, all right. I mean, it was obvious we had to do something to increase the population and to improve medical care, and no one wanted any of those high-tech weapons anymore, even if we could afford them. But mostly the idea was to make sure that people recognized the government in Atlanta as *the* government, and to prevent all these little dictatorships and kingdoms and whatever from taking root."

"And you think we can get beyond that now?"

"Ann Kramer thinks so. And really, it's all a matter of attitude. If she can convince enough people to agree with her then, yes, the future is ours for the taking. We can rebuild the nation, and then we can help rebuild the world."

He picked up his briefcase, and we started walking toward the house we shared with Gwen on Beacon Hill. We passed a mutant sitting cross-legged on the sidewalk, his stumps extended in a plea for coins; we tossed a few into his cap. A VOTE YES poster was plastered on the wall of the building behind him. Stretch's optimism was as puzzling to me as his love of exercise. Where did it come from? Probably some sort of mutation; surely it wasn't rational.

"And the referendum is the start?" I asked.

"The president has already started, Walter. But the referendum will make her success inevitable, if enough people vote for it."

"Do you think enough people will?"

Stretch nodded, his eyes gleaming. "Now that Ann Kramer is coming, I'm sure of it."

I couldn't help being a little envious of Stretch. Certainty must be a very soothing state of mind. We were silent for a while as we headed home.

Gwen, Stretch, and I live in an old town house in Louisburg Square—once one of the toniest addresses in Boston, and still in possession of a certain Brahmin grandeur. But like everyplace else, our home has suffered the depredations of time and neglect, and is now just one more symbol of what has been lost. Unlike the Feds, we no longer have electricity or central heat, and, despite Stretch's best efforts, our sewer system is at best problematic. But people have survived before electricity and central heat, so who are we to complain? We aren't bluebloods, but we are alive, and that is more than can be said for the rich folks whose home we have usurped.

Stretch and I smelled boiling chicken as we entered the once-elegant foyer. Gwen was home already, and it was her turn to make supper. "Hello," we called out, and she hurried from the kitchen and kissed us both. She lingered in my embrace and smiled at me. "How are you?" she asked.

"Just great." Gwen felt good in my arms. We have been together for a long time. I may not be the most faithful fellow in the world, but I'm smart enough to know I'm one of the luckiest.

"Walter got a case today," Stretch said.

"True?" she asked, her smile widening.

I nodded. "You may not be too happy about it, though."

"Come to the kitchen and tell me."

We followed her to the rear of the house and sat at the kitchen table while Gwen busied herself preparing the meal. Stretch poured a glass of cider and looked very pleased with himself. I was working for the government now. If only he could convert Gwen...

"You've probably heard that the president is coming to town," I said.

Gwen nodded. "They announced it this afternoon, but there were rumors before that."

Bolton had been right, then: people outside the government could have known the president was coming. "Someone made a threat against her," I said. "A group called 'The Second American Revolution.' Ever hear of it?"

Both Stretch and Gwen shook their heads. "There are a lot of bad people around," Stretch murmured. His tone suggested that this was a source of perpetual amazement to him.

"Anyway, Governor Bolton wants me to find out about these guys, see if we can round them up before they do anything to President Kramer."

Stretch was impressed. "I thought you were just going to be part of her security," he said. "But this is much more important."

Gwen, with her reporter's training, started quizzing me on the details as she put out the boiled chicken and boiled potatoes and boiled carrots. She is not a very inventive cook. I felt a little uncomfortable giving her all the information—a private eye owes his client some confidentiality, after all, even if he doesn't like his case— but I found it impossible to hide anything from her. She's too good a reporter, I guess. "So you think it could be someone inside the government?" she asked after I had laid out what I knew.

"Well, at least the hypothesis fits the facts," I said. "Someone goes to the records department and slips a folder into the file cabinet. Lo and behold, TSAR exists. He can't put anything into the folder, since nothing else exists but the name—and maybe he's afraid to forge any notes or reports, because it'd be easy for him to get caught. So meanwhile everyone starts looking for a phony group."

"But the other hypothesis also fits," Stretch noted, loyal as always to his employer. "Someone started the folder because he'd heard the name of the group, and then there was nothing to put in it because nothing else came up. And that makes a lot more sense, doesn't it? I mean, why would someone in the government threaten President Kramer?"

Bolton had asked me the same question. This time I just shrugged and ate a mouthful of carrots.

"Of course," Gwen said, "there are plenty of Feds who think this referendum is a bad idea. And Governor Bolton is one of them."

That was news to me. Stretch looked uncomfortable; it apparently wasn't news to him. "Why?" I asked Gwen.

"Don't you read the *Globe*?" she asked.

"Only your articles. The rest is too depressing. I'm apolitical, or haven't I mentioned that to you?"

She smiled. "Well, surely you know the criticisms people have made of the referendum."

"Who gets to vote," I responded. That was a tricky one for the Feds. Basically, there are three classes of people the Feds have to deal with. There are taxpayers—people who work for mainstream businesses or the government and have taxes withheld from their pay just like the old days; Stretch and Gwen were taxpayers. And there are the people on the census rolls who don't pay taxes: the government knows these people exist, but has no way of extracting money from them, generally because they don't work for a business that has to depend on the government for services, and that therefore has to do the government's bidding; I am such a person. And then there are the rest—the people who have nothing to do with the government, who live shadowy lives in the suburbs or on farms far away from Bolton and his minions, and just want to be left alone.

In the past, taxpayers have been the only ones who could vote, and then only for legislatures that had limited authority over purely local matters. But what good would the referendum do if voting was limited to this minority? Ideally it should be open to all, but if people weren't on some kind of government list, how could the Feds prevent them from voting more than once? So they opened up the voting to people on the census rolls But that left them vulnerable to the criticism that they were excluding a large segment of the population who would undoubtedly VOTE NO.

"Who gets to vote is certainly a problem," Gwen agreed. "And there's also the problem of interpreting the results. People who oppose the government aren't going to believe the government isn't cheating, so what's the point of the Feds running this big campaign and then announcing that they received ninety-eight percent of the vote? Does anyone really expect the Feds to tell us if they lose?"

"They've offered to let the opposition participate in counting the ballots," Stretch pointed out.

"But even if the opposition were organized enough to run the referendum with the Feds, why should they bother?" Gwen replied. "They're better off simply ignoring it. For the referendum to have any value, people have to believe in the whole process. Otherwise it's just a public relations gimmick—and a pretty pitiful one at that."

I was impressed with Gwen. Usually she says so little that you might forget how much she knows. "So the Feds win only if people think they've won," I said.

Gwen nodded. "And a lot of Feds—like Bolton—think the whole thing isn't worth it. The referendum will make them look weak, as if they're begging people to believe in them. Bolton's from the old school. Before anything else, you have to consolidate your power and impose order. Then you can fool around with democracy."

I recalled the speech Bolton had given me about the importance of the referendum. It hadn't sounded quite right. I had thought his audience was the problem, but apparently the problem was with Bolton himself. I finished off my chicken.

"Still, that's no reason for someone to threaten the president," Stretch argued. "Governor Bolton and the rest of them have been doing all they can to make the referendum a success. You should have heard the speech he gave today to the government employees. Maybe he's not totally behind the idea, but so what? I mean, everyone has disagreements with his superiors from time to time."

"It does seem like overkill," I agreed.

"You'll get to the bottom of it, though, won't you, Walter?"

"You bet, Stretch."

We were silent for a while as we finished our meal. Then Gwen changed the subject slightly. "Um, Walter, about The Second American Revolution?"

I looked at her. She sounded ill-at-ease. She almost never sounds ill-at-ease. "Yes, Gwen?"

"This is sort of a scoop. Would you object if I wrote a story about it?"

I smiled. Sometimes I forgot that Gwen had ambitions too. She has wanted to be a writer for far longer than I have wanted to be a private eye; perhaps, I've sometimes thought, it's easier for her to put things down on paper than to say them. At any rate, she was much more successful at achieving her dream than I have been at achieving mine. But there seemed to be a conflict here. I didn't mind telling my little pseudo-family about my case, but I doubted that Bolton and Cowens would approve if Gwen told the world about it. On the other hand, I couldn't remember anyone prohibiting me from mentioning TSAR, and I liked Gwen a lot more than I liked the Feds. "How about a compromise?" I suggested. "You can write about TSAR's threat, but don't bring up my name or what I found out in the government records."

"Perfect," she said. She leaned over the table and kissed me. "I'll also ask around at the Globe and see if anyone has heard of TSAR."

"Okay." I tried to sound enthusiastic, but I'm sure I failed. Gwen gave me a puzzled look, then seemed to decide not to worry about it. She had a story to write.

We cleaned up the dishes, and then Gwen bicycled back to the *Globe* to write up her scoop. Stretch changed his clothes and went off to one of his endless sewer meetings. I was left alone to ponder my case.

I climbed the stairs to the third floor, to the musty room where I felt happiest—where I kept my books.

I read too much. It's an addiction. Words are a narcotic; stories dull the pain of existence. Words also teach you things, of course: how to cure disease and build elevators and rule the world. All very interesting, all very helpful. Mainly, however, I'm interested in the narcotic angle.

I stared at the titles that thronged my shelves, and I recalled getting my first case—the pride and satisfaction it had given me, and the need I had felt to give it a title of its

own. I was part of the tradition now, following in the line
of Chandler and Hammett and the rest. My first case had
deserved a title as good as any of theirs.

I didn't feel that way about this case, however. It wasn't
just that I didn't like working for the Feds, I realized as I sat
in my broken leather recliner. It wasn't just the threat from
General Cowens, and my lack of interest in the referendum.
There was something more basic going on.

I had given my first case a lot of thought (not having had
much else to do lately). My attitude toward it was about as
changeable as my attitude toward the government.
Sometimes I thought I did a pretty good job, all things
considered, and at other times I was amazed at my
incompetence. But there was one thing that bothered me
about the case: it was bogus. Oh, there was a real client
with a real problem, but I wasn't getting anywhere in
solving it, until Gwen and my friend Bobby Gallagher
conspired to manufacture some evidence; their evidence led
me to England and, eventually, to a solution.

I figured out what they had done finally but, as usual, I
didn't know how to respond. Still don't. On the one hand, it
was a wonderful thing they did. It got me to England, the
promised land, where things still work, where Bobby and
Gwen fully expected me to remain, because when you get
out of hell it only makes sense to stay out. On the other
hand...

On the other hand, I kinda wanted for this dream of mine
to be real. I didn't appreciate having to rely on my tolerant
friends to come up with my cases for me and provide the
solutions for them and generally act as if I were a dotty old
uncle whom everyone has to humor. I was being unfair, I
knew, but I couldn't help it. It annoyed me that Bolton
found out about me through Gwen's article (even though I
had agreed with her that it would be good publicity); it
annoyed me that he then went to Stretch to get a personal
recommendation; it annoyed me that Gwen wanted to help
me out by asking her sources at the Globe for information
about TSAR. The more people helped, the less real my

profession seemed to me, and the more I wondered why I was doing what I was doing.

I am not naive, I think. I do not actually believe that mysterious blondes will knock on the door of my office. But I do believe that, in a land where the fabric of civilized society has become somewhat tattered, a service such as mine can be quite valuable. So far, I seemed to be alone in that belief. Maybe people are too used to handling their troubles themselves to come to a stranger with them. Maybe I should run my ad somewhere besides the *Globe*. Or maybe I should get a job in the sewer department.

When I fall into moods like this, the only thing I can do is to get out the drugs. I took a book down from a shelf and tried to dull my pain.

Stretch returned after a while and yelled good-night up the stairs. Gwen didn't come back until long after my oil lamp had been lit and I had started worrying about her.

She came up to the third floor and stood in the doorway. She looked beautiful in the flickering lamplight--her long brown hair framing her thin face, with its sad eyes and knowing smile. Maybe she isn't beautiful. We're both young, but I've known her for too long to be able to separate out what is emotion and what is objective reality in my perception of her. Reality doesn't matter in these things, I think. "You okay?" I asked.

She nodded and smiled.

"They like your story?"

"Sure. Wolsey loves scoops." Wolsey was Gwen's editor; like Spenser, he apparently had no first name. She came into the room and sat on the floor in front of my chair. She leaned back between my legs; I reached down and stroked her hair. She closed her eyes and sighed with pleasure. "No one there has heard of TSAR." She paused, then added, "I had to find out for my story."

"Of course." I felt a pang of remorse. Why should she have to apologize for trying to help me?

"Wolsey suggested that it could be an old group who gave themselves a new name—to keep the Feds from knowing who they are."

"That makes sense. But we still don't know what old group it might be."

"I'm sure you'll find out."

"Um," I replied, not at all sure I agreed with her.

I could feel Gwen smile her knowing smile. "Do you think you'll meet the president?" she asked.

"Doubt it."

"I'd love to interview her. I'd love to find out what she's really like, what she really thinks about things."

"Maybe you will. It sounds like she's eager for publicity."

Gwen shook her head. "She'll stay away from the *Globe*. We're too open-minded for the Feds."

She sighed, and I thought of her ambitions once again. Stretch wanted to improve the world, but Gwen wanted simply to understand it. Neither goal was particularly easy to achieve, however. I had set my sights a lot lower than both of them, I thought, but even I was having my problems.

After a while we went downstairs to our bedroom, even though I knew that tonight, as usual, sleep would not come easy for me. We paused as we passed Linc's room. "He wouldn't have approved of me working for the Feds," I whispered.

"Still, he would've been proud of you."

I knew, as usual, that Gwen was right. Linc's pain had been a lot more real than my psychic discomfort, and he had never found the narcotic that would dull it, the ambition that would drive him to ignore it. Finally he had been forced to end the pain in the only way he knew how. He had committed suicide while I was in England.

Gwen and I got into bed together and held each other close. At such moments, we used to whisper to one another about dreams coming true someday. But that had stopped since I came back from England. Now we knew that dreams can come true, but that life goes on, and more dreams are required. I guess maybe we were still growing up. Someday, maybe, we would stop dreaming, and then, like Linc, we would have nothing to hold onto but the pain.

"You're going to crack this case," Gwen said.

"And you're going to interview the president," I replied.

Gwen fell asleep in my arms then, and I was lost in a waking dream until morning.

CHAPTER 4

"**S**o how are you going to find out about TSAR?" Stretch asked me at breakfast the next morning.

I smiled what I hoped was a Gwen-like knowing smile. "I have my sources," I said.

"I hope this won't be dangerous."

"Oh, I know how to take care of myself."

I noticed Gwen staring at me; I looked away.

After breakfast we all left for work. Despite my misgivings about the case, it felt good to have something real to do for a change. I carried my bicycle down the front steps of our town house and, with a wave to the statue of Christopher Columbus at the far end of the square, I set off. I was going to Charlestown, on the other side of the river from Beacon Hill.

I felt a little nervous about Charlestown. It was Jim O'Malley's territory, and Jim O'Malley doesn't like me. O'Malley is a businessman, a competitor (and occasional partner) of my friend (and occasional employer) Bobby Gallagher. As Bobby's employee, I have had my share of battles with O'Malley's men—most of which I have won. O'Malley remembers things like that.

He is also much more powerful than Bobby, who is content to work with a few helpers out of a warehouse in

South Boston. O'Malley is practically the emperor of his community, and the Feds tend to give it a wide berth. I'm sure this situation doesn't please them, but there is little they can do about it; they have the resources to defeat O'Malley, perhaps, but they don't have the resources to govern a town that hates them. So they don't bother trying.

One result of this was that Charlestown became the ideal home for radicals and malcontents of the sort who might want to threaten the president. I had decided to take the straightforward approach, and assume that TSAR was real; Charlestown, therefore, was the place to begin. I wanted to talk to one malcontent in particular. His name was Henry Fisher, but it was hard to think of him without using Linc's title. Linc had dubbed Henry the Angriest Man in America.

Henry Fisher is a tailor, like his father before him.

Unlike his father, who died long before the War, Henry is successful. Times have changed, of course, and what had been a luxury in the old days is now a necessity. Old clothes need to be repaired until they fall apart; new clothes have to be made by hand, instead of appearing miraculously on the racks in shopping malls whenever you needed them. But success has not made Henry content with our brave new world; it has just given him more time to feed his anger.

Henry is working on a book. It is going to be an important book, a vital book, a book that future generations (should there be any) will have to read and ponder and discuss. It is going to explain the causes of the War. Henry is forever searching out books and documents, interviewing old-time government officials who have managed to survive, marshaling his evidence, honing his theories, structuring his arguments. And all of this activity keeps him in a constant state of wrath against the government, against the military, against Western civilization—against all the forces that have contributed to the virtual destruction of our planet. *How could they have done this to us?* It is a strange way to live, if you ask me, but I suppose his anger is what keeps him alive.

Despite his anger, Henry was not a suspect. He was going to be a source—although an unwilling one, I was sure.

Charlestown seemed just like all the other sections of Boston as I pedaled through it—except for the absence of Feds and VOTE YES posters. The weather was warm and sunny once again, and I had to keep reminding myself that I was in enemy territory. The house where Henry lived and kept his shop sat in the shadow of the Bunker Hill Monument, a gray obelisk commemorating the start of the first American Revolution; I was pretty winded by the time I had struggled up the hill to it. I chained my bike to a wrought-iron fence, and I went inside.

The shop, as usual, was crowded. A few customers were waiting in line to talk to a salesman, who was displaying a swatch of fabric to a hunchbacked woman who looked like a witch. Even witches need clothes. Beyond the counter, three women sat at manual sewing machines, busily stitching away. Those sewing machines were more valuable than the house, I figured. There are plenty of houses.

The youngest and prettiest of the women looked up finally and noticed me. "Walter!"

"Hi, Ann." She was Henry's daughter, a dark-eyed girl of about seventeen; despite the genetic influences on her, the only thing that made her angry was her name. Her full name, she had confessed to me once, was Anarchy, and every time she heard it she felt a profound urge to murder her father. "Is the AMA in?"

Ann laughed and stood up. "I'll go get him." She thought Linc's title for her father, and especially its abbreviation, were hilarious. I admired her figure as she walked through some dark curtains into the back room.

A few minutes later a little bald man with thick glasses perched on the end of his nose stuck his head through the curtains. "Walter Sands," he said. "What are you doing here?"

He sounded angry. "I've come to ask for your daughter's hand in marriage," I said.

"Phooey," he replied.

"Well then, how about a friendly conversation with my old pal?"

He looked put out. "I can spare you a few minutes, I suppose."

"Thanks."

The salesman opened a section of the counter and let me pass through. Beyond the curtains, Ann was standing next to her father. "Come on," Henry said to me. "And you get back to work," he growled at Ann.

"Yes, master." Ann grinned at me as she walked past.

Henry led me up a flight of stairs, then down a short hallway to his study.

The study looked a bit like my third-floor library, but I had a feeling there was no overlap between the contents of his groaning bookshelves and my own. "Have you ever read a novel?" I asked him.

"No time," he snapped. He sat down at a table piled high with papers. On the wall behind him, a couple of old Sierra Club posters showed the world as it once was. I sat in an uncomfortable ladder-back chair opposite him. "I haven't seen you in a while," he said. He sounded like a probation officer in one of the novels he had never read.

"I was away. I came back."

"So I heard."

"And Charlestown isn't my favorite place."

"That's not my fault."

Conversation with Henry isn't easy. I changed the topic. "So, how's the book coming?"

Henry eyed me suspiciously, as if probing for some ulterior motive. I tried to look interested. "Slowly," he admitted finally. "It's vital that I get everything right. It's vital that I make people *understand*." He bent over and picked up a large stack of paper from the floor. "I do have an extra copy of what I've completed so far," he said, "if you'd like to—"

"No, no, that's okay," I said quickly. "I'd prefer to wait for your final word on the subject."

Henry put the stack down. I tried not to look relieved. I don't think I succeeded. "You're never going to read it, are you?" he said.

"Of course I am," I lied.

He shook his head. "You just don't care. Remember, Walter, those who ignore the past—"

"—are condemned to listen to people who are obsessed by it."

"I may be obsessed," Henry said, "but it's an important obsession."

"Depends on the outcome," I replied. I thought back over the years I had known Henry and watched his stacks of paper grow. "I may never start your book, Henry, but have you considered that you may never finish it? I think your anger means too much to you; you can't let it go."

"You don't think I have reason to be angry? The governments of the world have poisoned us and all our descendants, and you expect maybe cheerfulness? I should whistle a happy tune and thank God they haven't exploded the rest of their bombs yet?"

"I just think your anger could be more productive," I said. "If the world never sees your book, how is it going to learn from its mistakes?"

"The world will see it all right," Henry replied, "if people would only stop interrupting me. Now, what can I do for you, Walter?"

I smiled my ingratiating smile. "I have a favor to ask."

I shouldn't have made him angry, of course, given the nature of the favor. But that would've been next to impossible. And I really didn't want to read his book. "Did you see the *Globe* this morning?"

Henry made a face. "The president is coming."

"And there's been a threat already."

He nodded. "Your friend Gwen's story."

"Right. She got her information from me. The Feds have hired me to track down this group called The Second

American Revolution." I kept smiling. "I thought maybe you might be able to help."

Henry erupted. "You want me to help you save the skin of the president of the United States, for God's sake? What do you think I've been doing for the past twenty-three years—writing a love letter to the government? Those people in Atlanta want to do it all over again—build up the nation-state so that they can have wars with other nation-states, so that people like you and me can end up rotting in a ditch from radiation poisoning or starving to death after another nuclear winter. I don't want to help you track down The Second American Revolution, Walter; I want to join it."

"Pretty please," I said.

Henry glowered at me. I knew what he was thinking. And he knew I knew.

He owed me.

I met Henry shortly after the Federal troops came up from Atlanta and put an end to the worst of that awful time called the Frenzy. Gwen and I were about fifteen, and we had just moved into our house in Louisburg Square and started to live some semblance of a normal life. It was a hopeful period for many people, but not for Henry Fisher. When I met him, he was in the process of trying to get himself shot to death.

Darkness was falling, and I was rushing home along Boylston Street in the Back Bay. The Feds had imposed a dusk-to-dawn curfew in the city, and they weren't interested in excuses if they caught you on the streets at night. So when I heard the shouted "Halt!" followed immediately by a gunshot, I wasted no time ducking into the shadows of an abandoned storefront, cursing my stupidity for staying out so late.

I turned to see a couple of soldiers, rifles raised, walking down the middle of the street. But they weren't walking toward me. They were headed toward a bald man, who held his ground as they approached. "Who do you guys think you are?" he demanded. "Is your only response to any situation to use your rifles? That's precisely the mentality that got us into this mess. I'm out here trying to find my child, and all you want to do is kill me. Can't you see that it's got to stop? How can you be so stupid?"

He kept talking like that, working himself up into his own frenzy. And then he started walking toward the soldiers. I could tell that this was a mistake. Even back then, before I had been a soldier, I could sense their fear and indecision. Here was a crazy man in a crazy city where they definitely did not want to be, and he was coming toward them, his right hand hidden beneath something (it turned out to be a bolt of fabric), and any second they could die a stupid, useless, painful death. It would be so easy to shoot the guy and get it all over with. No one would mind. No one would question them....

"We just want to be left alone," he ranted. "Haven't you done enough to us? Can't you just go away and let us solve our own problems? Can't you just go away?"

The soldiers would have liked nothing better. But they were here, for better or worse. They raised their rifles, but the bald man didn't notice, lost in his own furious world.

"Daddy!"

The bald man stopped his harangue. The soldiers lowered their rifles. "Daddy! I've been looking all over for you!" I ran out of the shadows and into Henry Fisher's arms. "Shut up, you dope," I whispered.

He looked at me. His glazed eyes seemed to refocus. He did as he was told.

"Better get your father indoors, kid," one of the soldiers said. "You don't know how close he came."

"Yes, sir. He gets excited sometimes, sir. Won't happen again, sir." I dragged the Angriest Man in America into the abandoned store and kept him there all night, despite his insistence that he had to go out and find his daughter. In the morning we went to the police station on Berkeley Street and found Anarchy happily playing with a holster in a pleasant cell where the nice men had put her until someone came for her. Henry managed to swallow his rage long enough to thank me for saving his life. I had made a grouchy but true friend.

So what are friends for? Sitting across from me in his study eight years later, Henry knew. "You're making a big mistake, Walter," he said.

"I know," I replied. "But here I am, asking for your help. What do you say?"

Henry shrugged. "How can I help? I can't tell you where to find The Second American Revolution. I've never heard of them."

Swell. "Do you think you would've heard of them, if they existed?"

"Any crazy person can give himself a name and make a threat," Henry pointed out. "But if the group is real, and their threat is serious, I think I'd have heard something about them."

I recalled the suggestion Gwen's editor had made. "Maybe some group is using a new name to keep the Feds from tracking them down."

Henry nodded, and thought for a moment. "If you want to assume that a group is really trying to disrupt the president's visit and the referendum, and they're using a pseudonym, I suppose you have to consider who has the intelligence and the resolve to pull it off. That narrows the choice down considerably. There's a lot of grumbling in this world, Walter, but precious little done about it."

I refrained from pointing out that he might be considered one of the inactive grumblers. "What groups would you suggest, then?"

"The only one that comes to mind is the Church of the New Beginning," Henry replied. "I don't think much of Flynn Dobler, but he has a following. And he isn't stupid."

I considered Henry's suggestion. I knew a little bit about the Church of the New Beginning. "I thought those people just ignored the government and everything associated with it."

"Correct. But that's a very foolish strategy, Walter. Because what happens if this referendum is successful?

Before long the government is in Charlestown and Concord and all the places it stays away from now. And then it'll demand taxes from Dobler's people, and force their children to go to public schools, and draft their young men, and then what's left of Dobler's new beginning? He knows all this. He knows he has a stake in what happens during the next couple of weeks. It wouldn't surprise me if he decided to do something about it."

Henry made sense. It wasn't much of a lead, maybe, but it was worth looking into. I stood up. "Thanks for your help, Henry. If you hear of anything, will you let me know?"

Henry didn't seem happy. "I suppose," he said. "But we're even now. Don't expect me to compromise my principles like this again."

"You're a sweetheart, Henry. I'll let myself out."

Henry grunted a good-bye, and I made my way back downstairs. Ann waved to me from her sewing machine. "How was he?" she asked.

"The usual. When are you going to run away from him and move in with a nice guy like me?"

She considered. "As soon as he finishes his book." I rolled my eyes. "What a waste. No wonder he's never going to finish it."

"Someday," she said. "Don't be a stranger, Walter."

"I won't."

I went out through the shop, unlocked my bicycle, and got on.

I hadn't pedaled fifty feet before I knew I was in big trouble.

CHAPTER 5

Rounding the corner on foot were two of O'Malley's lieutenants: Pete Santoro and Eddie Grimes. They recognized me as soon as I recognized them. They smiled. I turned and started pedaling in the opposite direction.

The opposite direction was uphill, however, and I didn't get very far before a large hand grabbed the back of my jersey and pulled me off my bike.

The hand belonged to Santoro. He was a big man with a black beard, glittering eyes, and a gap-toothed grin. With an earring and a sword he would have made an excellent pirate. His friend Eddie Grimes was also big—O'Malley liked the brawny type—but he had red hair and so many freckles they looked like a disease. Maybe they were a disease. He stood in front of me while Santoro twisted the neck of my jersey. "What're you doing here, asshole?" he said.

"Arrgh rend," I replied. Santoro's hold on my jersey made conversation rather difficult.

"What, asshole?"

Santoro eased off a little. "I'm visiting a friend," I said, gasping for breath. "Just leaving."

"Oh, I don't think so," Santoro said. "I think you'll probably wanna visit Mr. O'Malley so long as you're in the neighborhood."

"I couldn't impose on such short notice. Some other time maybe."

"Mr. O'Malley won't mind," Grimes said. "He likes surprises."

"If you don't wanna visit," Santoro said, "we'll have to punish you for trespassing. Right here. Right now."

They were certainly enjoying themselves. Nothing like a little power to brighten a person's day. "Whatever you say," I muttered.

"That's more like it," Grimes said. He grabbed my bike. "Let's go, Pete."

"Wait. We gotta pick up the boss's suit."

"Oh. Right."

Santoro let go of me and hurried into Henry's shop. Grimes held onto the bike and grinned, daring me to try something. I didn't bother. Santoro came back out of the shop a couple of minutes later carrying a long garment bag. Just my luck I visit the Angriest Man in America the day Jim O'Malley's suit is ready.

And then the three of us marched through the sunny streets of Charlestown to O'Malley's place. I felt frustrated and a little frightened. I didn't imagine O'Malley would have me killed, but he might want to teach me a lesson. And if Santoro and Grimes had anything to do with it, I knew the lesson would be painful.

Most of the people we passed had a smile and a greeting for the two thugs. Everyone knew whose suit was in the garment bag. Everyone wanted to be friendly with the people who worked for him.

We ended up across town from Henry's shop, at a grand old Victorian home complete with turrets and a widow's walk and stained glass in the front door. I could imagine an Irish doctor living in it in the old days with his wife and ten kids, the richest family in the neighborhood and happy to flaunt it. Jim O'Malley was also happy to flaunt it. The place looked as if it hadn't aged a day since the doctor's family disappeared from it; it had a new coat of paint, the windows were unbroken and sparkled from a recent washing, the lawn was green and weedless. Two more thugs sat on the front porch and watched us approach. They too grinned when they recognized me. "If it ain't the Sandman," one of them said.

"Mr. Sands wants to call on the boss," Grimes said. "Is he in?"

"Sure. Leave the bike here. We'll keep an eye on it for him."

Santoro and Grimes led me inside. The interior was even more impressive than the outside. There was plenty of good furniture to be scavenged, of course, and O'Malley had clearly kept the best of what came his way. I felt as if I had entered a museum. My two captors led me to a pair of large oak pocket doors at the side of the foyer. Santoro knocked softly.

"Who is it?" a loud, deep voice called out.

"It's Pete, Jim. Eddie and me ran into a piece of scum we thought you might wanna see."

"Did you get my suit?"

"Sure thing."

"All right. Come in."

They slid the doors open and pushed me into O'Malley's office. I noted the sculpted ceiling moldings, the flocked wallpaper, the polished parquet floor. It occurred to me that O'Malley had a better office than the governor. He even had an air conditioner running, although it wasn't particularly hot out; this was the kind of guy who believed in conspicuous consumption.

O'Malley was tall and sandy-haired, with thin features and penetrating blue eyes. He was wearing a three-piece suit, a starched white shirt, and a silk tie. I thought he looked silly. He smiled at me. He was missing a couple of teeth. I suppose he could have had them replaced; maybe he thought the gaps made him look dangerous. "Walter Sands," he boomed. "What a pleasure to see you."

The funny thing was, he sounded as if he meant it. "Great office," I said.

"We found him over by the Monument, Jim," Grimes said. "Sneakin' around."

"Just visiting a friend," I explained. "Didn't mean any harm."

"I think we oughta show him what happens to people who sneak into Charlestown," Santoro said.

O'Malley glanced at his bearded lieutenant. "Bring my suit upstairs," he ordered.

Santoro's face clouded over for a brief moment. When he was a young boy, had he dreamed of growing up to run errands for a hoodlum? The cloud passed. "Sure thing, Jim," he replied. He hurried out of the room.

"Get Mr. Sands a chair," O'Malley said to Grimes.

Grimes also did as he was told, bringing me an elegant carved oak chair from a corner of the room. "Thanks so much," I murmured to him as I sat down. He muttered a naughty word.

O'Malley's gaze returned to me. "I read that article about you in the paper," he said. "Going to England and all. I didn't think you had it in you. You were stupid to come back, though."

"That's what everyone keeps telling me."

"Still working for Gallagher?"

"Off and on. Not today, though," I hastened to add.

O'Malley shrugged. "Bobby Gallagher and I go back a long way. Back when things were a lot wilder than they are now. Two micks on the make." He grinned a gap-toothed grin. It made him look a bit like Santoro, but not much. "One time we got in a shootout together—did he ever tell you? Down on the South Shore somewhere, Weymouth maybe. We heard there was an auto supply store that hadn't been touched. Bobby and I weren't going to steal anything, mind you, we just wanted to do business with the owners. But this bunch of cavemen opened fire on us as soon as our van turned the corner. Shot out a tire, so we couldn't get out of there.

"So we're shooting back and forth for a while, and things are getting pretty tense because we're running out of ammo, okay, and then what are we gonna do? But then I got an idea. This van had a terrific stereo system, see? So I put in a disk, and I crank up the volume, and all of a sudden 'Stairway to Heaven' is booming out so loud I think I cracked an eardrum.

"And the cavemen stop shooting. After a minute they start crawling out of the auto parts place, and we kinda put up our hands—you know, we come in peace—and pretty soon we're having a great time. CDs were harder to come by than auto parts, see—a lot more fragile. These guys had alternators up the wazoo, but the only CD they had left was, I dunno, Jerry Vale's Greatest Hits or something. So we were like bringing gifts from the gods. Probably the only time Led Zeppelin ever contributed to peace and mutual understanding—and saved a couple of lives. Also, we got a great deal on the alternators." O'Malley smiled and leaned back in his chair. "Bobby ever tell you that story?"

I shook my head. "It's quite a story," I said. Bobby had told it to me maybe forty or fifty times. Except in his version, he was the one who thought to play the Led Zeppelin CD and thereby saved the day. Memory is a tricky thing.

"Yeah, those were the days," O'Malley said. "There was scope for the individual entrepreneur back then. You know what I'm saying?"

"Things just aren't what they used to be," I agreed.

He nodded. "Bobby's problem is that he hasn't changed with the times. He wants to keep on being an individual entrepreneur, but it isn't gonna work. You gotta operate on a larger scale nowadays, or you get squeezed out by the big boys—like me. You gotta grow or die. Right?"

"Uh-huh." I was now more bored than frightened. I didn't really need a lecture on economics, any more than I needed a history lecture from the Angriest Man in America.

O'Malley regarded me. "My operation is growing, Sands," he said. "I'm big now, but I'm only gonna get bigger. That means I'm gonna need good people. People with intelligence. People with management skills. Like you."

Uh-oh. "Me?" I managed to say.

"Sure. You're a smart guy, even if you did come back from England. Muscle is easy to find," he said, gesturing in the direction of Eddie Grimes, who didn't look happy. "Intelligence isn't. So waddaya say?"

"I'm flattered," I replied carefully. "But I'm kind of a loner. I don't think I'd fit in."

"Why don't you let me be the judge of that?" O'Malley shifted in his chair. "Look," he went on, "I'm talking about the future here. People who don't come onboard are gonna get left behind. People like Bobby Gallagher. You say you're a loner—well, you don't know how lonely things can get. Everything in this city is mine for the taking—and believe me, I'm gonna take it. You know what I'm saying?"

I supposed I did. "I guess I'm going to get left behind," I said.

"Think about it," O'Malley insisted.

I shook my head. "Nothing to think about."

There was a moment of silence, and then O'Malley's expression went blank. It was scary. I wondered how many people said no to him in the course of an average working day. "Throw him out," he murmured to Grimes, and he turned away.

I stood up. Grimes was grinning. Santoro was standing by the sliding doors to the office, minus the garment bag. He was grinning too. I walked out of the office, with the two flunkies following close behind.

"For a supposedly intelligent guy, that was a pretty stupid thing to do," Santoro said as we reached the porch.

I shrugged. "I don't feel like picking up some thug's laundry," I said. "Did you hear the way he talked about you in there?"

The two men exchanged a glance. "We do important things too," Grimes said.

"Very important things," Santoro agreed.

"It's your life," I murmured. I went to get my bike.

"Not so fast," Santoro said. "The bike stays here. We're confiscating it."

"Oh, come on. I haven't done anything." Taking someone's bike was a big deal. Like clothes, bikes don't appear in shopping malls by magic anymore.

"You've pissed us off," Grimes said. "That's enough. You got a complaint, go talk to Jim."

I looked around. Grimes, Santoro, the two guys on the porch—everyone was grinning at me. It was a wonderful joke. "At least give me a ride out of Charlestown?" I asked.

They thought that was pretty funny too. I sighed and started walking.

CHAPTER 6

The Church of the New Beginning is northwest of Charlestown, in Concord. It would've been a long trip even on a bicycle; on foot it was impossible, unless I wanted to spend the night on the road. So instead, I reluctantly headed south. It wasn't far to South Boston, but the distance seemed immense to me; I wasn't headed in the right direction, physically or professionally, and that made every step a chore. I was exhausted (and very hungry) by the time I reached my destination.

It was not a pretty street. No trees, no grass, no flowers, just an endless stretch of cracked asphalt lined by rusty warehouses with ancient trucks pulled up to them. Most of the people you see on this street are in a hurry, and armed. It is the kind of street you stay away from unless you are up to something illegal or dangerous.

But the weather was apparently too nice for anything illegal or dangerous to be happening on this particular day. Outside of the warehouse that was my destination, a table had been set up, and three men were playing cards. One was a fat, middle-aged fellow who didn't see very well; his name was Bobby Gallagher. To Bobby's left was his driver, a short man named Mickey with a shriveled arm. Seated with his back to me was a black kid named

Doctor J. He did a little bit of everything for Bobby. I was sure he was winning the card game.

"I see that business is booming as usual," I said as I approached them.

Bobby looked up from his cards and squinted at me. "Great," he said. "We could use a fourth. Sit down."

"Hey, Wally," Doctor J said.

"Hey, Doctor J."

Mickey waved his good hand at me. I waved back. "Got any food?" I asked.

Bobby motioned to a half loaf of bread, a slab of cheese, and a pitcher of cider on a blanket next to the table. "We had a picnic," he explained.

"Beautiful spot for it," I said. I pulled up a chair and began to eat.

"No bike," Mickey noted.

I nodded and immediately changed the subject. "Anybody here heard of a group called The Second American Revolution?" I asked, not very hopefully.

"Just what we read in the paper this morning," Bobby said. "Why?"

I summarized my case and my first less-than-spectacular morning on it, omitting O'Malley's version of Bobby's favorite story.

"Jesus, Wally," Bobby said, "mixed up with the Feds and O'Malley. You're doin' great."

"Thanks a lot."

"Why don't you come to work for me full-time and get these other guys off your back?"

"You can protect me from the Feds?"

"I have some small influence," Bobby replied, his dignity wounded.

"Watch out, Wally, or you'll be back in the army scavengin' copper wire in DC," Doctor J warned me.

I tried to smile. It wasn't all that funny. Everyone had a better idea about what I should do with my life. And now, half a day into my case, I already needed help. "Bobby, what are the chances I could rent your van for the afternoon?"

"Are you shittin' me?" Bobby asked. "You can't even drive."

"Well, I guess I have to rent Mickey too. I want to check out this lead in Concord, and O'Malley's thugs took my bike, and besides, you guys don't look like you're doing anything today. I'll pay you whatever you think it's worth."

Bobby looked very uncomfortable. You don't use motor vehicles for just any old activity. "Maybe we can find you another bike," he suggested.

"It's getting pretty late," I said, "and Concord is pretty far from here." I hated this. Asking favors from my friends was exactly what I didn't want to do.

"Let's go," Mickey said to me.

"It's not your van!" Bobby shouted.

"I'll get the gas," Doctor J said, and he went into the warehouse.

"You're both fired!"

Mickey and I followed Doctor J into the warehouse, leaving Bobby fuming at the card table. He didn't have quite the authority Jim O'Malley did. On the other hand, I had a feeling Santoro and Grimes wouldn't have crossed the street to save O'Malley's life, while Doctor J and Mickey would've crossed the continent to save Bobby's.

Bobby's warehouse was mostly filled with junk from the old days; the valuable stuff—the weapons and the computer parts—he wisely kept locked and hidden upstairs, past a dog named Brutus who despised me. Just inside the doors sat the gray Ford van that was Bobby's prized possession. Mickey started doing a final check of the van while Doctor J poured precious gasoline into it. Mechanically ignorant, I kept away from the van (and Brutus) and felt uncomfortable.

"This isn't funny, you know," Bobby said, following us inside.

"We'll be back by dark," I said. "Promise."

"You aren't gonna be in any danger, are you?"

"Oh. Right. Can I rent a couple of guns, too?"

"Not funny," he muttered. But he went to get the weapons. By the time he returned, Mickey and Doctor J were finished. I got in the passenger side next to Mickey. "Name your price," I said to Bobby. "I'm serious."

"You're an asshole," Bobby said.

Mickey backed us out into the street. Doctor J waved. Brutus barked. I could feel Bobby glaring at us until we turned the corner.

"I really want to pay him," I said to Mickey.

Mickey just laughed. I gave up.

We crossed into Boston proper, drove through the city, then over the Charles River into Cambridge. From there we made our way through Cambridge and up the old Route 2. Mickey whistled as he dodged the craters and the boulders and the assorted debris in the roadway. He enjoyed this; I didn't. I said a please-don't-collapse prayer each time we approached a bridge; I watched out for police who might stop us to ask for a permit that we didn't possess; I wondered what would happen if we had a mechanical problem that Mickey couldn't fix. In the old days, of course, there were tow trucks to call and service stations to walk to; now there is only you and your ingenuity to keep you from disaster. Lacking the ingenuity, I couldn't do anything but worry.

"Where exactly are we going?" Mickey asked.

"The Church of the New Beginning," I said. "It's up by Walden Pond, I'm pretty sure."

"Weirdoes," Mickey said.

I smiled. Mickey was not the kind to be in sympathy with the church. "Ever hear of Walden Pond?" I asked him.

He shrugged. "Know how to get there."

"In the old days a guy went there to get away from civilization, and he wrote a famous book about it. I'll lend it to you, if you like."

"That's okay." Mickey isn't much of a reader. "Sounds stupid, actually. What's wrong with civilization? I mean, you'd have to be pretty strange to want to drive on a road like this instead of buzzin' along one of them old superhighways at seventy miles an hour."

I couldn't disagree. "I suppose it's easy to criticize civilization," I said, "if you know it's there when you need it. After a tough day of criticism, you can leave your hut in the woods and go back to your high-rise condo and have a hot bath and cook up a frozen dinner in the microwave and watch TV all night. It'd work out pretty well, I bet."

Mickey laughed. "Sure was different back then, Wally. You watch TV in England?"

"A little."

"It was really strange of you to come back, you know that?"

"Um."

"If I made it to England, you better believe you'd never see me in Boston again."

"Well, I hope you get the chance."

We were silent for a while, as Mickey dreamed of England and the old days and I worried about flat tires and broken axles. We turned off the highway by Walden Pond, traveled a bit further, then stopped when we ran into a boy in a homespun robe leading a flock of sheep across the road. I asked him the way to the church, and he pointed us in the right direction.

We ended up jouncing along a dirt path through sparse woods until we reached a large new wood-frame building on a rise overlooking acres of farmland. On top of the building was a cross, tilted to the right, with its arms bent slightly down, so that it looked a little like an arrow pointing off into the sky. "I guess this is the place," Mickey said. He didn't sound glad to be here.

People were staring at us. You didn't have to be a private eye to figure out why; you only had to look at their homemade robes and leather sandals and horse-drawn carts and the rough-hewn construction of the building. The Church of the New Beginning had turned its back on high-rise condos and frozen dinners for good.

"You stay here in the van," I said to Mickey. "This probably won't take long."

"Okay, Wally." He reached for the shotgun that Bobby had given us.

"There won't be any trouble," I said.

"You never can tell."

You never could. I opened the door and climbed down from the van. "Hi," I said to no one in particular. "Anyone know where I can find Flynn Dobler?"

A bearded man who looked like he'd stepped out of the Bible pointed to the building.

"Thanks a lot," I said, and I went inside.

The place looked solidly built, but strange. Where were the light fixtures and the electrical sockets and the radiators? No one built new buildings anymore. What was the point, with a population that could fit in one-tenth the available housing? The entrance hall in which I was standing was high-ceilinged and airy, and smelled of the woods. It made me nervous.

A woman appeared at the end of the hall and walked toward me. She was wearing a powder-blue robe and leather sandals, and she was gorgeous, with long, straight black hair and piercing blue eyes. She made me nervous too. "Can I help you?" she asked. Her accent sounded strange—not foreign, not local, as if she had learned how to speak English from a book.

I thought about using my ingratiating smile, but gave up the idea. Her gaze was too direct, her eyes too honest. "I'd like to talk to Flynn Dobler," I said.

"Why?" she asked. From her, the question didn't sound rude.

"I—I'm thinking of joining your church."

She nodded, although I doubt that she believed me. "Wait," she said, and walked away.

I waited. There were no chairs. No decorations on the walls—no paintings, no old posters. No books to read. It was as if these people had just moved in and hadn't gotten around to unpacking yet. After a couple of minutes the woman reappeared and gestured for me to follow her.

"My name's Walter Sands. What's yours?" I managed to say as she led me up a twisty flight of stairs to an open gallery.

She stopped and glanced back at me. "Marva," she said. Her tone suggested that this was information I was entitled to have, but that no further information would be forthcoming. I followed Marva along an open gallery. We passed through a small room with an uncomfortable-looking bed in it, then out onto a balcony overlooking the farmland.

On the balcony, a man was sitting at a simple wooden table. He too was wearing a robe and sandals. He was writing on a sheet of paper with a quill pen. "Brother Flynn," Marva said, "this is Walter Sands." And then she left us, shimmering away in a powder-blue haze.

Brother Flynn put the pen down, blotted the paper, and looked up at me.

I have a friend who thinks he is Jesus Christ. He wanders through Boston with long hair and a beard, wearing a robe and sandals and carrying a cross. He looks a bit like Flynn Dobler. Except that you take one look at my friend, and you know that something is not quite right inside him. Looking at Flynn Dobler, I wasn't at all sure. His dark eyes were alive with a vision, but I couldn't tell whether it was a vision of madness, or whether he was viewing a truth no one else had yet seen.

"Please sit," Dobler said. I obeyed. "Marva says you want to join our church." His eyes seemed to be sucking everything out of my brain.

"I'm thinking about it," I said.

"I don't believe you." That made me very nervous. "You came in a motor vehicle," Dobler pointed out. "The man who came with you has a gun."

"Well," I said, "you're not that easy to get to from the city. And I'm not real sure about joining. So when I had a chance to get a ride, I thought I better take it."

Dobler continued to gaze at me. I was pretty sure he didn't buy my story, but at least he didn't throw me out. "What do you know about the Church of the New Beginning, Walter Sands?" he asked.

"Well," I said, "you're trying to purify yourself, to get rid of everything from the past and make a fresh start. The old civilization got us into the mess we're in, so you want no part of it. You're trying to develop your own instead."

Dobler nodded. I felt as if I had gotten back on track. "There are many who curse the War," he said. "Many who waste their lives crying over what has been lost. But we see the War as a blessing, an opportunity that will not come again. Look." He gestured to the farmland that stretched out in front of him, freshly plowed and ready for planting. "Much of what you see used to be a golf course, where men would come and hit little balls while people starved and went homeless, while our air and water were being poisoned, while governments plotted to destroy each other. Now it is part of a community in which all care for each, in which we strive to find what is most important in life and to live in accordance with Nature, not with the artificial customs and duties that have been imposed upon us by our culture. We try to use nothing that comes from the old days. We do not read their books, we do not live in their buildings, we do not wear their clothes. Someday we will speak our own language. The new generation will have no memories to torment them, and nothing at all will remain of the past. We have lost our golf balls, Walter Sands, but we have gained our souls."

I had the feeling he had said this sort of thing many times before, but still it made a powerful impression. I could see why Henry Fisher thought Dobler was the most capable opponent of the Feds. I could also see why Henry didn't like him. Here was a guy who was ignoring the past with a vengeance—who was making a religion out of it. To Dobler, Henry's book was not just a mistake; it was heresy. "You make a lot of sense," I said. "And your community looks quite impressive."

"We have been here seven years. There were just a few when we began, but now we are many."

Seven years, I thought. Since just after the Feds moved in and made it possible for people to do what Flynn Dobler had done. "And the government leaves you alone?"

Dobler stood up. His robe flapped in a sudden breeze. I could imagine a cheering throng beneath the balcony, taking in his every word as if it came straight from God. If he had a military-style crew cut and wore clothes from the Salvage Market instead of a robe and sandals, would he have looked so impressive? "The government cannot defeat us," he said, "because we possess the truth, and the truth is the most powerful weapon in the universe."

I wasn't at all sure that this was true, but I let it pass. "Does the government try to defeat you?" I persisted.

He glanced down at me. Had the question seemed suspicious? "It makes an effort once in a while," he replied, "but we pay no attention. The government is part of the death throes of the old civilization. If the War had only been more destructive, we would not have to put up with those death throes now."

If the War had been more destructive, I thought, none of us would be around to put up with anything. "But the government worries me," I said. "There's this referendum, you know."

Dobler smiled. "Oh, you needn't worry about the referendum, Walter Sands."

Oh? "Why not? If the referendum succeeds, won't the government be stronger—more capable of forcing its will on you?"

Dobler continued to smile. Had he seen through me? Or was the idea just too absurd for him to contemplate seriously? "The government cannot succeed, Walter

Sands," he said. "It cannot rule people who refuse to be ruled. It will crumble like its monuments in Washington, and we will be here to build on the ruins."

That wasn't what I wanted to hear. "How can you be sure?" I said, pressing the issue.

"Walter Sands, you seem more interested in the government than you are in our Church," Dobler observed. "Why is that?"

"Maybe I'm less convinced than you are in the inevitability of your triumph," I said. "I don't want to join you and then have the Feds come and draft me into their army, or make my kids go to their schools. I think we have to do more than just ignore the government and hope that it goes away."

Dobler nodded, and then abruptly sat down. Had he tired of the game, or finally made up his mind about me? In any case, it was clear that I had lost. "I don't think you're the type to enjoy our simple life of manual labor."

"Perhaps you could convert me."

"I'm sure I could. But right now I prefer to have you go away."

"Why is that?"

"Because it is better if the conversion comes from within."

"How does that happen?"

Dobler shrugged. "Stop riding in motor vehicles. Stop having friends with shotguns. And stop worrying about the Feds. Concentrate on what really matters. Then come back, and perhaps we can talk some more." He picked up his pen and started writing again. I hesitated for a moment, then left the balcony and went back inside the building.

Marva was nowhere in sight. Time to do a little snooping, I decided. I started down the hallway, not sure what I should be looking for, and opened a door at random. I saw what appeared to be an empty classroom, with about a dozen small chairs and desks facing me. There were plants on the windowsill, and several child-like watercolors on the wall; a couple were dim likenesses of Flynn Dobler. I felt a pang of regret: my experiences of school had been few and unpleasant. On the wall next to me was a hand-lettered sign:

Brother Flynn Says: Tomorrow Is Another Day!

I guess you don't have to be original, if nobody is allowed to read books.

I shut the door and continued down the hall. I heard some noise behind another door, and I opened it slowly. I couldn't be sure, but this room looked like some sort of chapel. Several people in the familiar robes and leather sandals sat on benches or knelt on the floor, their faces in their hands. At the front of the room was the same bent cross I had seen on top of the building; this one was surrounded by flowers. A couple of the people were muttering to themselves—praying for amnesia, perhaps?

A hand pulled me back. "You can go anywhere else you like, Walter Sands, but you are not allowed in the meditation area unless you are one of us."

It was Marva. She quietly shut the door. She didn't look distressed or angry at my snooping, but it was clear I wasn't going to see any more of the meditation area. "Sorry," I said. "Just curious."

She nodded and led me back downstairs. I decided to find out if I could extract some information from her. I wasn't optimistic. "Been with the church long?" I asked.

"All my life."

That confused me. "But I thought Flynn Dobler said the church has only been going for seven years."

She stopped and looked at me. "Before I came here, I wasn't alive," she replied simply.

"Oh. Why does it mean that much to you?"

"You've seen the world out there," she said. "By comparison, this is paradise. Don't you agree?"

She had a point. "You may be right," I said. "Brother Flynn suggested I should purify myself before I can enter paradise."

Marva nodded. "You'll be back," she said, with the certainty of the true believer.

She stopped at the front door and watched as I walked over to the van, where Mickey was waiting nervously for me. "Can go?" he asked.

"We can go."

She was still watching as Mickey started the van and quickly headed down the dirt road toward the ruined highway.

CHAPTER 7

The sun was setting as we made our way slowly back down Route 2 toward Boston. It had been a long day.

Mickey and I discussed the Church of the New Beginning as he drove. The very idea of the place appalled him. "*Nothing* from the old days?" he asked in disbelief. "No motors or anything?"

For Mickey, a world without motors is a world without meaning. "I guess maybe if someone there invents a motor on his own, it'd be okay," I said. "If he could prove it wasn't something he remembered from before."

"Weirdoes," Mickey muttered.

I thought of Marva: *By comparison, this is paradise.* "They seem happy."

"Well they shouldn't be."

There didn't seem to be any response to that. I thought about Flynn Dobler. Henry was right: Dobler certainly seemed smart enough to pull off something against the president, and he certainly had the motivation. He hadn't taken the bait when I started bad-mouthing the government, but no one with any brains would have, I supposed. And if Marva was any indication, he had followers who would be more than willing to do his bidding.

Unfortunately, none of this added up to very much. Maybe he was a fiendish plotter against the government, or maybe he was just another one of the many sincere people around nowadays who carry their ideas a little too far. I had no real basis for deciding which was the truth.

And I also couldn't decide how I felt about his ideas. *And all our yesterdays have lighted fools/The way to dusty death*, I thought. But would Flynn Dobler's tomorrow and tomorrow and tomorrow be any better? I had no idea.

Mickey turned on the headlights. "Didn't get very far on your case, huh?" he remarked.

"Afraid not. But I've got time."

"I know you can do it, Wally. And look on the bright side. You've got Bobby all worried. You told him we'd be back by dark."

I smiled. "There's that," I said. But if driving in general made me nervous, driving after the dark outside the city terrified me. And it didn't make me any calmer when Mickey pulled the van over to the side of the road and stopped. "What's the problem?" I asked.

"Oh, I dunno. Radiator hose, maybe."

"Can you fix it?"

"Have to take a look."

Mickey didn't sound worried, but his response wasn't particularly encouraging, either. He got out of the van and went around to the back, where he rummaged for tools and parts. I Picked up the shotgun and stared out into the darkness. Shortly before I went to England, Mickey and Bobby and I had been ambushed by a couple of O'Malley's men on another highway.

It had not been a pleasant experience. I doubted that anything so well planned would happen out here, but there were enough crazies lurking in the woods and the abandoned suburbs to make me long to be anywhere else— even Charlestown.

Mickey came around to the front of the van and started tinkering under the hood. His flashlight cast a feeble gleam in the darkness. "How's it going?" I called out to him.

"Okay, I guess," he said.

This did not greatly encourage me. Wild dogs started howling somewhere nearby. And then a car approached, chugging mufflerless along the road. It slowed as it pulled alongside us, and I tensed. Then it speeded up and roared past, leaving us to our fate. That was okay with me. I had a feeling I would have done the same thing, if I had been in the car. Good Samaritans can too easily end up dead Samaritans.

"Going any better?" I asked Mickey.

"Maybe."

He tinkered for a few more minutes, then closed the hood and got back into the van. "Fixed?" I asked, daring to hope.

"Well, let's give it a try." Mickey started the van, and we headed slowly forward. After a couple of minutes he said, "I guess we'll make it," and I allowed myself to exhale. We crept back to the city without incident.

Mickey dropped me off in Louisburg Square. "Thanks, Mickey," I said. "I owe you one."

"Happy to help. Those people gave me the creeps, though."

"Try not to think about them. And tell Bobby I'll pay him for the use of the van."

Mickey merely grinned. I got out, and Mickey drove off to South Boston.

It felt good to be back in the city, on my home turf. The square was deserted and dark, except for the flickering yellow beams of lamps in a few windows; but the square was not the wilds of Concord, and my town house and my little family were just a few steps away. I turned to take those steps, and perhaps I relaxed a little too soon—you should never relax in this world—or perhaps it was a little too dark.

Whatever the reason, I didn't see the two men until it was too late.

They came out of the shadows by the front steps. They wore masks. They were silent and very efficient. One of them grabbed me from behind, clamped a gloved hand over my mouth, and twisted my right arm behind my back. The other set to work on me. I tried fending off his blows with my free arm and even kicking out at him, but the first guy just increased the pressure on my arm, and pretty soon it seemed easier just to take my punishment.

I don't know how long the punishment lasted—a few seconds, a few years. But when it was over, the square was still dark and silent, and the men were gone, and the steps to my house seemed like a mountain I would never be able to climb.

I tried to call for help, but all that came out was a kind of strangled whimper. I thought about staying where I was; perhaps I would get lucky and die soon. But finally I decided I would probably linger in agony for hours, so I started up the mountain. In a way, this was even harder than the attack, because the pain was self-inflicted: my ribs didn't have to feel quite this bad; a little rest would do my shoulder a world of good. But somehow I made it to the top.

And then what? Reaching the knob was out of the question; the door would have been locked, anyway. I knocked, but my knuckles barely had the strength to scrape the wood. So I lay on the cold stone and started to think about whimpering in earnest.

And then I heard someone whistling "Good Day Sunshine."

It could only have been Stretch, home from another sewer meeting.

"retch," I managed to mumble.

I heard light footsteps, and then saw Stretch's tiny form hovering like an angel of mercy above me. "Holy Jesus," he gasped. Stretch never swears. And that swear was the last thing I heard for quite a while.

I opened an eye and saw Gwen staring down at me. "wen," I said.

"Soon," she replied. "You'll be better soon. Nothing's broken."

That wasn't what I meant. I tried to shake my head, but that didn't turn out to be such a good idea. Gwen leaned over and kissed my cheek, and that was a very good idea indeed. It didn't matter what I had meant. I closed my eye.

"Is he conscious?" I could hear Stretch whisper.

"Yes."

"Should we show him?"

"Not now, Stretch."

I reluctantly opened the eye again. "Wha'?" I asked.

Stretch came into view. "It's just, well, this paper was tacked to the door, Walter."

He held up something white in front of my face. I opened my other eye and tried to focus. Finally the piece of paper came clear, along with the message typed on it.

Stop meddling, or next time you die.

Boston is ours.

THE FEDS MUST GO!

The Second American Revolution

I closed my eyes once more. I was not happy.

"I guess you made too much progress on your case, Walter," Stretch said.

Funny, I hadn't noticed much progress myself. I tried to think, but my brain wasn't interested. I felt myself drifting away—from the pain and from the thinking. I would have to face it all soon enough, but not now, not now.

When I awoke again, Gwen was still there, and my brain seemed to have returned as well. I was lying on the sofa in the downstairs parlor. Sunshine streamed in through the bay window. I tried to move. I failed.

"Take it easy, Walter."

"There were two of them," I explained, feeling a need. At least I was talking better. "I didn't have a prayer."

"Don't think about it. You're safe now."

Was I? I felt safe enough in daylight, with Gwen by my side. But my bruises were happy to tell me the kind of trouble I was in. Whoever had beaten me up knew where I lived; if they had come here once, they could come here again. Gwen held some juice up to my lips, and I managed to swallow a little. "Maybe I'm not cut out for this kind of work," I said.

"No one's cut out to be beaten up."

"I should've known I was in danger." But how? Between sips of juice I told Gwen what had happened. "So who could have done it?" I asked her. "For that matter, who knew I was on the case? Henry Fisher, of course, but he isn't going to hurt me. And Flynn Dobler suspects I'm not really looking to be a convert, but how could he know where I lived—and how could he get his people down from Concord before Mickey and I got here in the van, if he doesn't believe in automobiles?"

"Well, he could've read my article about you," Gwen suggested. "And if he really is behind TSAR, he's obviously willing to bend his religious beliefs to fight the government."

I thought about that. And I thought about Mickey's problem with the radiator hose, and the car that had passed us in the night. Someone could've gotten from Concord to Boston ahead of us. What was a clue, I wondered, and what was just life happening to you?

"Or," Gwen went on, "if your theory is right about someone in the government being involved, it might be easy enough for whoever it is to find out you'd been put on the case, and arrange to give you a warning."

I closed my eyes and half-sighed. Sighing hurt. Gwen was just trying to help. But instead she was just depressing me. "What do you think I should do?" I asked.

"Rest."

"Will you—"

"Don't worry. I'm not going anywhere."

"Thanks," I said. I held her hand, and I tried not to worry.

Gradually I improved. By the end of the day I was able to sit up. By the end of the evening I was able to stagger upstairs to bed. By the next morning I was able to shoo Gwen and Stretch off to work and face the day alone. There was nothing to be afraid of, after all. TSAR had no reason to beat me up again, because I had stopped meddling.

Hadn't I?

I was not in a particularly good position, I realized. Bolton would not be happy if he found out I was sitting at home all day staring out my bay window instead of carrying on the investigation. In fact, I should already have reported the incident to him. I didn't relish the thought of becoming Private Sands again.

On the other hand, I didn't want to die.

If I went back to work, there were things I could look into, I supposed. And a private eye has his professional ethics. I had taken Bolton's ten dollars. I owed him more than one day's work (no matter how difficult the work had been). Still, I couldn't see putting my life on the line for the Feds. I could always refund them the eight dollars I hadn't earned.

This was not an easy decision.

At supper that night Gwen helped me make up my mind. "Two masked men beat up a soldier early this morning," she told Stretch and me. "He was off-duty, going back to the compound after sneaking a visit to his local girlfriend. They left a note pinned to his jacket. It had the usual message: Boston is ours. The Feds must go."

"Those—those—" Stretch couldn't find the words to express his anger.

"Is the *Globe* running a story about it?" I asked Gwen.

"Front page," she replied.

"Um, it doesn't mention what happened to me, does it?"

She shook her head. "Of course not, Walter."

I looked down at my scrambled eggs. "I think," I said, "that I'm going to take a vacation from being a private eye."

Gwen reached out and covered my hand with hers. "Are you sure?" she asked.

"No," I said.

"But Walter, someone's got to stop these people," Stretch said. "We're talking about America here. We're talking about the president."

"All she has to do is stay home in Atlanta," I pointed out.

"But then what happens to the referendum?"

"That's her problem, not mine."

Stretch looked disappointed in me. "It's everyone's problem, Walter."

We let it drop. You don't argue with Stretch about something like that. Gwen and I lay in bed together later, staring into the darkness and thinking. "If I were working for anyone but the Feds," I said, "I wouldn't be doing this."

"Bolton will come and get you, you know."

"I know." Damn case. "Are you ever assigned stories you just don't want to write?"

"All the time. No one threatens my life, though."

There was that difference. But having your life threatened came with the career I had chosen. If I didn't like it, I had made the wrong choice. We were silent for a while.

"How are your bruises?" Gwen asked.

"Getting better, I guess."

"Do you think they could stand some kissing?"

I smiled. "I think kissing would do them a world of good."

Gwen rustled in the darkness, and suddenly she was naked. I lay back and let Gwen take care of what ailed me. She gently kissed the bruises on my face and chest, then moved down and started licking some parts of me that hadn't been bruised. I groaned with pleasure. Her treatment was doing wonders for me. Pretty soon I pulled her over onto her back and did some licking of my own, until we were both so wet and slippery that the next step in the treatment seemed to come on its own. Her legs were wrapped around me, and I was thrusting into her, and for a few moments there were no problems, there were no threats, just Gwen and me—one single point of fire in a dark, cold world.

The next day I stayed at home again and waited for the summons that would end my brief vacation. I didn't have to wait long. That afternoon an ancient jeep pulled up outside, and my buddies Danny Smith and Gus Ziegler got out. They climbed the front steps and pounded on the front door.

I heaved myself off the sofa and went to let them in.

"We've been looking for you, Mr. Sands," Danny said. "You weren't at your office."

"Lucky thing you knew where I lived, then. Call me Walter, by the way."

"W-w-what happened to your face?" Gus asked from behind Smith.

"You know the soldier that got beaten up?"

Both men nodded, and their faces darkened with anger.

"Same thing happened to me."

Sympathy immediately replaced the anger. "That's terrible, Walter," Danny said.

"We've gotta c-c-catch those guys," Gus added.

"Yeah, I guess we do."

"Governor Bolton told us to come and—" Smith started to say.

"Right," I interrupted. "Hold on a sec." I got the eight dollars and the sheet of paper with TSAR's threat on it. "Okay," I said. And I followed the two soldiers out of my nice safe house back into the real world.

CHAPTER 8

There was lots of activity in Government Center. Crews were out scrubbing everything in sight, replacing bricks in the wide plaza, putting up the stage, stringing red, white, and blue bunting. The VOTE YES posters were suddenly outnumbered by "See Your President Speak Thursday" posters. Thursday was the day after tomorrow. "What's her security going to be like?" I asked.

Danny shook his head. "She wants it low-key, they tell me. Doesn't want people to get riled up."

"The g-governor said he might assign me and Danny to her," Gus mentioned as he drove the Jeep. "Says she n-needs all the help she can get."

"Well, if she gets you two guys, she'll be fine."

Gus and Danny smiled. As before, they stopped in front of the JFK Federal Building and brought me up to Bolton's office, where they left me with more smiles and best wishes for my recovery. My relationship with them was progressing.

My relationship with Lisa, the governor's attractive blond secretary, was going nowhere, however. She glared at me as I approached her desk. "Sands," I said, smiling. "Walter Sands. The governor wants to see me."

She murmured something into her phone, then hung up. "Have a seat," she ordered.

I kept smiling. "You going to see the president speak Thursday?"

She ignored me, so I took the hint and sat down. I think I understood her. Like Bolton, she was probably a local who had cast her lot with the Feds. Undoubtedly she had taken some abuse for that, and this had made her suspicious and resentful of people like me. She imagined I was judging her, despising her because she had sold out for chocolate bars and lipstick and aspirin. I was doing nothing of the sort, of course. I was simply admiring what the chocolate bars had done for her figure.

"You can go in now," she informed me after a brief wait.

"Thanks, Lisa," I said.

She ignored me. I went into Bolton's office.

Bolton looked up. General Cowens half-turned in his chair to face me. "I've been waiting for a report," Bolton said. As I sat down, he noticed my face. "What happened to you?" he asked.

"I got warned." I showed them the message from TSAR and described the beating I had received.

"This is outrageous," Bolton said. And then he seemed to focus his anger on me. "How long ago was this?"

I shrugged. "A couple of days."

"Why didn't you tell us about it right away?"

"I was recovering."

"And meanwhile precious time has been lost."

"And one of my soldiers has been attacked," Cowens pointed out. This was clearly a matter of much more consequence than my trivial injuries.

"I don't see how I could have prevented that," I said.

"Perhaps if you hadn't told a reporter about this group in the first place, they wouldn't have felt so powerful and important."

"That's absurd," I said. "No one said I wasn't supposed to talk about TSAR. And you're much more likely to find out about them if you don't keep their existence secret."

"If that's your theory," Cowens said, "it hasn't proved to be true. We've learned nothing about TSAR as a result of that article."

I stood up and took out the eight dollars. "I guess my performance has not been satisfactory," I said, with an air of injured innocence. "In that case I have no choice but to refund your—"

"Sit down," Bolton thundered.

I reluctantly did as I was told.

"Now tell us everything that happened to you. Let's see if we can get anywhere in figuring this out."

I summarized for them what I thought was relevant about my day on the case.

"So there's a possibility that the Church of the New Beginning is behind this," Bolton said.

"It's conceivable," I replied. "I didn't really think so at the time I talked to Flynn Dobler, but—"

"But maybe you asked the wrong questions," Cowens said. "I'll have my people look into Dobler."

"I don't want any indiscriminate roundups of suspects, Bob," Bolton warned. "Just because they dress funny and don't like us doesn't mean we can arrest them. That's just the kind of publicity the president doesn't want."

"My duty is to keep her alive, not to worry about publicity," Cowens muttered.

"Your duty is to obey lawfully appointed civilian authorities," Bolton responded.

There was a brief silence. The rebuke hung in the air like a thundercloud. I decided to change the subject. "I wonder if any progress has been made on the government angle," I said.

Both men looked at me. "What government angle?" Cowens demanded.

"The file on TSAR. Did you find out who started it?"

Cowens gave me his usual frigid stare. "That has not yet been determined."

"Well, it could be important," I said. "When I was in your records department the other day, I noticed that the

TSAR file wasn't dog-eared and faded like all the others. That suggests to me that it was put in there very recently."

"Yes? So what?"

"If no one 'fesses up to starting the file, that means we're not talking about a case of faulty memory. Someone may be lying because he started the file to divert attention from the real conspirators—but he just didn't do a very good job of it. And that would explain why I got beaten up: he saw me here and figured out what I was up to, and he decided he had to make his point again."

"But who are these 'real' conspirators?" Bolton asked. "Why bother with this charade?"

"Well, it's my understanding that a lot of people in the government are opposed to the referendum. If these threats get the president to cancel it and they can blame the opposition, I guess that would make them very happy."

Bolton shook his head. "I don't buy it. They beat up one of our soldiers. No one in the government would do that." He didn't sound too sure of himself, though.

"The stakes are pretty high," I pointed out.

"I wonder why you're so insistent on suggesting that someone in the government is to blame," Cowens said.

"I'm not insisting on anything. You can believe me if you want. I don't care." This was as bad as I had expected.

"Well, Bob, I think you should continue to look into who started that file on TSAR," Bolton said. "And you, Sands, should assist in the president's protection when she arrives tomorrow."

"Now wait a minute, Frank," Cowens said. "I don't want this person underfoot. It's going to be hard enough as it stands protecting her, with all the limitations she's put on us."

"He won't be underfoot if you utilize him properly," Bolton responded. "She's put limits on you. All right, I understand that. So why not take advantage of what's available to you? Sands here knows the locals. He might recognize one of the men who beat him up, or some radical who might be associated with TSAR. He could be invaluable to us. And because he's from around here, the president won't mind our using him. She'll welcome it, in fact. A fine example of federal-local cooperation. That's what the future is all about."

Cowens looked unconvinced. In fact, he looked very unhappy. I hoped he would put up more of a battle. But he didn't. "All right," he said, a soldier grudgingly obeying orders.

"Fine. You two can take care of the details, then. Thanks for coming in, Sands." Bolton picked up some papers and pretended to be busy. He was good at that. Cowens and I were dismissed.

We walked out of his office. My body was still sore; I noticed that I wasn't walking much better than the old general. "I don't want to work for you any more than you want me working for you," I said.

His watery blue eyes gazed at me with distaste. "But you are working for me nevertheless," he said. "And you'll obey orders. Report to Major Fenneman at 0:10:100. And don't make any mistakes. Understood?"

I stared back at him. "Uh-huh," I said.

The elevator came, and we didn't say anything more to each other.

At home, no one seemed surprised that I was back on the case. Stretch was excited that I was still involved in the great mission of protecting the president.

After supper, I studied a photograph of President Kramer in the newspaper. I realized that I hadn't really looked at her before. For all that she was supposed to represent the new era, she certainly looked like someone from the old days, with her makeup and jewelry and her professional hairdo. "She's kind of attractive," I said.

That was probably not a smart thing to say, I understood immediately. "She's ancient," Gwen responded.

"She's not even forty," Stretch said defensively.

"That's ancient."

"Not if you have good medical care."

"Why does she get good medical care and the rest of us get nothing?"

"She's the president. She's important."

"Oh, that's right. I forgot."

Stretch looked uncertain. He knew that Gwen was often critical of the government, but he hadn't encountered quite this attitude before. He decided to change the subject. "Do you think you'll meet her?" he asked me.

"Absolutely not," I said, having smartened up. "No chance whatsoever."

"Oh, I bet you will. She's eager to meet locals."

"Not me, though. I'm nobody. Cowens isn't going to let me anywhere near the president."

"You can never tell," Stretch said. "President Kramer doesn't take orders from Cowens, or anybody. She's her own woman. She's not married, you know."

Swell. "Well, if I meet her, all I'll do is tell her she should have an interview with Gwen."

"I think that would be a very good idea," Gwen agreed.

Stretch seemed puzzled by the whole conversation, but luckily he had a meeting to go to, so he didn't have to continue it. Gwen and I remained behind. She played the piano while I listened and worried.

I have mentioned one problem I have had with my first case: that it was bogus, that without the help of my friends it would scarcely have existed. Here is another problem: I was unfaithful to Gwen in the course of it. This seemed like a good idea at the time. I was a private eye, after all, and that was what private eyes did. Besides, I was in a foreign land, and I was pretty sure I was never going to return to Gwen and the rest of my friends in Boston.

But here I was, back in Boston, and I had to face the consequences of my actions. I had never exactly admitted my indiscretion—but Gwen had never exactly asked me flat-out, so I had never exactly lied. Gwen knew, though. I was certain of that.

I would have hoped she'd take such things in stride, knowing me, knowing my dreams. But that, perhaps, was just another one of my dreams: the private eye's girlfriend who understands all, who forgives all. Perhaps Gwen did forgive all, but that didn't seem to keep her from being jealous when she encountered another woman in another case. Even if that woman was the president of the United States. It seemed a little silly to me, but I was not the one to judge her.

"I don't want any part of this," I said as we went upstairs together.

"I don't want any part of living after a nuclear war," she responded. "But that doesn't change reality."

"What do you want me to do?" I asked her.

"I want you to hold me," she said. "I want you to make the world disappear."

"Will you take one out of two?"

She stopped and gazed at me as we entered our bedroom. "I'll take whatever you give me, Walter."

We got into bed then, and I held her until she fell asleep. Then I wandered upstairs to read and ponder and await the dawn.

CHAPTER 9

In the morning I walked back to Government Center. The sky was overcast after a week of sunshine. The red white and blue bunting looked a little bedraggled, the "See Your President Speak Thursday" posters looked a little pathetic. Who would bother obeying such a command in such lousy weather?

A guard at the entrance to the JFK Federal Building was dubious about my appointment with Major Fenneman, but a phone call confirmed how important I was. I was escorted to some sort of command center, where I sat and waited while soldiers rushed in and out and phones rang and people shouted orders at one another. It was almost noon before I was finally summoned.

I entered a small, cramped, windowless office dominated by a beefy soldier with short gray hair and a Cowens-like cold stare. He looked me over for a moment before he spoke. I had a feeling that, like his boss, he didn't approve of what he saw. "You're the guy the governor stuck us with, right?" he asked.

"Uh-huh." I knew by now that this was not an officer's favorite response, but I couldn't seem to help myself.

His small eyes seemed to get even smaller. "This is no time for games," he warned me. It wasn't exactly clear to me what he was referring to.

"Look," I said. "I've been hired to help you guys. Just tell me how you want me to help."

"I want you to stay out of the way," Fenneman said. He unlocked a drawer, took out a yellow clip-on badge, and tossed it to me. "Wear this," he said. "Hitch a ride to Logan with one of the escort cars. They're leaving about now. Make sure Governor Bolton sees you. That's all you do. Clear?"

"What if I notice something suspicious? Who do I talk to?"

"Talk to one of your reporter friends. Just don't bother my people while they're trying to do their job."

Cowens had obviously told Fenneman I had leaked the story about TSAR to the *Globe*. And that didn't endear me to him. I put on the badge and stood up. "I'll do my best," I promised the major.

Fenneman ignored me.

I walked back to the command center and found out from a helpful secretary where the escort cars were. I followed his directions to the garage, where my yellow badge got me a seat in a comfortable old full-size Chevrolet next to a couple of security people, who decided after a brief exchange that I was not worth talking to. We left the garage before very long, and I stared out the windows at the drizzly cityscape as the driver made his way to the airport.

Logan Airport is another one of those places that hit you over the head with the contrast between the old days and the new. Where once, I have heard, there were so many flights that people worried about mid-air collisions and all-day traffic jams and no parking spaces, now there were empty runways and deserted terminals and crumbling garages, with just the occasional flight to keep the place's pulse beating. For many people, that feeble pulse was the only symbol of hope they could find. There was a world beyond this dismal one they inhabited, and it was possible—just possible—to reach it.

I was one of the lucky ones who had reached it. And yet I had come back. So the airport for me was not a symbol of hope but of confusion. The confusion between dreams and reality, perhaps—between what you think you want and what you find out really matters. There was joy here, and there was regret, and it was impossible to determine which was stronger.

The airport looked different from the way I remembered it. There had been no brass bands for me, no floral arrangements and American flags. No soldiers, no dignitaries, no reporters. Gwen hadn't been waiting for me in the terminal, wearing a red badge and a green raincoat and looking a little bored. I walked up to her. "My badge is better than your badge," I said.

She smiled. "It won't matter what kind of badge you have if the weather gets any worse. They won't try to land in a storm."

"Wouldn't that be nice?"

"But they'd just get here tomorrow," she said.

"Maybe it'll keep raining until after the referendum."

"And maybe the world will disappear," she murmured. She wandered off to interview the governor finally, and I stood by myself, nose pressed against the glass, looking out at the runway.

The plane arrived an hour and a half late, by which time the band was tired and the dignitaries were worried, and the soldiers and reporters were very bored. There were no suspicious characters that I could see, except maybe for me; the president would be safe here.

Bolton and Cowens and a few others went out with their umbrellas to greet her. A stairway was rolled up to the plane. The door opened and a couple of aides hurried down, and then President Kramer came into view, breathing the fresh wet air of Boston for the first time.

She waved and descended. She smiled and shook hands. She chatted briefly with Cowens and Bolton, and then everyone headed inside the terminal. The band started to play. The soldiers stood at attention. The reporters scribbled.

Inside, the president shook some more hands, and I got my first close-up look at her. If anything, her photographs in the *Globe* hadn't done her justice. Her hair was a richer shade of auburn than I had ever seen before—dyed, I supposed, but that didn't seem to matter. She wore a lot of makeup as well, but it accentuated her assets rather than hid any deficiencies. She had deep brown eyes and high cheekbones and a wide mouth that seemed to break easily into a toothy smile. She was tall—taller than Bolton, who stuck close by her side—and she wore gold bracelets that clanked on her arm as she shook hands. Everything about her seemed a bit much, a bit larger than life—at least, a bit larger than the life I was used to. I was impressed.

When the band stopped playing, Bolton stood on a platform and made a brief welcoming speech. Perhaps a little too brief? He said all the right things, but still managed to convey a lack of enthusiasm. Everyone applauded, at any rate, and then President Kramer replaced him on the platform.

"Thank you for that gracious introduction, Governor Bolton," she began. "The weather may not be ideal, but it hasn't dampened my excitement at coming here. It really is wonderful to finally be in Boston—a city that has done so much to help build and sustain our great nation. All of you should be very proud to be part of Boston and New England, with their great traditions—just as I hope you are proud to be part of America. America has suffered much, but at long last it is starting to recover. I am here to ask for your help in speeding that recovery. I am here to see if we can't join together and overcome the tragedies that have befallen all of us.

"The referendum we have put before you asks a very simple question, but your answer to it is vitally important to the future of our nation. If we continue to be a house divided, if we continue to bicker about petty issues, the tragedies we have suffered will diminish the lives of our children and our children's children. But if we can come together, future generations may look back at this moment as the turning point—when despair turned to hope, when anger turned to understanding, when hatred turned to love. While I'm here, I intend to do my best to help make this such a turning point. Thank you very much."

Loud applause, and then shouted questions from reporters. But President Kramer wasn't answering questions just yet. Everything was behind schedule, Bolton explained; the president had to get downtown; the press would have its chance later. The band played another number, and we all headed back to our cars.

The president's words replayed themselves in my mind as the old Chevy joined the motorcade back to Government Center. Her voice had been surprisingly soft, so that you had to strain to hear what she had to say. But the effect was that her words insinuated themselves into your consciousness much more completely than those of an orator like Bolton. She hadn't said anything I hadn't already heard, and upon reflection I thought her remarks were a bit too pat, too balanced, too speech-like; but still the words were there in my mind, and I had been affected in spite of myself.

I wondered what Gwen thought.

The president rode ahead of us in the largest, shiniest car I had ever seen. Not many people were lining the streets to see it, however. I wondered how many would show up for the speech tomorrow. Of course the Feds would dragoon whomever they could, so that at least the space would be filled up; but what mattered was whether people would show up on their own, out of curiosity or loyalty or hope or nostalgia. Would they ride their horses in from the farms? Would they make the trek down from New Hampshire and up from Connecticut? Kramer couldn't get them to support her unless she could first get them to listen.

When we reached Government Center, I thought about going home. Bolton had seen me at the airport; that was all Fenneman had required of me. But I decided instead to hang around a while longer. I was intrigued.

The present's first stop was City Hall, across the plaza from the JFK Building. She was going to preach to the converted, at an indoor rally for Federal employees. My yellow badge got me backstage, into a crowded meeting room where everyone seemed to be talking at the same time as they tried to thrash out a revised schedule. President Kramer seemed unconcerned. She chatted with everyone and smiled her wide smile and looked as if she was enjoying this chaos. I noticed a couple of large men near her whom I took to be bodyguards or Secret Service men or whatever such people were called nowadays. Their eyes swept the room and occasionally gazed at me. I stayed in a corner and tried to be invisible.

I failed. Eventually President Kramer made her way over to me, her bracelets jangling. "Hello," she said. "I'm Ann Kramer. You're Walter Sands, aren't you?"

I shook her hand. It was cool and soft: the hand of a ruler , not a worker. I inhaled her perfume. I had never smelled anything so rich in my life. Her eyes gazed at me as if no one was more important in this world. Her personality seemed to envelop me, like a fog. "Um, that's right," I replied. But how in the world had she known?

She smiled, noticing my puzzlement. "General Cowens told me on the way in from the airport that a local fellow had been hired to help protect me. I approve, although you certainly don't look like a security person." She gestured at the two hulking guys behind her, who appeared to have been born for their roles.

"That's why I'm such a good security person," I said.

"There have been threats, haven't there?"

I nodded.

"Do you think there's anything behind them?"

I saw no reason to hide the truth from her. "Some masked men beat me up while I was investigating the threats, so yes, I think you've got something to worry about."

President Kramer looked chagrined. "Oh, I'm so sorry. General Cowens didn't mention that. Was it awful?"

I shrugged. "Part of the job," I said.

"Tough guy. Well, I certainly appreciate what you're doing for us. You're a supporter of the government, I take it?"

Once again, no reason to lie. "I'm apolitical," I said.

"But how are you going to vote on the referendum?"

"I don't know. I'm not even sure I'll vote."

"It sounds like you're one of the people I'm here to convert."

"I guess I am."

"Do you think I'll be able to do it, Mr. Sands?"

I considered. "I think you can probably do anything you set your mind to."

She gave me a brilliant smile. "As long as I have people like you to keep me safe, right? Thank you for all you've done, Mr. Sands." She jangled away; her perfume lingered. My narrowed eyes scanned the room, and I saw General Cowens staring at me. I smiled back. His stare hardened for a moment, and then he looked away.

So now the president of the United States knew me. I wasn't so sure this was a good thing. Eventually the schedule got straightened out, and President Kramer went off to talk to the Federal employees, who had been waiting for a couple of hours. Once again, I tagged along.

The Federal employees—including Stretch—were delighted to see her. They would have cheered her even if she had simply read from an ancient phone book. But she gave another speech like the one she gave at the airport, only longer this time, and tailored to her audience. The microphone she used amplified her soft voice but did not destroy its insinuating, seductive quality. You government workers are the guardians of the flame, she told them. It is because of you that we have come as far as we have. It is because of you that the forces of anarchy and despair have been held at bay. But our work is only beginning. The flame must burn brighter, until it can light up our entire nation once again, and then the world....

And so forth. Pretty good stuff, and they loved it. They stood and cheered at the end, and then President Kramer shook more hands. I hung around while the press conference was being set up. Stretch noticed me and walked over. He was glowing with excitement. "Wasn't she wonderful?" he said.

"She gives a good speech."

"I bet even Gwen was impressed."

I glanced at Gwen, who was scribbling in her notebook while the president talked to a knot of supporters. "Gwen isn't easy to impress," I pointed out.

"Still, that kind of eloquence has to move you."

I saw Governor Bolton approaching us. "Let's talk about it at home, Stretch," I said.

Stretch nodded his understanding. "Okay, Walter." And he went away, still glowing.

Bolton was not glowing. He looked harried; his scar throbbed. "See anything?" he asked.

I shook my head. "Not likely something would happen in here, is it?"

"How would I know?" he snapped. "It's not likely someone would tack a threat to my door, but someone did."

No, the governor was not enjoying himself. "What's up after the press conference? Do you want me to stick around?"

Bolton considered. "There's a formal dinner, but I suppose you don't need to attend. The danger's at the speech tomorrow. Just make sure you're there. And don't bring a weapon. She doesn't want any weapons."

"Cowens isn't paying any attention to me," I pointed out.

"That doesn't mean you can slack off," Bolton said. "I hired you, and you'd better do the job." He stalked off before I had a chance to reply.

I wasn't enjoying myself very much either, I thought.

Then I thought some more, and I decided that maybe I was. It was interesting to watch the president in action. And as long as nobody tried to beat me up or throw me in the army, there were worse ways of spending the day. I moved to the front of the auditorium to listen to the press conference.

About thirty news people, including Gwen, were crowded into the first couple of rows of the auditorium. I was a little surprised that there were so many—but then, I didn't pay much attention to the news. There were a few low-power radio stations on the air, I knew, and a lot of smallish local newspapers. All apparently had reporters here.

Their questions ranged from the fatuous to the obnoxious. Kramer answered each of them with charm and wit. Gwen's questions, of course, were the best. "Madam President," she said, "the post-War Federal government has adopted a new constitution, abolished political parties, restricted the right to vote, imposed controls on internal travel, and essentially eliminated state government. And yet you are asking people to vote yes on the referendum, among other reasons, because your government is the legitimate successor to the one that was destroyed during the War. How can you expect people to believe this?"

President Kramer smiled. "I don't want to give a history lesson, but let me just say that I was there, in Atlanta after the War. What took place in Atlanta wasn't easy, and what came out of the deliberations wasn't perfect, but it was a miracle that anything was accomplished at all. You may not consider that the soldiers and civil servants and congressmen who met there fairly represented the United States of America, but who do you suggest would have been better? The constitution they wrote was different from the old one, but it had to be. These have been extraordinary times, and extraordinary measures have been required.

"Now the times are changing, and the government must change with them. That's why we're having the referendum. That's why I'm here today. In my speech tomorrow I hope to outline some of the ways in which the government is going to change—and that's why everyone should come and listen."

"There has been at least one threat of violence against you if you came here," Gwen said. "How do you respond to such threats, and do you think that they represent deep-seated resistance to the government?"

"We cannot allow such threats to interfere with our goals. To do so would be to give in to the basest elements in our society. And no, I don't think the threats are at all representative of the feelings of the people of New England. Of course many people have grievances against the government—and I'm sure some of these grievances are legitimate. But I don't think any responsible person advocates or condones violence against me personally or against the government. If anyone is considering such violence, let me warn him now that I am extremely well-protected."

President Kramer smiled at her two bodyguards. And then she smiled at me.

Gwen had no further questions.

The press conference ended soon afterward. I went over to Gwen, but she had no time. "Stories to write," she said. "Deadlines to meet. I'll talk to you later."

"Um, about the way she smiled at me—"

"Oh, Walter, don't be silly. I've got to run." She kissed me on the cheek and left with the other reporters. The president had already disappeared. I was alone in the auditorium with nothing to do. So I took off my badge and went home.

Stretch wanted to rehash every microsecond of the president's visit, so I did my best to satisfy his curiosity. He was particularly impressed that I had actually had a conversation with her. "She just seems so warm and outgoing, doesn't she?"

I couldn't disagree. "It won't make any difference, though," I pointed out, "if no one's going to listen."

"They'll listen," Stretch said earnestly. "They have to listen."

It was long after dark when Gwen got home from the newspaper. She looked tired.

"Wasn't the president wonderful, Gwen?" Stretch said.

Gwen looked down at him. "I need to eat before we get into this."

We waited expectantly while she ate. It seemed important to both of us to find out what she thought about President Kramer. When she had finished her stew, we all adjourned to the parlor, and Gwen delivered her opinion. "She's a very slick politician," Gwen said.

Stretch looked distressed. "You don't think she really means what she says? You think this is an act?"

Gwen shook her head. "No, it's not an act, exactly. But it isn't real either. Maybe we don't see enough politicians nowadays to recognize this type of person very easily, but I think I understand her. Everything she does is calculated to help achieve her goals; but at the same time she's sincere in everything she does, because she's done these things for so long that they've taken on a life of their own. I think she'd be legitimately upset if someone accused her of being less than completely honest when she talks about the wonderful, hard-working, generous people of New England. But I bet in some sense she also couldn't care less about us.

"I think she probably also has the same kind of attitude toward her goals," Gwen went on. "She can't tell the difference between what's good for the country and what's good for her, because she's so convinced of how indispensable she is to her cause."

Stretch, of course, jumped to President Kramer's defense. I wasn't interested in what he had to say, however. I was too busy thinking about Gwen's little speech. I didn't necessarily disagree with it; I too had sensed that odd mixture of artificiality and sincerity in the president. But it worried me that Gwen, normally so laconic, had so much to say about Kramer. Maybe it was just a reporter's interest in an important public figure. Or maybe it was a woman's irrational fascination with a potential rival. And I didn't feel like having to deal with that.

One more day, I thought. The president would be gone, and the case would be over. Just let me make it through one more day.

"What did you think of the president, Walter?" Gwen asked me.

I had learned my lesson. "Oh, I'm with you a hundred percent, Gwen. She's slick. Shifty. Paranoid."

"But is she as attractive in person as she is in her photographs?"

"Absolutely not. The *Globe* must have retouched those photos to make her look younger. The poor woman's almost in her grave."

Gwen smiled. "But you seem to have made an impression on *her.*"

"That was just more of her slickness. She found out I was undecided about the referendum. Every vote counts."

"Did she persuade you?"

"Not at all. I can see right through someone like that." Stretch started to remonstrate with me, but he didn't get very far before we all heard the noise. He fell silent, and the three of us sat tensely, listening.

A car had pulled up outside our house. We heard the car doors slam, then footsteps. Gwen clutched my hand. Had TSAR returned to punish me for ignoring its threat? There was a pounding on our door.

Stretch looked at me. "Don't answer," he whispered. But what was the point? We couldn't keep them out if they were determined to get in. I extricated my hand from Gwen's and went to the door. I took a deep breath and opened it.

"Hi, Walter. We're back."

It was Danny Smith and Gus Ziegler.

"Well hi there," I said. I had never been so happy to see Federal troops. "What can I do for you?"

"The p-p-president wants to see you," Gus said. My happiness faded. The soldiers didn't seem to notice. Too excited by their lofty responsibilities, I suppose.

"Bolton told me I didn't have to go to that formal dinner," I said. "She'll be safe until the speech tomorrow."

"The dinner's over, Walter," Danny said. "This doesn't have anything to do with the governor. President Kramer just told us she wanted to talk to you. Privately."

"Oh. Right." The three of us stood there while I tried to think.

"Um, Walter?" Danny said.

"Right." Thinking seemed to be difficult. "Well, I guess I don't have much choice, then."

Danny and Gus just looked at me. What was there to choose? It was an order from the commander-in-chief.

"I'll just go and get my jacket, okay?"

"Sure, Walter."

I got my jacket and went into the parlor. "You, uh, heard what's going on?"

Stretch and Gwen nodded. Stretch looked very impressed.

I've seen Gwen look happier.

"I imagine I won't be long," I said.

"Stay as long as you want," Stretch said.

"We'll be here when you get back, Walter," Gwen reminded me.

"Right." There didn't seem to be anything else to say, so I put on my jacket and went back to the soldiers. "Take me to your leader," I murmured, and we walked out into the damp night.

CHAPTER 10

"Any idea what she wants?" I asked Danny and Gus as we got into the jeep.

"We're just soldiers, Walter," Danny replied. "No one tells us anything."

"But you must be p-p-pretty important, right, Walter?" Gus asked.

"I'm just an independent local subcontractor. Is she staying in the compound?"

"Uh-huh."

The government compound is an old-time apartment complex called Charles River Park, a short walk away from Government Center. Keeping the Feds in one place makes protection easier. I recalled that Governor Bolton was one of the few Feds who didn't live in the compound, preferring his own home in the Back Bay. I wondered if TSAR had caused him to think twice about that. "Has Bolton moved into the compound, what with all the threats going around?"

Danny shook his head. "They've asked him to, but he won't."

"Isn't he worried that they'll come after him? He'd be an easier target than the president, after all."

"I dunno, Walter. I think he likes being a little different from the out-of-state people."

"Does he think being a local will protect him from TSAR?"

Danny considered, and then shook his head. "He knows that folks don't much like him around here. Maybe someday they'll respect him, though."

So Bolton had his dreams too. I let it go. If TSAR came after Bolton in the Back Bay, that was his problem, not mine. I looked out into the night. There was no traffic, of course. For once I felt safe driving after dark. TSAR might attack an individual soldier, sneaking back to the compound before dawn, but no one was likely to mess with the three of us. One of the benefits of working for the government.

I wondered what President Kramer wanted with me. Despite Gwen's unspoken fear, I thought it highly unlikely that the woman had an uncontrollable desire for my body. I'm just an average-looking guy, not the kind women hunger for at first sight. But what then, if not that?

Maybe, for all her brave talk, she'd decided she needed more security, and wanted my advice. Or she wanted to give me a medal for having been beaten up. That would be okay. I could handle that.

"What do you guys think of the president?" I asked.

"She's a lot better-looking than her p-p-predecessors," Gus said with a grin.

"Yeah, yeah. But what about her policies? As far as I can tell, this referendum has just stirred up a lot of trouble for the Feds."

"But she's the president," Danny pointed out. "A soldier is supposed to obey the president."

"You're not always gonna be a soldier," I pointed out in turn.

Danny shrugged. "Then ask me again when I'm a civilian."

Gus came to a stop in front of the compound's gates. The guards checked us over, then let us pass. Gus parked the jeep in front of a big high-rise. There were more guards to inspect us—and frisk me—before we could go inside. "Pretty good security," I said.

"Too bad it won't be like this at the speech," Danny muttered.

The lobby was as fancy as anything I had seen in England. Plush carpeting, indirect lighting, a floral arrangement on either side of the elevator. The elevator came right away, and Danny pushed the button for the top floor. "She's staying in the p-p-p-" Gus tried.

"Penthouse," Danny said.

"It's spectacular up there," Gus added, with no difficulty this time.

"I bet."

When the elevator stopped, we stepped out into a softly-lit foyer, where one of Kramer's bodyguards stood facing us. "You're Sands?" he asked me.

"Uh-huh."

He turned away and muttered into an intercom by a door. A few moments later, the door opened, and President Kramer was smiling at me. "Hello, Mr. Sands. Thank you for coming."

"My pleasure."

She held the door open for me. I went inside. She closed the door on Danny and Gus and the guard.

She was wearing gray slacks and a white cashmere sweater.

Same jewelry as this afternoon. Same perfume. She had a good figure, and I was sure she knew it. She led the way into the penthouse. It too was dimly lit, with white walls, thick gray carpeting, low couches that looked too soft, and chrome chairs that looked too hard. Piano music wafted to us from hidden speakers. A silver vase of flowers sat on a glass-topped coffee table.

It was strange to think that a place like this still existed in Boston; stranger still to be in it.

"Can I get you something to drink, Mr. Sands?"

"Um, no thanks. Call me Walter, um, Madam President."

The president walked up a couple of steps into a gleaming white-and-black kitchen and poured herself a glass of white wine. "Are you sure, Walter?" she called out. "It's French. I doubt you get anything like it around here nowadays."

"I don't drink," I said. For once this felt like a vice.

"Ah. Good for you." The president returned from the kitchen. She had the self-confident stride of the doubt-free; she was the kind of person who would have been successful even without a nuclear war, I realized. Her bracelets jangled. She joined me in front of a large picture window. There wasn't much to see—no panorama of city lights to admire, just darkness speckled with an occasional dull glow. "The whole world is dark," the president murmured in her soft voice. "Will it ever be bright again?"

"I was in England once," I said. "Plenty of electricity there." I didn't feel like getting philosophical.

She smiled. "At the dinner tonight Governor Bolton told me about your adventure. You must be a resourceful fellow to get over there."

I shrugged. "'Stupid' is the adjective most people use. Stupid to come back." Why was she talking about me with Bolton?

"I don't think that's stupid. I think it's admirable."

"Why?"

"Because you cared about your country. You couldn't leave it behind."

I shook my head. "I cared about my friends. My country had nothing to do with it."

"Well, your friends are your country. Don't you think that's true?"

"I don't know." And what business was it of hers?

She seemed to sense my impatience, because she smiled again and turned away from the picture window. "You probably want to know why I asked you to come here."

"Take your time," I said. "I'm in no hurry."

She went over and sat on a soft couch. I sat on a hard chair. "Remember this afternoon I told you that you were one of the people I was here to convert?" she said. "Talking about you with Bolton tonight made me feel that even more strongly. You came back. For your friends, you say—all right. But still, you came back. And yet you're not sure about the referendum, not sure whether you support the government. I wanted to see if I could convince you."

"But why?" I said. "I'm just one vote. I have a friend who's a reporter—she was at your press conference this afternoon. Why don't you talk to her? You could reach a much larger audience."

President Kramer shook her head. "Reporters aren't interested in listening; they're interested in writing stories. You seem like a person who'll listen. If I can convince you, perhaps I can convince the rest of New England in my speech tomorrow."

"So I'm a test case?"

She smiled and sipped her wine. "Something like that, Walter."

"But what makes you think I'm representative of the rest of New England?"

"Oh, I don't know. A certain independence of spirit, perhaps. Combined with a certain loyalty. I could be totally wrong, of course."

I thought about it. I hardly considered myself a typical New Englander. Or a typical anything. But maybe I was wrong too. And anyway, it was her problem if she had picked the wrong guinea pig. "Okay," I said. "Convert me. Madam President."

President Kramer put her glass of wine down on the coffee table and leaned forward. "Tell me what you don't like about the government, Walter."

I laughed. "Where should I begin? You know all that stuff about taxes and the draft and so on. But I suppose what really bothers me is the way you people invoke the old government—you know, you're the successors to Washington, D.C., and therefore we owe you our support. I mean, maybe you are the successors, but so what? Look what the old government helped do to the world. It seems to me that after a nuclear war all bets are off. We should be looking for change, not continuity. Let's see if we can do things right this time around."

The president pondered my response. "I agree, Walter," she replied finally, "but surely your experience will tell you that a utopia doesn't appear by magic. In the kind of world we lived in after the War, anarchy or repression was much more likely. You're old enough to remember what it was like, aren't you?"

I remembered a childhood in Maine filled with grim long winters and perpetual hunger and marauding gangs and death.

And then I came to Boston, and had to face the Frenzy. "It sucked," I admitted.

"Yes," she agreed softly, "it did." She leaned back on the couch, and she got the familiar glazed look of someone remembering the old days. "I grew up in Washington, Walter. My father worked for the Environmental Protection Agency." She laughed humorlessly. The name was one of those jokes that weren't very funny. "We survived because we were on vacation when it happened. But of course before very long we were wishing we hadn't survived. My mother died of typhus, and my younger brother was shot to death by a gang looking for food. Then my older sister just disappeared one day, and we never found out what happened to her.

"That left my father and me. Somehow he'd heard about what was happening in Atlanta, and decided that we had to go there. It was a long and dangerous trip. All I can remember was how terrified I was—not so much that I would die, but that my father would die, and I'd be left alone in the world. I was twelve, Walter, and I didn't know anything.

"We almost made it. He died of an infection just after we reached Georgia. I managed to find a nice group of people, none of whom wanted to rape me or make me a slave. They took me in, and I could've stayed with them until they started dying too. But it was in my head that I had to get to Atlanta. I didn't know why, but it had been important to my father, so it became important to me. Everything would be fine if I could get to Atlanta. So I went off again, on my own this time. It was awfully stupid of me, but I made it.

"And then when I got to Atlanta, I wondered what was so magical about the place. Like everywhere else I'd been, there wasn't enough food and there were more than enough diseases, and people were very interested in a stupid twelve-year-old girl." She fell silent for a moment, as people often do in these reminiscences, overcome by what they have endured.

"But you changed your mind about Atlanta," I prompted.

She nodded. "I found a friend of my father's, and he took me in. It was an absurd coincidence, I suppose—I was begging on a street corner when he walked by and recognized me. Maybe it was fate. At any rate, it was the happiest day of my life, at least since the War. He had been a congressman, and now he was involved in setting up the new government. I couldn't have cared less about that at first—I was too happy just to have a roof over my head and someone to take care of me."

"And you stayed on in Atlanta?"

"That's right. And without realizing it, I was getting a first-hand view of what people like my father's friend had to go through in rebuilding America, the unimaginable problems they had to try and solve. Before long I went to work for the government—it was far better for me than any schooling I could have gotten—and I've worked for it ever since.

"But I'm not telling you all this to make you admire me or feel sorry for me or anything like that. Everyone has similar stories. I just want you to understand that I haven't been cloistered from the real world—I haven't always lived in fancy places like this and drunk French wine. I know what it's like out there. And I know what the government had to go through to make things even a little bit better. I don't want people to turn their backs on those accomplishments. If you were to start fresh, I doubt that you'd do any better. And you could do much worse."

That was true, I supposed. I had no more confidence in Flynn Dobler than I did in the Feds. But still, something about her argument didn't convince me. I wished Henry were with me; the Angriest Man in America would have known how to respond. I gave it a try. "I'll grant that the Feds have done some good things," I said. "But I just think their premise is wrong. They're trying to preserve the old-fashioned nation-state"—thanks for that term, Henry—"when the War has made the nation-state a bad idea, if it was ever a good one. I mean, Florida has different problems from ours. We don't care about Florida, and Florida certainly doesn't care about us. So why not just go our separate ways? Florida won't have to support us with their taxes, and we won't have to be ruled by southerners. Everyone's happy, and no one's big enough to get involved in another nuclear war."

The president went into the kitchen and poured herself another glass of wine. "Were you happy during the Frenzy, Walter?" she asked in her soft voice as she returned.

I had to admit that the Frenzy did not rank as one of the high points of my life.

"Florida helped stop the Frenzy. I'm sure a lot of people in Florida felt the way you do: who cares about those Yanks? Let them kill each other off; we'll still be okay. What saved you was simply the idea of the Union—the idea that we can accomplish more together than we can on our own. Even if that means that some of us have to make a sacrifice in the short run so that we can all eventually benefit. You've heard of Abraham Lincoln, haven't you, Walter?"

"Of course."

The president put her feet up on the coffee table and stared into her wineglass. "I think about Lincoln a lot nowadays. He believed in the idea of the Union. He believed in America. A lot of people died because of his beliefs—but it was worth it."

"He was one of the ones who died," I noted.

She looked at me and slowly nodded. "I think America is worth that kind of sacrifice, Walter. And more. Because America is not just another nation-state. It is the best expression of the highest ideals of which mankind is capable.

Not perfect, mind you—and we've had to compromise some over the past twenty years just to keep the dream alive. But the best anyone has been able to put into practice. And that makes America vitally important."

The president put her feet down and leaned forward, her eyes boring into me. She suddenly seemed ready to let me in on the deepest secrets of her life. "We live in terrible times, Walter. No one can deny that. But out of the despair and the misery comes opportunity. Russia is back almost to feudalism, in the places where things haven't broken down completely. Europe is limping along, but it lacks the resources and the will to make any progress. The rest of the world is a mess. Everyone is tired of war and tired of anarchy and ready to change. I can feel it.

"How many people over the centuries have dreamed of a universal government, Walter? But here we are—here I am—with a chance to do something about it. One government, Walter, embodying America's ideals and America's dreams. One government, to ensure peace and freedom and justice for every human being.

"You know, a lot of people disagree with me about this. I was appointed president because Congress thought it was time for new blood, new ideas—someone who would look to the future instead of the past. But a lot of people in Congress are worried now; they think I'm moving too fast, endangering the progress we've made already. I respect their opinion, but I can't agree with it. I respect what they've done, but I want to do more. And we have to start now, because the opportunity may never come again. We have a duty to humanity."

Now normally this kind of talk would provoke nothing more than a cynical private eye's smile from me. *Peace, freedom,* justice…lovely words, but I hadn't seen much of them lately. It was tough enough getting peace and freedom and justice for one person, never mind all of humanity.

But somehow, listening to Ann Kramer, I seemed to have temporarily misplaced my cynicism—despite knowing clearly how she was trying to manipulate me. As Gwen had said, the president was both calculating and sincere; and as a result, I found myself not believing...and believing. Her words, like her perfume, seemed to surround me, tantalize me, entice me. Peace, freedom, justice. Sure, they were a dream, but they were a dream worth having—weren't they?

"And you think the referendum is the start for all of this?" I managed to say, since she seemed to be waiting for a response.

"Yes," she agreed quickly. "It's the key. America isn't complete without New England, and New England simply isn't cooperating like the rest of the country. Perhaps it's that independence of spirit I mentioned. Perhaps the British occupation after the War still rankles, or I suppose the Frenzy just took too much out of you. Whatever the reason, I need to know that you people are on my side before we move ahead. If all Americans aren't united, we simply won't have the moral strength we need."

"So what happens if you lose the referendum?"

"But I'm not going to lose, Walter. I'm not going to lose." She suddenly stood up and paced with her determined strides through the soft light of the room. "You can accomplish anything you want if you're willing to risk everything you have. And I am willing to do that, Walter. New England will support me, and a united America will support me, and then we can take our message to the other nations. We can show them what faith in your fellow man can achieve. We won't conquer them by force of arms; we'll convince them by force of example."

Baloney, I thought.

Inspiring, I thought.

And then she was standing behind me as I sat on the hard chair. She put a hand on my shoulder. I looked down at the manicured nails, the expensive gold bracelets. I felt the warmth, the pressure. I listened. The music had stopped; when had it stopped? There was only her voice. "Can you see it, Walter? Can you see the world I see? It will be the best that we can create. We won't make everyone rich or abolish crime or cure all diseases, but what it is possible for humans of good will to accomplish, we will accomplish, because we will be working together. Because we are all part of America."

She fell silent, but she did not remove her hand.

I felt weak. I felt empty—ready to be filled. *America. Perfume. Peace. Bracelets. Justice. Warmth. Freedom.* America coming together. I had returned for my friends. But weren't my friends a part of America? *Can you see it?* Well, yes, maybe I could, somewhere in the soft light, shimmering just out of my grasp. Why hadn't I seen it before?

Because I needed this woman to show me. Why not believe in it now?

Because...

I couldn't think of a reason.

Perha*ps I should reach up and grasp her hand. Perhaps I would feel better if I turned and lost myself in her. Put an end to thinking entirely.*

But before I could do that, I had a final thought. No not even a thought. An image, a fleeting memory—of a gorgeous woman in a blue robe standing in the doorway of a newly built building, watching me leave, confident that I would return.

Before I came here, I wasn't alive.

Without thinking, I had pitied Marva, pitied the mindless life she must have been living, caught in the spell of Flynn Dobler's soulful eyes. Her happiness did not make her less pitiful.

So what was the difference between her and me?

The pressure of the president's hands suddenly felt like the weight of history on my shoulders. How many people had stopped thinking through the centuries, losing themselves in the warm, comforting world of someone else's dream? It was probably easier to count the number of people who hadn't. And look where it had gotten us.

Private eyes aren't supposed to stop thinking. Private eyes are loners; they live by their own code, not someone else's. They seek justice one case at a time, and let the rest of the world take care of itself. Of course, it wasn't clear that I was much of a private eye. But if I had any aspirations to become a better one, it was time to shape up.

Can you see it?

"I dunno," I said.

The president's hand tightened its grip. And then she placed her other hand on me, and she began gently massaging my neck and shoulders. "It's important to me, Walter," she murmured. "Important that you understand. Important that you believe."

She certainly knew how to give a massage. I suddenly wondered to what lengths she was willing to go to get my vote. We have a duty to humanity. I decided I didn't want to find out. I stood up and turned to face her. "Well, I certainly appreciate your taking the time to talk to me like this," I said.

She stared at me. "What's the matter, Walter?"

"Nothing. It just seems as if you've made your case, and now I have to take some time and think about it."

"You're not convinced?"

"Well, you certainly are persuasive, and I'm sure your speech will be a great success. But I guess I'm just going to keep an open mind."

The president couldn't seem to believe what she was hearing. "This is important, Walter."

"I understand." I started backing toward the doorway. I didn't want to listen anymore to that low, persuasive voice, to inhale that perfume, to feel those hands on me.

"Are you at least interested in hearing about some of the political reforms we're considering?" she persisted. "They may help change your—"

"No , no, I don't think so. I'll wait for your speech. I really have to go now."

I was at the door. I looked at her, and she finally seemed to accept her defeat. "You'll be there tomorrow?" she asked.

"I've got a job to do," I said. "I'll be there."

"Good," she replied, suddenly smiling. "I'll feel much safer."

I couldn't tell if she was kidding. I opened the door and went out into the foyer. When the door was closed behind me, I too felt much safer.

Gwen was in bed when I got home, but she wasn't asleep. I lit the oil lamp and sat across the room from her. "How is Ms. Kramer?" she asked.

"A little disappointed, I think. She tried to get me to vote for the referendum, but she failed."

"And how are you?"

I considered. "I feel—not guilty." I liked the sound of the words, so I repeated them. "Not guilty." I looked at Gwen. I thought this would please her, but it didn't seem to. "We just talked, Gwen," I said. "She talked, mainly, and I listened. And then I left. Everything's all right."

She turned her face away from me. "I worry," she whispered. "Our world is so fragile, Walter. So fragile."

It was true. Linc was gone now; who would be next? Gwen had made her sacrifice in getting me to England. Now I was back, and she could feel relieved for a moment. But how long could the relief last? I had been unfaithful to Gwen in England; couldn't I leave her for good in Boston? I had dodged bullets there; couldn't one hit me here? Her sacrifice really had changed nothing. Life was still hard and capricious, and we still had to live.

There was no comfort I could give her except myself. I went over and lay next to her. She put her head on my chest. I could feel my heart beating under her, and I wondered if its sound was soothing or frightening to her. Its rhythm was strong and regular, but someday that rhythm would falter and stop. And then what?

I held her in the flickering lamplight. Neither of us spoke, and it was a long time before she fell asleep. I never did.

CHAPTER 11

The next day dawned dark and threatening. Even Stretch seemed depressed by the weather. "Today is too important for rain," he said. But the Feds didn't control the weather, so there was nothing to be done.

We all walked over to Government Center together. It was early, but there were already people heading to the speech, including families in horse-drawn carts who had obviously come in from outside the city for the big event. This made Stretch feel a little better. Gwen took notes.

The plaza was not crowded when we got there. Martial music blared over the loudspeakers. There were soldiers around, but not many, and none were armed. Stretch found some of his buddies from work and stayed with them. Gwen wandered off to get some interviews. That left me alone to search for suspicious characters.

I didn't find any. Or rather, all the characters were equally suspicious, except perhaps for Stretch and his pals, and maybe some of the teenagers, who didn't know any other world and therefore had only a vague idea of what they were missing. Everyone else had the sullen, dubious look of people whom life has let down once too often; everyone else appeared to have a grudge against the government. And these were the ones who had enough faith left, or enough interest, to show up for the speech.

I ran into an acquaintance named Charlie DePaso. We had survived the youth camps together, and this creates a bond that nothing can quite sever. He was a fisherman now, a gnarled little man with bad teeth and skin like shoe leather. "Why'd you come, Charlie?" I asked him.

"Dunno, Walter," he said. "Better'n mending nets, I guess."

"Gonna vote yes on the referendum?"

He shrugged. "Never voted in my life. Don't see why I should start now."

"But no one has asked you to vote before, " I pointed out. "I hear the president's pretty persuasive."

"Well, I'm gonna need a lot of persuadin'."

My friend Jesus Christ—the one who looks like Flynn Dobler—was also there, dragging his cross and urging people to repent. His little son trailed behind, passing out hand-scrawled biblical slogans. "Do you support the government?" I asked Jesus.

"Render unto Caesar," he replied.

"Think people will vote yes?"

He sighed and readjusted the cross on his shoulder. "The things of this world don't matter, Walter."

"Don't peace and justice and freedom matter? What if the president can bring them to the world?"

Jesus just looked at me and shook his head. His son handed me a piece of paper. I read the message on it:

For Thine Is The Kingdom

I stuffed the paper into my pocket. "See you around," I said to Jesus.

"Repent, Walter," he replied.

The plaza slowly filled. I was impressed by the number of people who had showed up, but I had a feeling that a moderate shower would scatter most of them in no time. I made my way to the front of the crowd and saw Major Fenneman, who was standing next to the roped-off section where the dignitaries would sit. He was listening with a glum expression on his face to someone communicating with him through bursts of static on a walkie-talkie. I figured maybe I should let him see me, in case there was any question about me fulfilling my professional obligations.

"Can't anyone talk her out of it?" Fenneman demanded as I approached. "Christ, we've got enough to worry about without her pulling something like this." He saw me and glared. "What do you want?" he said to me.

"Just to say hi. I'm here if you need me."

Apparently I was the last thing he needed at the moment. He dismissed me with a quick gesture and went back to his conversation on the walkie-talkie. I wandered away—to the edge of the plaza this time—wondering what Fenneman wanted her talked out of; I figured I knew who he was talking about. I stood on a little stone bench to get a better view of the proceedings.

In a few minutes I saw flashing blue lights in the distance, and then the president and her entourage came into sight—jeeps and shiny cars and motorcycles, with the president waving from the back seat of a convertible. The motorcade circled around the edge of the plaza, coming within ten feet of me. The president brightened when she saw the familiar face and gave me a special wave. I didn't wave back.

"Did you see the bracelets on her?" a kerchiefed woman standing next to me on the bench said to her friend. "I wonder how much she gets paid."

"Too much," her friend replied.

The motorcade pulled up behind the platform, and the martial music stopped. President Kramer appeared on the platform, along with Bolton and Cowens and a bunch of officials. More waving, and then Bolton approached the microphone and spoke. "My fellow citizens, it has been a long time since we in New England have been honored as we are today, by the presence of the chief executive of our great nation. Far too long. This is a day that will live in our memories. It is a turning point in our history…." And so on.

"I've never trusted that one," the kerchiefed woman said.

"I've never trusted any of them," her friend replied.

Bolton's introductory remarks were, as usual, irreproachable yet unconvincing. The crowd responded in kind, with tepid applause at all the right points, but without ever showing any real excitement. Finally he finished, and the moment had arrived. President Kramer stepped up to the microphone; the applause was somewhat more enthusiastic now.

"She is pretty, though, you've got to give her that."

"We could be pretty, if we had her money."

"Do you think she dyes her hair?"

"The hair's phony. The tan's phony. It's all phony, every piece of her. A phony president and a phony election."

She's not going to win, I thought suddenly. She can't convince me, and she can't convince Charlie DePaso or Jesus Christ or these women. It's over.

"Thank you, Governor Bolton, for those kind words," the president said. "My friends, I am here today to ask you to support the government of the United States of America in the referendum next week. I recognize that you may not find this support easy to give. I understand the issues you have with the American government. But I'm asking you to have faith. Faith in the government. Faith in the future. And faith in me. Of course, it's difficult for you to have such faith unless you know me. So let me first take a few minutes to tell you about myself…."

And she launched into the story of her life, with which I was already familiar. Much of what she said after that was familiar as well. Oh, she changed an emphasis here and there, and sometimes she anticipated objections I had made. But basically she was repeating her performance of the night before.

But if I had been the test case, the dress rehearsal, why did she think this approach would succeed? If she couldn't manage to convince me, how was she going to convince

Charlie DePaso and the two women next to me? She couldn't exactly go around massaging everyone's neck and shoulders. And we weren't in a beautiful pre-War apartment, listening to music and sipping wine. We were huddled under leaden skies, cold and suspicious. What did we care about her experiences in Atlanta? What did Lincoln matter to us? Could we see the world that President Kramer saw? Not today, I'm afraid.

But then she went further. This was the part that I hadn't wanted to stay and hear in her apartment, too afraid that I would succumb to her the way Marva had succumbed to Flynn Dobler. "All of this is nothing but words, I admit," the president said. "Perhaps some of you have heard too many words over the years, and seen too little improvement in your lives. Perhaps some of you think the referendum is pointless, because it won't put more food on your table or give you better health care. Well, let me tell you here that I am prepared to stake the future of the Federal presence in New England on the results of the referendum.

"If you give us your support, we will immediately take steps to institute direct election of all local officials, up to and including governor, by vote of the entire adult population, not just taxpayers. Individual state legislatures will be re-established, and New England will return to being six separate states once again. As they did before the War, the new state governments will control policies and laws within their borders, and the Federal government will handle interstate issues. Federal troops will stay in the states at least until the elections are over; after that, the new governments will decide individually what role, if any, they want these troops to play within their states.

"Now I must be honest and tell you that not everything will change. Conscription will continue, as will Federal taxation and restrictions on interstate travel—we can't allow unlimited exit visas to the South. But what we are proposing is, I believe, a major step toward giving the brave people of New England what they need and deserve: a chance to determine their own future within the framework of a system that will preserve and extend our great American ideals."

The president paused, and people applauded—rather warmly, I think. "That seems like a good idea," the woman next to me said.

"I'll believe it when it happens," her friend replied.

"What if you lose?" someone shouted.

The president waited for silence. "If we lose," she said softly, "we leave. It's as simple as that. The reduction of the Federal presence will be gradual, in an attempt to prevent chaos, but within two years we will be gone. We hope the two-year time period will be sufficient to allow some sort of peaceful evolution of new political entities to take place—and we will do our best to help that process—but ultimately you will be on your own—your own borders, your own soldiers, your own laws. New England will no longer be part of the United States of America."

There was no applause at this, only a kind of buzzing silence as people tried to come to terms with this new prospect. No one had believed that anything would change if the referendum lost; the Feds would just continue with business as usual. But on the other hand…

"Why should we trust you?" someone else shouted.

"We recognize that the results of the referendum will only be valid if people think they are valid," the president said. "Therefore we have asked well-known opposition groups to join with us in supervising the balloting. We renew that request today. Now if, under those circumstances, the government—win or lose— subsequently reneges on any of the commitments I have made here today, do any of you seriously believe that we could continue to govern? Any credibility we have with you, any respect we have from you, would be gone, and this whole effort would have been worse than useless. No, this is for real, my friends. You have your future in your hands, and I pray that you make the right decision.

"The right decision, of course, is to vote yes—vote to support the government—vote to stay part of the United

States. Such a vote entails responsibilities, but with those responsibilities comes the possibility of renewed greatness. You will remain a vital part of the adventure that is America, and you will help our nation take its place once more at the forefront of human progress. And perhaps a hundred years from now people will look back on this day, and say that it was then that the tide turned, it was then that the long darkness ended, and the new day began to dawn."

The president stopped speaking. The applause that followed seemed genuine, but it also seemed tentative, and a bit confused. She had offered people what they had always said they wanted: freedom from the Feds. But did they really want that freedom if the Feds were also offering to give them a say in the way they were governed? After all, that was something else they were always complaining about. They couldn't have it both ways.

All of a sudden the referendum was no longer a joke.

The president waved and shook hands with the people on the platform and waved some more. The music began again. And before long the applause faded. People were going to have to go home and do some thinking.

The president came down off the platform and started shaking hands with the dignitaries in the roped-off section. The crowd began to drift away. It started to rain.

And then the president walked past the dignitaries and the guards who protected them, into the milling crowd, reaching out physically to the people she had just tried to reach with words. I looked back to the platform. General Cowens was still there, staring at her with his arms folded. Major Fenneman stood next to him, gesticulating with his walkie-talkie. This, apparently, was what they had been unable to talk the president out of.

"Want to try and shake her hand?" the woman next to me asked her friend.

"What's the point?"

"Well, she's the president, after all."

"So what? Come on. It's raining."

A lot of people seemed to feel the same way. There was no surge to greet her, no spontaneous outpouring of respect and affection. The weather was more important than Ann Kramer.

Still, there were hands to shake and an occasional baby to kiss, while her grim-faced bodyguards stood by and reporters struggled to record what was happening. I stayed where I was and watched her progress across the plaza. She was progressing, I noticed before long, toward me.

I got down from the bench. I saw Gwen among the reporters. I wondered if I should leave. It was raining, after all. President Kramer smiled at me. "Well, Walter, what do you think?" she called out as she approached.

"Great speech," I said.

"Did I convert you?"

I shrugged. "You certainly gave me a choice to make."

"But you haven't made it yet?"

I shook my head. "Maybe I'm too—"

The gunfire interrupted my reply.

For a moment I didn't understand. What was that noise? Why were people ducking and sprawling and screaming? I turned and saw a large green car come roaring out of the crescent of abandoned shops and offices beyond the plaza. Two masked men leaned out of the front and rear passenger-side windows. They were firing submachine gun rounds into the air. The car was heading right at us.

I reached for my gun. No gun.

I turned back to the president. Her bodyguards were pulling her down to the ground. She stared at the car as if she couldn't believe it was real, as if this were just a nightmare that would soon pass. The gunfire stopped and I heard the squeal of brakes just behind me. I turned once again. The masked men were out of the car and coming toward me. It occurred to me that I was literally the only person standing between them and the president. Not a position I would have chosen, but here I was.

I tried to think of something to do. Nothing came to me. I wanted to fight, but fists can't accomplish much against submachine guns.

So I stood where I was and wondered if I was going to die as I watched the men approach. I noticed their black masks, their shapeless tan jackets and dungarees. And— and—

I didn't have time to finish my thought. One of the men pushed his machine gun into my midsection. I clutched my stomach and gasped for breath. Then the other man swung his weapon at my head, and all thinking ceased.

When I opened my eyes, the first thing I saw was an out-of-focus General Cowens. He was conferring with Major Fenneman. I tried groaning to see how it felt. It felt awful. Cowens turned and looked down at me. "He's conscious," he said to Fenneman.

"What do you want me to do?" Fenneman asked.

"Take him to Nashua Street. Find out what he knows." Fenneman made a gesture, and a couple of soldiers came into view. They reached down and picked me up. I glanced around. No green car. No president. Plenty of soldiers— with weapons now. And there was Gwen—standing just beyond a line of troops, gazing anxiously at me. I tried a smile for her. It felt awful.

The soldiers tossed me into a jeep and sped away from the plaza. I closed my eyes as we bounced along and felt my head throb. I had a feeling things were not going to get any better for me. Apparently I was being taken to jail, although I couldn't for the life of me figure out why.

CHAPTER 12

The Nashua Street Jail was a brick pre-War monstrosity on the Charles River, not far from the Federal compound. It had survived the Frenzy, but just barely. Entering it felt like entering a mausoleum. The soldiers handed me over to a fiendish-looking old man with a limp, who led me through dark corridors, meanwhile muttering unintelligible phrases that could have been prayers but were more likely curses. He deposited me in a small dark cell, where he left me to ponder my fate with the part of my brain that was still able to ponder.

I didn't like being in jail. There are drawbacks to growing up after a nuclear war, I grant you, but it does give you a good bit of freedom in many ways. And you grow fond of your freedom, because you don't have that much else going for you. I hadn't enjoyed the youth camps; I hadn't enjoyed the army; and I certainly didn't enjoy being locked in a prison cell with a splitting headache and no idea what was going to happen to me.

I tried to think about what had happened back in the plaza. It was mostly a blur and a roar in my memory, but some things stood out: the green car appearing out of nowhere; the approach of the masked men, their little eyes fixed on me; the president's expression as she was dragged to the ground. Was she all right? It didn't seem likely; her bodyguards weren't armed, and everyone else was too far away to help. *If she comes, she faces our wrath,* TSAR had warned. That made me feel even worse. It seemed so stupid, so preventable.

It had been my job to prevent it.

I closed my eyes. There was nothing I could have done, right? If there was something, I would have done it. Right?

There had been something, it occurred to me. Not something I could've done, but something I could've...I tried, but I couldn't bring it back. And then it was too late.

"Sands?"

I opened my eyes. A soldier was peering in at me. The fiendish old man was unlocking the cell. "Uh-huh?" I said.

"Let's go," the soldier said. "Major Fenneman wants to talk to you."

The soldier escorted me through more dark corridors to a small, windowless room. There were two wooden chairs and a table in the room; Major Fenneman sat in one of the chairs. A naked light bulb hung down from the ceiling. "Sit down," Fenneman said.

I sat in the other chair. I didn't like this room any more than the cell. Fenneman regarded me from across the table. "What happened?" I asked. "Is the president all right?"

"I'll ask the questions, if you don't mind," Fenneman said. Uh-oh, I thought, he'd been studying his tough-guy lines. "Why were you eavesdropping on me before the speech?"

It took me a moment to figure out what he was talking about. "What do you mean, 'eavesdropping'? I went over to let you know I was there, in case it mattered to you. Then I left."

"But you stayed long enough to find out what the president was planning to do after her speech."

"No, I didn't. All I heard was your end of the conversation, and you were just complaining about how annoying she was being." What was he getting at, anyway?

"And then afterwards it was merely coincidence, I suppose, that you stopped the president and talked to her at the exact spot, at the exact moment that TSAR struck—and in an ideal location to make their getaway."

Oh, Lord. I had known the Feds could be stupid, but not this stupid. "Are you suggesting that I set this up somehow? Look, the president came over to talk to me. Ask anyone who was there. And take a look at this bump on my head. This isn't a fake. One of those guys really did whack me with his machine gun."

Fenneman wasn't interested in examining my bump. "Maybe that was just a way of diverting suspicion. At any rate, we need the truth. Now."

That didn't sound encouraging. I stared at Fenneman. He was an awfully big man. His hairy hands flexed on the table. My head throbbed. "I can't tell you anything more than I've already told you," I said. "I had nothing to do with this."

Fenneman glared. Had he really expected me to confess to something? He got up and came around to my side of the table. He reached out and pulled me up from my chair. His hand was around my throat. His face was close to mine. I could see the broken veins in his cheeks, the hairs in his nostrils; I could smell his sour breath. "Now," he repeated.

"This is all a mistake," I tried to say.

His grip tightened.

"Excuse me, sir?"

It was a timid voice coming from the doorway. "What?" Fenneman demanded.

"Could I just have a moment, sir?"

Fenneman glared at me, then thrust me back down into the chair and went out into the corridor, shutting the door behind him. I closed my eyes. I could hear the murmur of voices. Fenneman's was loudest; he sounded angry. Finally the door burst open and Fenneman reappeared. I tensed. "Get up," he ordered.

I got up.

"Bolton wants to see you," he said. "But you'll be back. And then you'll talk. Understand?"

"Uh-huh." I saw a soldier standing in the open doorway. I walked toward him. Fenneman didn't stop me. "You'll be back," he repeated as I left the room.

"Let's go," the soldier said, and he hurried off down the corridor. I struggled to keep up; I sure didn't want to get left behind. After a few turns and a couple of staircases, I found myself outside once again. Rain had never felt so good.

"Walter! Over here!" It was Danny, standing next to a jeep across the courtyard. Gus waved from inside the jeep.

I hurried over to them.

"I heard they conked you on the head," Danny said. "How are you feeling?"

"I'd feel a lot better if Fenneman didn't think it was all a trick."

Danny looked puzzled. "What sort of trick?" he asked.

"To keep people from suspecting me, I guess."

"But that's crazy."

"Tell Fenneman." I got into the jeep. "Why does Bolton want me?"

"To have you help find the president, I guess."

"She's alive?"

Gus started up the jeep, and we headed away from the jail. "No one told you?" Danny asked. "They kidnapped her. Apparently got away clean." He shook his head. "Isn't that something?"

"Oughta k-k-kill the bastards," Gus muttered.

"Gotta find 'em first."

Jeeps and police cars rushed past us, and I heard the distant wail of sirens. I was glad she was alive. And I thought: surely, with every soldier and policeman in Boston looking for her, she shouldn't be that hard to find. But then I thought: if TSAR gets her out of Boston, and no one snitches on them, she'd be almost impossible to find. It was a big country out there, and the Feds controlled only a small portion of it. There were plenty of places to hide a single human being. "What do you think'll happen if we don't find them?" I asked.

"I think things will get very bad, Walter," Danny said.

I couldn't disagree.

As usual, Gus parked outside the Federal Building and they brought me up to the governor's office. The VOTE YES signs and the "See Your President Speak Thursday" signs in the lobby looked grim to me now, but no grimmer than the guard who searched me before letting me enter Lisa's waiting area. "Hi. Um—"

"Sit," she said. She looked grim, too. People rushed in and out. Phones rang. My head hurt. And my ribs too, I suddenly noticed. The headache had masked the other pain until now. I bet I looked as grim as everyone else.

Finally I got the word from Lisa, and I entered Bolton's office.

The governor was in his shirtsleeves, tie askew, and he was pacing in front of his flags. He didn't look grim, exactly; he looked intense, energized, ready for battle; his scar seemed to glow. It occurred to me that his opposition to the referendum and Kramer's visit to Boston had been vindicated; that probably helped his mood, no matter how bad things got. "Sit down, Sands," he said as I entered. "How's your head?"

I sat down. "Apparently I'm going to survive," I said bravely. "But my health has certainly gone downhill since I started this case."

"I'm sorry that Fenneman carted you off afterward. That was stupid."

"He and Cowens apparently think I had something to do with this. I didn't."

"Of course not. But you're a local, you see, and that automatically makes you suspect." He paused and looked reflective. "I've had to face that kind of attitude for years," he continued finally. "You can be both a local and a patriot. Why does that have to be a contradiction? But they can't see that—it's us against them in their book. They're the occupying force, and their job is to make the locals knuckle under." Bolton paused, and then sat down behind his desk.

I felt a twinge of sympathy for Bolton, a traitor to many of his fellow locals, but at the same time still a suspicious character to hard-line Feds, unappreciated by everyone while he struggled to keep things going in New England. But I had my own problems. I waited for Bolton to come to the point.

Apparently he wasn't quite ready. He sat down, but he continued to be reflective. "President Kramer was different," he said. "She wanted to get past these Federal-local problems. She wanted everyone to share the same dream. But she pushed too hard too fast; she wanted everything to happen yesterday. And now you see what we have to face. She was quite interested in you, incidentally. We talked about you at dinner last night. People like you are the future, she said. I don't know about that, but at least she saw you as something more than a problem to be solved."

That was nice. But my head hurt, and I didn't really care about what had happened at dinner last night.

Bolton finally stopped dithering and pushed an envelope across the desk to me. "This was found taped to the outer door downstairs about forty-five minutes ago," he said. I stared at it. "To The Fed Bolton" was typed on the outside. I turned it upside down, and a gold bracelet fell out. It didn't take Sam Spade to figure out whose bracelet it was. I took out the sheet of paper that came with the bracelet and read what was on it.

We have the Fed Kramer.

The Feds must withdraw from Boston. Now.

When the withdrawal is complete, you get her back.

If you disobey: first torture, then painful death.

The Second American Revolution

Beneath the typed threat was a handwritten message:

Francis: They mean what they say. Oh God, it's begun already. Please help!

AK

"This is her handwriting, huh?" I asked Bolton as I handed the letter back to him.

He nodded.

"Any leads on where they have her?"

"We found the car abandoned in an alley in the Back Bay. We're searching the area, but I'm not hopeful. They probably just switched cars, and now they could be anywhere."

"But one of them was in town forty-five minutes ago."

"True, but how much should we read into that?"

I didn't know. "Do you have roadblocks set up, things like that?"

"I'm sure General Cowens is being very efficient and thorough. But let's face it, there's only so much his people can do. That's why I need you to stay on the case."

I closed my eyes. "I haven't accomplished very much so far," I pointed out.

"Well, here's your chance to make up for it. There's a thousand-dollar reward, incidentally."

That didn't excite me, for some reason. A part of me—maybe most of me—wanted to go home and get into bed and rest my aching head, and let somebody else worry about finding President Kramer. But another part of me wanted to solve this damn case. To prove that I was not as incompetent as I felt right now. And to get back at those bastards who beat me up every chance they got. "Can you keep Cowens and Fenneman off my back?" I asked Bolton.

"I can do my best. But you've got to understand how hard they're taking this—especially General Cowens. He's not likely to care who he disobeys, or what rules he breaks, if he thinks it might help him get Kramer back. So just try to stay clear of him."

Reasonable advice. "Okay," I said. I considered. "What will you do besides offer a reward? I take it you're not going to give in to TSAR's demand?"

"Of course not. The American government does not give in to terrorists. The president must be returned unharmed. If she is not, there will be serious consequences for the people of New England."

He sounded as if he were rehearsing a statement for the press. "Um, what would those consequences be, exactly?" I asked.

Bolton folded his arms. "If you were a member of Congress down in Atlanta, what would you want to do, Sands? Kramer talks them into radical changes in how we run things up here, just the way she talks everyone into everything. They give in reluctantly, because they risk losing New England altogether if the referendum fails. And this is the result. So how do you think they're responding right now?"

I didn't need to know much about the Feds to come up with an answer. "I think they'll probably want to nail New England to the wall. Back to the old days—martial law, troops on every corner, no local say in anything. Show us who's boss."

Bolton nodded. "You get the picture. So find her, Sands. Fast. This isn't just a Federal problem. It's everyone's problem."

I stood up. "I'll do my best."

Bolton picked up a pen and started scribbling. I walked out of his office.

I trudged home in the rain from Government Center. Even though it wasn't dark yet, the streets were practically deserted, except for the occasional jeep rushing by. The people I did see seemed stunned and nervous. They averted their faces as they passed, as if afraid that someone would detect some glint of guilt in their eyes and turn them in for the reward. If my experience was any indication, the Feds would be pulling in a lot of people with little more justification than that.

Bad news. I didn't know if Kramer's speech would ultimately have turned the tide in favor of the referendum, but it would certainly have improved people's perception of the Feds. Now, as Bolton pointed out, the Feds wouldn't care about anyone's perceptions. And that would make life worse for everybody.

Unless somehow the case was cracked before anything bad happened to the president. Well, maybe it could be cracked. TSAR couldn't be operating in a total vacuum, I figured. They had to have friends and relatives and neighbors. Maybe the Feds would get lucky and pull in the right people. Maybe the reward would make someone rethink his loyalties. Maybe a passerby would notice something out of the ordinary and dutifully report it to the authorities.

What role could an independent local subcontractor play in all of this, I wondered. Not a very large one, I decided, unless his head stopped hurting enough so that he could get some bright ideas. I slowed down. There had been something...but it disappeared in the mental fog once again, and there was nothing to do but keep on walking and hope the fog would lift.

Stretch was home cooking supper. I hadn't realized how hungry I was until I walked in the door and smelled his stew. Stretch came running from the kitchen when he heard the door slam behind me. "Walter! Are you all right? Gwen said you'd been—"

"I'm okay. Is she here?"

Stretch shook his head. "She's off trying to track down what happened to you after the soldiers took you away. What an awful, awful day."

"Tell me about it. But let me eat first."

Stretch insisted on cleaning my head wound first, and then I ate some of his stew. It felt good to be sitting at our old table in our old kitchen, with the pot simmering on the stove and Gwen's plants thriving on the windowsill above the sink and the useless electric light hanging from the ceiling. Nothing like the threat of torture to make you appreciate unthreatening everyday life.

I even enjoyed listening to Stretch, who was frightened and confused and looking for reassurances that I was unable to give him. "It's just some thugs, right, Walter?

The government will understand that. It won't allow all the progress President Kramer has made to disappear overnight. Right, Walter?"

"I guess so, Stretch. But I'm not the one to ask."

"But maybe you'll find her—and then everything will be okay. Do you think you'll be able to find her, Walter?"

"I'll try, Stretch. I'll try."

After supper I went upstairs to lie down and await Gwen's return. I could imagine how worried she was; it was a nightmare come true for her. But at least it had a happy ending: here I was, safe and sound, instead of dead or in the clutches of the fiendish Feds.

I wondered if anything else would have a happy ending. *If you disobey: first torture, then painful death.* And the Feds were going to disobey—that was clear. It was unlikely TSAR would kill the president for a long time; she was their only bargaining chip, after all. But they could certainly make her suffer. And the rest of us would suffer along with her.

I closed my eyes, wondering if the day's excitement would bring the sleep that almost always eluded me. No such luck, I decided soon enough. My memory kept replaying the scene in the plaza: the gunfire; the green car appearing out of nowhere; the president's expression; the masked men approaching; the attack; the pain. It was as if the events themselves had been too much to comprehend at the time, and now my brain had to view them over and over again in order to get them under control; and it had to control them before I could rest.

The president talking to me.

The gunfire, the people screaming and sprawling.

The car roaring out of the darkness.

The bodyguards dragging the president down.

The masked men getting out of the car and walking toward me. And—and—

And the fog suddenly lifted, the events were under control. I opened my eyes. What did it all mean? *What was a clue, and what was life just happening to you?*

I sat up. It wasn't much to go on, but it was something. Was it worth the hassle and the danger of investigating?

This isn't just a Federal problem. It's everyone's problem.

Apparently it was. I thought about waiting for Gwen. Maybe I could talk it over with her. Maybe she could help. But no, I would need help enough as it was. It was my case; I would solve it—or try to solve it—without her.

I got my gun, which I had left on the night table when I had left for Government Center. It occurred to me that if I had brought it with me I'd probably be dead—the masked men would certainly have used the other end of their submachine guns if I had tried to fire at them. Didn't matter. I went downstairs and found Stretch brooding in the parlor. "I'm going out to do a little investigating," I said. "Tell Gwen I'm okay. Tell her I love her."

"Sure, Walter." Stretch brightened. "Do you have a theory?"

"I dunno. Maybe. Is Linc's bicycle still in the basement?"

"I guess so."

I took a lamp and went into the basement. Sure enough, it was still there. I felt a twinge of guilt. Linc would not have wanted his bike used in trying to save the president of the United States. On the other hand, he would've done anything to help me be a private eye. It was okay. I brought the bike back upstairs. "Wish me luck, Stretch."

"Good luck, Walter. And please be careful."

"I'm always careful," I said, patting my wounded skull. I went out the front door and carried the bicycle down the steps. Stretch waved to me from the doorway as I pedaled off in the darkness in pursuit of the president.

CHAPTER 13

Riding a bicycle at night is not something I recommend. I had a little flashlight with some precious batteries, but it couldn't do much to dispel the darkness. Still, I didn't have time to walk—and walking is not much safer.

The streets were entirely empty now; everyone was indoors, trying to stay out of the way of the Feds. I was reminded of the awful time of the Frenzy, when to go out after dark was to risk death—or worse—at the hands of mobs whose every inhibition disappeared when the sun went down. Perhaps this fear was not quite as bad—the Feds weren't crazy, after all—but it was bad enough. I was careful to duck out of the way the few times I heard a car approach. I had no desire to get hauled back to the Nashua Street Jail to explain why I was out on the streets.

Bobby Gallagher's warehouse in South Boston was locked up tight. I pounded on the metal door. "It's Walter," I called. "Lemme in."

Eventually the door swung open and Doctor J peered out. "Gee, Wally," he said. "Whatcha doin' here?"

I brought my bicycle inside. Brutus started barking at me. "I've got a business proposition for your boss. And Mickey. Are they in?"

"Of course they're in. Where else would they be?"

"Are you crazy, Wally?" Bobby called down from the top of the stairs.

I went up the stairs to him while Brutus went wild with indignation. "I need to talk to you and Mickey," I said.

"Couldn't it wait till morning? This ain't the night to be cruising through the city."

"I understand. But no, it can't wait."

"Geez. Must be important. Step into my office."

Bobby's office was a tasteful blend of used office furniture and orange shag carpeting and fake-wood paneling and water-stained acoustic ceiling tiles. I sat on a gray metal folding chair and waited while Bobby collected Mickey from somewhere in the warren of rooms on the second floor. Doctor J also came upstairs, and in a couple of minutes the meeting was ready to convene.

"You don't look so hot, Walter," Mickey noted.

"Things haven't been going well," I said. And I summarized for them my run-ins with TSAR and the Feds.

"Hey, Wally, this private eye shit has gotta stop," Bobby said when I had finished. "You're safer gettin' into shootouts with O'Malley's gang."

"You're probably right. But I've got this case now, and I'd like to solve it."

Bobby shrugged. "All right. So where do we fit in?"

"Well, I've got this theory." I took a breath as I considered my meager evidence. "See, there were a couple of things about what happened on the plaza today that I sort of half-noticed. They finally came back to me after I'd gone over it in my mind a hundred times or so, and I think maybe they're important. First of all, there was the car. It was awfully loud—it didn't have a muffler. Remember when we were stopped on Route 2 that night, Mickey, and a car passed us?"

Mickey nodded.

"This car sounded a lot like the car that night."

"Flynn Dobler," Doctor J said.

"Well, his followers, anyway. What if Dobler is really TSAR, and he sent people to beat me up and get me off the case? Maybe he recognized my name from Gwen's article in the *Globe*, and the article would've told him where I lived too, and he was stringing me along the whole time I talked to him."

"Lotsa cars don't have mufflers," Mickey noted.

"Yeah, I agree. But there was this other thing, too. The guys I saw in the plaza—the guys in the masks—were dressed pretty normally. You know, old jeans and jackets. Except that they were wearing sandals—just like Flynn Dobler's followers. Maybe that's just a coincidence. Or maybe they knew they'd have to move fast, and they didn't want to risk putting something on their feet that they weren't used to. So they wear the same sandals they wear all the time, and they figure no one will notice."

Bobby shook his head. "That's it? I ain't convinced. Like Mickey says, lotsa cars don't have mufflers, and lotsa people wear sandals."

"Okay, the evidence isn't overwhelming, but I think it's worth checking up on. After all, Dobler does have a motive: he's about as anti-government as you can get. If the government goes away, there'll be no one to bother his church. And he's smart enough to pull this off. I can vouch for that."

"So I take it you wanna borrow Mickey and the van again?" Bobby asked. "Go up to Concord and be a hero?"

"I don't expect any favors," I said. "I want to offer you a business proposition. There's a thousand-dollar reward for getting the president back. If Mickey drives me up there and I find her, you and Mickey can split the reward."

"Nothing for you?"

"Nope. I'm in this to get TSAR. I don't care about the money."

"But you want us to go out on the most dangerous night of the year," Bobby protested. "Why don't you just tell Bolton your theory, and let the Feds handle it?"

"Because *I* want to handle it. Maybe troops'll stop us, but I don't think anything bad will happen. Bolton's on my side, and I'm just following his orders. Mickey, you won't have to get involved in anything. Just park out on the highway, and I'll take it from there."

"Can I come?" Doctor J asked.

"Now wait a minute," Bobby said. "No one's agreed to anything yet. Mickey, do you wanna do this?"

"As long as I don't have to deal with those weirdoes up there, I don't mind."

Bobby considered. "Well, all right," he said finally. "But Doctor J, you've gotta stay here and help protect the warehouse."

"That's no fun," Doctor J grumbled.

"I don't think this trip'll be any fun either, Doctor J," I said. I stood up. "Thanks, Bobby. You won't regret this."

"I'm regretting it already. Now get out of here before I change my mind."

Mickey and I headed back downstairs. "And be careful," Bobby called out to us.

Brutus lunged at me as we walked past.

"You scared?" Mickey asked as we headed into Cambridge in the van.

"Yup."

"I think you'll do okay."

I hoped he was right. "Don't sit there all night if I don't come back," I instructed him. "Two hours, maximum. No sense you getting into trouble too."

Mickey looked pained at the thought of abandoning me to the weirdoes, but he didn't object.

We didn't see another vehicle on the road; everyone else had more sense than we did. But we were lucky: the van didn't break down, no bridges collapsed, and the Feds were nowhere to be seen. Before long we were up near Walden Pond once again, and it was time for me to be a private eye.

Mickey parked the van by the side of the road and shut off the ignition. The darkness was total. "Kinda spooky," he muttered.

I turned on my flashlight and checked that my gun was

loaded and ready for action. "Think of the five hundred dollars," I said.

"I could buy my own car with that much money."

"That's right. Think about cars."

Mickey grinned. "Good luck, Wally."

"Thanks, Mickey."

I got out of the van. We had stuck Line's bicycle in the back, but I decided it would be easier to walk, so I headed off on foot toward the Church of the New Beginning, gun in one hand, flashlight in the other.

It had been a long time since I'd taken a walk in rural darkness, and it awakened memories I'd just as soon have let sleep. Memories of my childhood, when the whole world seemed hostile and terrifying, when the darkness hid bears and wildcats and the usual nighttime dangers, but also desperate gangs of men and women, crazed with hunger and disease and hopelessness, ready to prey on any ignorant little boy who wandered into their path. And who could tell what else was out there? Obscene mutants, formed in the radioactive fury? Or perhaps ghosts—the ghosts of the millions who had died, sweeping over the continent in search of a reason for their death? My father and I would barricade ourselves in our farmhouse at night and sleep with shotguns by our sides; or rather, he would sleep, and I would lie awake, my fear too strong to let me rest. I greeted each dawn with gratitude and relief; each dawn was a small victory in our battle to survive.

I stifled those memories finally. Living in the past does not help you survive the present. Now I had to worry about Flynn Dobler and his minions, not the shadows of my youth. Certainly there would be sentries on duty here. How was I going to avoid them and still make my way to the president (wherever she was)? The beam of the flashlight made me conspicuous, but if I turned it off I was helpless. There was nothing to do but forge ahead and hope they didn't notice me.

After a brief trek I found myself on the path leading up to the main building. There were no lights on in it. I wondered if I should scout around, looking for a car or some other evidence that Dobler was involved in the kidnapping. I decided not to bother. It wouldn't change what I had to do.

I had a theory. I figured they were holding the president in their meditation area, up on the second floor of the main building—the area that Marva had forbidden me to enter. Of course they could have put Kramer anywhere, but I thought perhaps Marva had been a little abrupt, a little anxious, when she had shut the door on my snooping. Maybe a room had already been prepared for the president there; maybe that's where they stored their masks and guns and did their plotting. It seemed like a good first place to check, at any rate.

I moved forward slowly now, ready to grapple with a sentry any moment. None appeared, however; there were only the night-sounds and me. I reached the front door of the building with no problem. I slowly turned the door's handle; it creaked open.

Why no sentries?

I slipped inside and shut the door behind me. I paused. The building was silent. I crossed the entrance hall and headed upstairs, smelling the new-building smells and listening for suspicious sounds. At the top of the stairs I turned left and made my way along the gallery to the door that led to the meditation area. Once again, I paused. Once again, silence.

I opened the door.

Darkness. I entered and shined the flashlight around the room. I saw the bent cross surrounded by flowers; I saw wooden benches and prayer mats and, in the corner, a pair of sandals; nothing else. I walked across the room and checked the darkness behind the cross. There were a couple of doors. I opened each of them. Closets. Empty.

I stood there and sighed. Now I would have to go to my backup plan. It was risky, but at least it would produce results—good or bad. Better than stumbling around the rest of the Church's buildings in the dark. I left the meditation area and continued along the gallery. I stopped in front of the room that led to the balcony where I had met Flynn Dobler. I was betting that it was Dobler's bedroom. I was betting that if I asked Flynn Dobler a straight question, he would give me a straight answer. Particularly since I had a gun in my hand.

I entered the room.

I won my first bet. Dobler was asleep in the narrow bed next to another, open door. He appeared to be naked underneath the thin blanket; he looked much less Godlike when one could see his scrawny white arms and hairless chest. He breathed softly as he slept.

I shined the light on his face. I left it there.

He stirred finally, grumbled, and opened his eyes.

He immediately shielded them against the light. "What's going on?" he demanded.

"Hi," I said. "It's Walter Sands. I talked to you the other day, about joining your church. Remember?"

"Get that light out of my eyes so I can think."

I shifted the light to one side. At the same time I held up the gun to make sure he could see it.

Dobler stared at me, and at the gun. "I remember," he said. "What do you want?"

"I want the president."

He looked confused. "I don't understand."

"You kidnapped her today. I've come to take her back."

He struggled to sit up in his bed. "This is crazy," he said. "What do you mean, I kidnapped the president?"

"You know what I mean. At the speech today. Your men ditched the getaway car in the Back Bay, then picked up another car and drove back here with her."

"Don't be ridiculous. I didn't even know she was kidnapped."

"I don't believe you. The men were wearing sandals, just like your people do."

My evidence didn't sound all that impressive, saying it like that; I didn't bother mentioning about the muffler-less car. Dobler rolled his eyes. "So what?" he said. "Look I haven't got her, and waving your gun at me isn't going to change that."

He sounded sincere, but he could also have been a good actor. Or, like President Kramer (in Gwen's interpretation), he could have been both sincere and insincere at the same time. "You better give that a little more thought," I said, "because I'm willing to use this gun if you don't hand her over." I hoped *I* sounded sincere.

"Brother Flynn?"

A shadow appeared in the far doorway, next to Dobler's bed. It was Marva, dressed in her blue robe. She stared at me, her eyes wide with fright. "I—I heard voices."

"Hi," I said. "We were just talking about the president of the United States. Do you know where she is?"

Marva shook her head.

"Would it help jog your memory if I threatened to put a bullet into Brother Flynn?"

Her knees appeared to buckle. "I don't know anything about the president," she whispered. "I swear. Please don't shoot Brother Flynn."

"Don't worry, Marva," Dobler said. "He isn't going to do anything. He's not the type."

How did he know my type? "Are you going to risk Brother Flynn's life, Marva," I said, "on the chance that I'm not the type?"

She looked at me, then looked at Dobler, sitting up in his bed. And then she leaped on top of him. "You'll have to shoot me first," she said to me over her shoulder. Her eyes were filled with tears.

Dobler seemed a little uncomfortable with Marva on top of him—and maybe a little disgusted. "Look," he said to me. "Search the place all you want. I'll come with you if you like, and you can hold your gun to my head and everyone will see you mean business. Will that satisfy you that she's not here?"

Marva continued to look back at me over her shoulder. Her hands were pressed against the wall behind the bed, and she was tensed to accept her martyrdom. Maybe she *wanted* to become a martyr. My head started to hurt. "Let's go," I said. Marva reluctantly got off Dobler. He got out of bed and put on a robe. Marva averted her eyes while he was naked. "Tell us what you want to see," Dobler said when he was dressed, "and we'll show it to you."

"This building first," I said.

Dobler nodded. "Marva, light a lamp," he ordered. Marva did as she was told, and we set out, poking our heads into the classroom, the meditation area (again), several offices, and other rooms whose purposes escaped me. No president. Nobody. "Where are all your followers?" I asked.

"They live in their own cabins around the farmland," Dobler said. "We'll visit every one of them, if that's what it will take to satisfy you. We'll visit the barns. We'll visit the outhouses. Whatever you want."

He sounded almost bored now. His boredom angered me. Why was he so sure of himself?

Probably because he was innocent.

"Let's go," I said.

We went outside: Marva in the lead with her lamp, then Dobler, then me, with my flashlight and gun. We walked along a rocky path that led from the main building back toward the farmland. We had gone maybe a hundred feet when I tripped over a rock and fell. My gun clattered away from me. I crawled quickly after it, but Marva was quicker. She stooped down and picked it up, then aimed it, trembling, at my face. "Don't move," she whispered.

I stayed on my knees. I glanced at Dobler. His arms were folded. He was staring at Marva. There was a moment of silence as I waited for him to decide my fate. "Give the gun back," he ordered her gently.

She looked at him in dismay. "But Brother Flynn—"

"Give it back," he repeated. "We don't use guns. Guns are part of the past. Guns are evil. You know that."

Marva hesitated for just a moment, and then put the gun on the ground in front of me.

"Shall we continue?" Dobler said.

I took the gun and stood up. My head felt awful. I didn't want to be here anymore. "I've seen enough," I said. "Sorry to bother you."

Dobler shrugged. "There's plenty left to show you."

"That's all right." I considered. "Do you have any idea who might have kidnapped the president? The group calls themselves The Second American Revolution, but no one seems to have heard of them."

Dobler considered in turn. "I suppose there's no reason why I should tell you if I did. It doesn't matter, though. I haven't heard of them either. The only person I know of who hates the government enough and is smart enough to be behind something like this is a man named Henry Fisher."

I would've laughed if I hadn't been so depressed, if my head hadn't hurt so much. "I've heard of the guy," I said. "Thanks." I turned to leave.

"Sands!"

I paused. "Yes?"

"Concentrate on what really matters, Walter Sands," Dobler said. "You are a very confused young man."

I guess you didn't have to be very smart to figure that out. I started the long walk back toward the van.

Concentrate on what really matters. What was that? People like Kramer and Dobler knew; apparently I didn't. All I knew was that I wasn't a private eye, I had never really been a private eye, my first case was a gift from my friends, and my delusions seemed to have permanently disabled me from carrying out Dobler's injunction. And my head hurt.

Mickey was waiting for me in the van, his shotgun at the ready. He looked at me with surprise as I climbed into the passenger's side, alone. "No president?"

I shook my head.

"Um, were you wrong about her being here, or did you just not find her?"

"I was wrong, I guess."

Mickey tried to hide his disappointment. No reward. No car. "Well, maybe you'll come up with another theory, Walter. It's tough being a private eye."

I turned away and looked out the window into the darkness. Mickey hesitated for a moment, then started the van and headed back to Boston.

In Louisburg Square, I asked Mickey to wait until I was safely inside my house. It had been such a wonderful day so far, I didn't want to spoil it for myself by getting beaten up again. I got the bike out of the van and walked carefully toward the front steps. Nobody was lurking in the shadows, however, and I made it inside without any further damage. Mickey gave a quick toot of his horn and drove off to Southie. I closed the door, turned, and immediately noticed the dull glow of lamplight in the parlor.

Gwen was sitting in a wing chair, half-asleep, a quilt wrapped around her. "Walter?" she murmured groggily.

"The one and only." I left the bike in the foyer and plopped myself down on the sofa opposite her.

"Are you all right, Walter?"

"I'll live."

She roused herself from her dreams and came over to see me. She examined the bump in my head, studied the expression on my face. "What happened tonight?" she asked. "Stretch said—"

"I had a theory. About Flynn Dobler. I got Mickey to drive me up to Concord, and I talked to the guy. My theory was wrong."

"I'm sorry, Walter. She sat beside me on the sofa and took my hands in hers. I was so worried about you."

I leaned back and closed my eyes. "I'm all right," I said.

"You really want to solve this case, don't you?"

"Of course I do. That's what I'm paid for: to solve cases."

"I'm on the case too," Gwen said. "Wolsey would love to have the *Globe* find the president. Why don't we work on it together? You could come with me tomorrow and—"

"No."

She hesitated. "No?"

"I'm gonna solve this case on my own."

"But I'm sure we'll do much better if the two of us—"

"Maybe we would. But I don't want any help. If I can't find her by myself, it isn't worth it."

I kept my eyes closed. Gwen took her hands away from mine. "Walter," she said, "this isn't one of the novels you're always reading. These people are real, they're dangerous, and you—"

"I'm what?"

"You're just one person. You've been hurt already. I saw them club you down on the plaza today. I don't think I could stand to see you hurt anymore."

"There's more than one kind of pain," I muttered. I opened my eyes. Gwen was staring at me in the dim light. She looked as frightened as Marva waiting for me to shoot her. "Trust me," I said.

She didn't reply. I stared back at her for a long moment, then got up from the sofa and went to the third floor—to my novels.

She didn't follow.

I sat in my sanctuary until daylight, brooding. And then it was time to carry on with my case.

CHAPTER 14

The three of us had a grim, silent breakfast together before going off to work. Stretch was eager to find out what I had accomplished the night before, but a couple of short answers from me quickly dampened his enthusiasm. Gwen just stared at me.

Stretch left first, glumly anticipating a tense day at City Hall. And then Gwen was ready to depart. "What are you going to do?" she asked me as we stood in the front hall.

"I don't know," I said truthfully.

"Will you be careful?"

"Of course."

She stared at me some more; her stares were more eloquent than Kramer or Bolton's speeches. Then she embraced me, pressing her head into my chest. She hurt my aching ribs, just a little. And then she was gone.

I hung around for a while, wondering what to do. Finally I decided to return to Charlestown and have another chat with the Angriest Man in America.

It wasn't that I shared Dobler's suspicion of my friend; I just had nothing else in mind. And after all, a case could be made against Henry: perhaps he had gotten tired of writing and researching and finally decided to do something. I hadn't visited him often enough lately to know if he had changed. Maybe the referendum was the last straw, and after all these years his anger found an outlet in action. So when I had come snooping around, he cleverly pointed me in the direction of his enemy Flynn Dobler, and had his henchmen wear sandals during the kidnapping as yet another way of diverting suspicion.

It made about as much sense as my theory about Dobler, I decided. So I took Linc's bike down the front steps and pedaled off to where I had begun my investigation.

The bad weather had disappeared along with the president, and sunlight sparkled in the puddles. Maybe it was the change in the weather, but the people I passed seemed to be in a slightly better mood today. They still looked somber, but a little bit of the tension was gone from their faces. The first night had passed, and nothing terrible had happened. There were still troops everywhere, of course, but I didn't witness any arrests or violence or even anger. Perhaps that would come with time, but for now we seemed to be in the eye of the storm.

There were even troops in Charlestown. I certainly would have expected an explosion from that, but an uneasy quiet prevailed there as well. I kept an anxious eye out for Santoro and Grimes and the rest of O'Malley's thugs, but they seemed to be lying low. I hoped none of O'Malley's suits were being altered today.

Henry Fisher's shop was deserted except for the women working at their sewing machines. Where would he keep the president, I wondered, if he was behind TSAR? And how could he get thugs to work for him, with his sour disposition? What if Ann hired them? That was even stupider than suspecting her father.

Ann came over and greeted me. "What happened to your head, Walter?" she asked.

"I had an accident."

"Soldiers?"

I shook my head. "Not this time. What does the AMA think about the kidnapping?"

Ann rolled her eyes. "I think it bothers him that someone actually did something, instead of just talking about it."

She could have been lying to protect her father, I supposed. "Can I talk to him?" I asked.

"Sure. Go on up, Walter. He needs friends like you."

"He needs a son-in-law like me."

Ann grinned and opened the counter to let me through.

I went upstairs, then down the hallway to Henry's library.

Henry was standing by the window, looking out. He turned when he heard me. "Walter Sands," he said. "We're getting to be best buddies."

"Hi, Henry. How're you doing?"

He shrugged and walked over to his cluttered table. "You look like shit," he remarked, peering at me through his spectacles.

"Yeah. I had an accident—while protecting the president."

"You do good work," he said.

"I'm trying to find her," I replied. I sat down opposite him.

"I hope your work improves."

"Do you mean that?"

Henry sighed. "I find in myself an aversion to violence of any kind. I don't want to be ruled by Kramer, but I don't want to be ruled by The Second American Revolution either. I just don't want to be ruled."

"You don't think TSAR is simply trying to free us from the yoke of Federal oppression?"

"Maybe. But who knows?"

"I was hoping you might. Haven't you heard anything? Any rumors on the street? Any hot tips from your radical friends?"

He shook his head. "Did you check out Flynn Dobler?"

I recounted for him my experiences at the Church of the New Beginning. And then I decided to get everything out in the open. "Dobler suggested that you might've done it."

Henry's face darkened, and I braced for an explosion. But it never came. Instead, he started to laugh. "I suppose I should be flattered," he said. "Someone actually thinks I could be a criminal mastermind. Do *you* think so, Walter?"

"If I can be a private eye, you can be a criminal mastermind."

Henry continued to grin. "Dobler still could've done it, you know," he pointed out. "He might have just been bluffing by offering to show you around."

"I know. You might be bluffing too. A fellow just has to go with his instincts."

"Well, my instincts tell me you better keep looking."

I had to agree. "The thing is," I said, "this couldn't have been pulled off by just anybody with a dislike for the Feds. There were at least three people involved, they had guns and cars, and they were very lucky or very smart or they had advance knowledge of the way things were going to happen at the speech yesterday. So why have none of your radical friends heard of them? I know things aren't as, well, *connected* as they were in the old days, but on the other hand there are a lot fewer people to keep track of. How did TSAR manage to come out of nowhere?"

Henry shrugged. "It's hard enough trying to understand the past, Walter. Understanding the present is impossible."

I pondered that for a moment. "But that's my job," I said finally.

"Maybe you need another job," Henry replied. "Write books. It's safer."

"You're not kidding." I stood up. "You sure you didn't do it, Henry? It'd make my life a lot easier."

Henry shook his head. "You know how much I like to oblige people," he said. "But some things are just impossible. I'll let you know if I hear anything."

I sighed. "Thanks, Henry."

I could've lurked around Henry's shop searching for clues, but it wasn't worth it. Flynn Dobler and Henry seemed to cancel each other out in my mind. Each had a motive and a few shreds of evidence against him, but not much else. I didn't quite understand either one's views or his approach to life, but that was hardly grounds for believing them guilty of kidnapping the president. For want of any other bright ideas, I returned to the scene of the crime, thinking I might find some clues there, or at least some inspiration.

I was surprised to discover that several hundred people had made it to the Government Center plaza ahead of me. They certainly weren't searching for clues—they were just sitting or standing or milling around, talking quietly. And they didn't seem to be under arrest, either. There were troops on the outskirts of the plaza, and particularly around the area where the president had been kidnapped, but they seemed to be ignoring the crowd.

I looked for a familiar face, and finally spotted Charlie DePaso sitting in the sunshine with his hands clasped around his knees. I flipped the kickstand of my bike and sat next to him. "Hello, Walter," he said. "What happened to your head?"

"Accident," I replied quickly. I was getting tired of that question. "What's going on, Charlie? Why are all these people here?"

"I don't know exactly. I just came over 'cause I felt so bad about the president. I guess a lot of people felt the same way."

Yesterday, I recalled, Charlie had been here simply because it was better than mending nets. "You didn't seem particularly sympathetic to the president before her speech," I said. "Was she that persuasive?"

Charlie scratched his chin. "I dunno, Walter. It just seemed like she was talkin' about making things better for everyone, and then all of a sudden we're back to the same old stuff again. Know what I mean? It's gotta stop sometime. Maybe now's as good a time as any."

I thought about Henry's similar response. *I find in myself an aversion to violence of any kind.* Unless he was a very good actor, he had hardly seemed like the Angriest Man in America when I talked to him. Maybe, I thought, something good would come out of this.

But then I thought of Bolton's threats, and the troops everywhere, and I paid attention to my aching head and ribs, and I realized that this was just another one of my dreams.

The Feds were going to get mean, and TSAR was already mean.

Charlie would leave this vigil and go back to his nets and his indifference. And Henry would return to his book and his anger.

"Any theories about where they've got her, Charlie?"

He shook his head. "I heard they found the getaway car in an alley off a Fairfield Street, but I doubt they'd keep her around there—too easy to search the neighborhood, right? So they probably took her out of town—and then what are you gonna do?"

"Beats me." I stood up. Charlie had gotten as far in his analysis as I had. "See you around, Charlie."

"Take care of your head, Walter."

I walked my bike over to where the kidnapping had happened. The area had been roped off, and inside the ropes a few soldier were standing around trying to look like they were doing something constructive. One thing they could do was stare at me, and when they started to do that I turned and walked away.

I wasn't getting inspired.

I decided to try the alley offa Fairfield Street.

It hadn't been very far for the kidnappers to drive—just a mile or two down Beacon Street, maybe a little longer if they stayed off the main streets. And then, while the Feds were still scrambling to get into their jeeps and follow, they were in the midst of the old brick town houses of the Back Bay.

Fairfield is a side street in the middle of the Back Bay. It was easy enough to find the alley where the car had been left; it too had been roped off. The green car was gone, but a couple of soldiers were still there, sifting through the debris for clues. Once again, I lingered outside the rope until I attracted attention, and then I moved on.

It was not, I decided, a particularly helpful spot for TSAR to leave the car. If they hopped into another car and continued along Beacon Street, they would quickly pass through the Fenway into Brookline, then a few miles later into the wilder suburbs beyond that. Or they could have turned right on Mass. Ave. and headed over the Harvard Bridge into Cambridge—the route to the Church of the New Beginning, but also to any location north or west of the city.

So now what? I bought some food from a street vendor on Boylston Street, then sat on a bench and pondered. Still no inspiration. I had no choice, then, but to do more legwork. To do, really, what Bolton wanted me to do—check out my sources, talk to the people that the Feds might not know about or couldn't get the truth out of if they did know about them. Henry Fisher had been my top prospect among those sources, but there were others, and now was the time to track them down and find out what they knew.

I finished my sandwich, hopped on my bike, and set to work.

It was a frustrating afternoon. I renewed many old acquaintances, but the conversations had a sameness that started to get to me after a while:

"Walter, good to see you. I heard you went away."

"Yeah, well, I came back."

"That was a stupid thing to do. Hey, you look terrible by the way. What happened to your head?"

"Accident. Have you heard anything about this group The Second American Revolution, by any chance?"

"Only what I read in the *Globe*. But isn't this kidnapping awful? Just when things were starting to get better."

"Yeah. If you find out anything, will you let me know?"

"Sure. Actually, there's this vigil or something over at Government Center. I think I might stop by, see what's going on."

It was strange, the changes in attitude I saw. I was superfluous; these people would have talked to the Feds anyway, if they had known anything. But unfortunately none of them knew anything. I returned home to Louisburg

Square no wiser than when I had left in the morning.

Stretch was already there. His mood was as bleak as my own. "Any news?" I asked him.

He shook his head. "What about you, Walter? Did you find out anything?"

"Nope."

"At least there hasn't been any violence yet," he said, always trying to look on the bright side.

"The Feds seem to be holding back," I remarked.

"I think that's smart," he said. "But if they get another message from these terrorists—if anything happens to President Kramer…"

He didn't have to finish the sentence. "Did you see the crowd in Government Center?" I asked.

Stretch brightened a little. "Isn't that wonderful? I thought I might go over there myself."

"Will they still be there after dark?"

"I'm pretty sure. I heard some people say they weren't going to leave until the president was returned unharmed."

I considered the vigil for a moment. "Do you think maybe the Feds are behind this vigil?" I said. "I mean, what if they're organizing it as a way of stirring up support and putting pressure on TSAR?"

Stretch gave me one of his how-you've-disappointed-me looks. "Certainly the government likes what's happening," he replied, "but don't you think people have minds of their own? No one told me to go, that's for sure."

And no one had told Charlie DePaso either. Stretch was right; the Feds couldn't force the population to feel bad about the president. And if they tried, people would be sure to notice, and everyone would react accordingly. I stared out the bay window into the square. "You think Gwen'll be home soon?" I asked.

"I don't know, Walter. I bet they're awful busy at the *Globe*."

I wondered if she was making any progress on solving the case. I doubted it. "Maybe we should wait a while before we eat, in case she shows up," I said.

"Fine with me."

We sat in silence. I read the *Globe* and Stretch studied sewer reports. Darkness fell; no Gwen. We decided to eat. Neither of us felt like cooking, so we had leftover stew. It wasn't very good. We talked for the sake of talking. "I wonder what they'll do about the referendum," I said.

"I heard it's still on," Stretch said.

"I'd think that Bolton would use this as an excuse to cancel it."

"I'm not sure it's his decision."

"Too bad for him. I bet he's even more anxious to cancel it, now that he knows Kramer will eliminate his job if it passes."

Stretch shrugged. "Oh, he knew that already. He mentioned all her proposals to the government employees back when he first announced that she was coming. Told us to keep them quiet, though, so we wouldn't spoil her announcement."

I considered this. "That was before he called me into the case—before he knew about TSAR."

"Well, I guess he knew about TSAR when he made his speech to us," Stretch said, "because it was right after the speech that he asked me about you."

I considered some more. I felt some things falling into place, but I had to be sure—I didn't want to run off the way I had last night, too eager to solve the case to really think everything through. "I know Bolton lives in the Back Bay, but where, exactly?" I asked Stretch.

"He's got one of those fancy town houses on Beacon Street. Corner of Fairfield, I think."

I stared at my stew. *What is a clue...* I wished Gwen were here. But no, I could do this myself. Maybe just go over it with Stretch, make sure at least that it sounded right. "Stretch," I began, "do you think it's odd that absolutely no one has heard of TSAR? No one at the *Globe*. None of my radical friends, not even the government security people?"

"There was that file you saw," Stretch pointed out.

"True, but there was nothing in it, and no one claims to have started the file. So what's going on?"

Stretch stared at me. "You've got a theory," he said excitedly.

He wasn't going to be excited for long. "Maybe," I said, "this case isn't about the future of America or anything as grandiose as that. Maybe it's just about a man who wants to hold onto his job."

"*Bolton*?" Stretch said, quick on the uptake. He didn't look convinced.

"Hear me out. Bolton has been opposed to the referendum from the start. He thinks Kramer is pushing too fast, jeopardizing the government's progress. He's sure of this when he finds out about the proposals Kramer is going to make in her speech. And now, no matter what the outcome, he won't be governor for much longer. If the referendum loses, he better head for the hills with all the rest of the Feds. If it passes, people get to elect their governor, and they're bound to choose someone else—he hasn't exactly made himself loved around here.

"So he thinks about what to do, and he comes up with this idea: Make up a terrorist group and have them kidnap the president. He must have some flunkies who'll do the dirty work for him, and he can make it easy for them because he knows all the plans for the president's trip, and he realizes she wants to go easy on the security. Anyway, once she's kidnapped, he's all set. He keeps her for a couple of days, then has her rescued. If this makes the president and the rest of the Feds change their minds about the referendum—fine, that's what he wanted in the first place. If they decide to go ahead with it, well, it has a better chance of passing now, because the government will get the sympathy vote. And then he's more likely to be elected, as the rescuer of the president. So no matter what happens, he's better off than he would've been if things had gone ahead the way they were supposed to."

There, it sounded okay. But Stretch was shaking his head vigorously. "I don't get it," he said. "If he's the villain, why did he hire you?"

That had been so obvious to me that I'd forgotten to mention it. "It's the oldest trick in the book," I explained. "Who's going to suspect you of committing a crime if you're the one hiring the private eye to investigate the crime? But once you've hired him, you can control the guy's investigation so that it never touches you. I started talking about an inside job right away when Bolton brought me in, but he didn't want me to follow up on that. He wanted me to find the file on TSAR that he had planted in their records. He wanted me to go out and look for radicals like Flynn Dobler. And most of all, he wanted General Cowens to see how concerned he was about TSAR—concerned enough to hire this local to help in the investigation."

"But Walter—"

I could feel myself getting carried away now. I didn't want any interruptions from Stretch. "And after I got started," I went on, "why would I think of Bolton? He has his thugs beat me up as a warning to get off the case. Why would the guy who hired me do that? I tell him I'm suspicious of Dobler, and he has his thugs wear sandals during the kidnapping so I'll go off on a wild-goose chase. He's counting on me to be stupid, to suspect everyone but him. I think maybe he's been a bit too clever for his own good."

"But Walter—"

"I mean, he has them leave the getaway car right there in the Back Bay, a couple of blocks from where he lives. Everyone thinks the kidnappers must've switched cars. But what if they didn't—what if the president is being held captive right there in the governor's mansion? They could be keeping her drugged or blindfolded or something so she doesn't know where she is. And of course it's the last place anyone would think to look."

"Listen, Walter," Stretch finally managed to say as I took a breath. "I don't know if your theory makes any sense or not. But I'll tell you one thing: Governor Bolton couldn't be behind this. He's just not that kind of person. I know he opposed the president on the referendum, and I know he might not be governor anymore if it takes place, but I still don't see him doing what you're accusing him of. He's a good man, Walter. He's worked hard for New England, and he's been loyal to the government. Why not accept what he's done at face value? He hired you because he was worried about the president's safety, and he thought you could help."

Well, maybe. But my theory explained a lot—a lot more than my Dobler theory or my Henry Fisher theory, anyway. It came down to what you thought of Bolton. Stretch saw him one way. But was that just Stretch being Stretch? And I saw him—how?

Not very clearly, it seemed. Obviously he was caught between the Feds and the locals, and he felt that conflict keenly. But was he a strong-minded patriot, or a self-seeking conniver? Did he become a Fed out of personal conviction, or because joining the people in power offered him food and shelter and a measure of security in an unsafe world?

The main difficulty with being a private eye, I realized, was not the danger or the lack of cases, but the need to make judgments about people, all of whom are too complex to be summed up in a phrase, none of whom are so obviously guilty or innocent that your job is just to catch them if guilty or protect them if innocent. My judgment of Flynn Dobler had been faulty. Could I do better with Bolton?

I wasn't sure. I had thought everything through, but I still didn't know Bolton, and until I did it was all just a theory.

I got up from the table.

"What are you going to do, Walter?" Stretch asked.

"I'm going to take a look at Bolton's house, see if there's anything suspicious happening."

"Walter, please be careful. Please don't do anything rash."

He sounded like Gwen. But he was right, I supposed. "I promise. But do me a favor, will you, Stretch?"

"What's that?"

"Don't tell Gwen what I'm up to. I don't want her worried, too."

"Well, okay, Walter."

I had a feeling Stretch wasn't going to do what I asked, but that couldn't be helped. I went to get ready for my stakeout.

CHAPTER 15

Stakeout. The word sounded terribly professional and dramatic to me, but I knew the reality would most likely be far from exciting. I packed some equipment, and I pedaled carefully down Beacon Street to the governor's mansion. The moonlight made travel a bit easier than it had been the night before. I parked the bike and lurked in the shadows of an abandoned building across the street. And then I waited.

Nothing happened. A couple of lights were on—electric ones, to judge from the brightness—but there was no sign of activity. It made sense that Bolton would try to keep people away from here if President Kramer was being held inside, and of course he'd order the thugs holding her not to show themselves. But it also made sense that there was simply no one home. Bolton might still be at his office, and as far as I knew nobody else was living in the mansion. He was a widower, after all, and he didn't have a family.

So what should I do? Wait all night? I was prepared to. I didn't need to sleep, and I didn't have anything better to do with my time. But what if nothing happened? That's the risk a private eye takes, I supposed, and I steeled myself for that possibility.

I waited. The lights stayed on. No movement inside. The moon climbed in the sky. The stars whirled. A dog barked. Something seemed vaguely familiar to me about all this; was it important? I searched my memory, and when I found what I was looking for, I realized that I shouldn't have bothered. It was simply the past, come back to torment me once more.

After my father died, I was taken in by an older couple who were as kind as could be expected under the circumstances. But the circumstances kept getting worse in Maine, so finally they decided to head for Boston in the slim hope that life would be better there. I don't know if it was the right decision for them; thugs took me away from them before they had even entered the city. It didn't take me long to leave the thugs, and then I was on my own in the city, a stupid boy in a cruel new world. I didn't stay stupid long. Couldn't afford to.

There were times, though...Smart people did not venture out at night, but I did sometimes, cold and hungry and lonely, wandering the dark streets and risking my life just to be somewhere other than where I was. I would see a house—like Bolton's—with lights on, and a silhouette or two passing through a room—and I would stop and stare at it, and I would try to imagine what life was like in there. Perhaps all was normal—parents cooking dinner for their children, then sending them up to their warm beds, where they dreamed sweet dreams that just might come true someday. Surely such houses existed somewhere! Was it my fault that I had never lived in one?

It was at times like those that I felt the pull of the Frenzy most strongly. My dreams would never come true, so why not substitute rage for hope? If I couldn't live in such houses, why not destroy them? Maybe I would be destroyed too, maybe we would all be destroyed, but what did it matter? What did anything matter?

I shivered and sent the past back where it belonged. I decided to recite Shakespeare to myself; my memory's good at such things. I picked *Richard II*; it's about a ruler who ends up in prison, so it seemed vaguely appropriate. I quickly transported myself from modern Boston to medieval England, and I stayed there for quite some time. I was midway through the play when it occurred to me that I should take a look around the rest of the mansion. This annoyed me. I should have thought of it right away. Private eyes shouldn't get tangled up in bad memories—or in Shakespeare. Who knew what was going on in the back while I sat staring at the front?

I made my way out onto Beacon Street. A dog started barking again, and I froze. I didn't want to deal with a dog just now. Eventually the barking stopped, and I continued.

The side of the building, on Fairfield Street, was dark. At the back, a high brick wall surrounded a small yard. I followed the wall around to the alley; in the alley the wall gave way to a locked gate, then began again. I looked up; there was a light on in a second-floor window. I stood in the alley and watched. The light was partially obscured by the budding leaves of a tree that had somehow managed to survive in the yard. Once again nothing was happening, but at least I had a different vantage point from which to see it not happening. I picked up where I had left off in *Richard II.*

...when the searching eye of heaven is hid

Behind the globe and lights the lower world,

Then thieves and robbers range abroad unseen

In murthers and in outrage boldly here...

And then there was a shadow moving through the light. I shifted a little bit to improve my angle. The damn tree made it difficult. The figure moved again, and I saw it more clearly this time.

It was a woman, black shadow against yellow light. I couldn't make out any more. And then the light went out.

So now what? I couldn't say for sure it was the president, but it was one more piece of evidence for my theory. Should I rush off and tell Cowens? Not likely to do any good, unless he disliked Bolton even more than he disliked me. Go get reinforcements of my own? A pitched battle wouldn't help the president, if she was inside. And, of course, I wanted to do this by myself.

As I considered the situation, I realized I might be able to take a closer look, if I cared to be a little athletic. I decided it was worth the risk.

I took out my flashlight, switched it on, and studied the wall. Some of the bricks were crumbling, and it was easy enough to get a foothold and climb to the top. Once there, I slithered quickly down the other side, landing on cracked asphalt. My aching ribs reminded me that strenuous activity wasn't a good idea. I paused to get my breath and shined the flashlight carefully around. A jeep was parked by the gate; that didn't bode well. It occurred to me that my pals Danny and Gus could be two of Bolton's henchmen. No, I didn't want to believe that.

I went over to the tree. It was a maple, tall and sturdy despite its unpropitious location. I put the flashlight away. Then I leaped, caught hold of the lowest branch, and pulled myself up onto it. As quietly as I could, I worked my way up till I was level with the second floor. Despite the moonlight, I couldn't make out anything in the room where I had seen the figure. I could hear something, though: a woman's low moans.

Just beyond the tree was a fire escape. I doubted that anyone had set foot on it in a quarter of a century, but I didn't know what else to do. I reached out and grabbed the railing, then gingerly put my weight on it. The fire escape creaked slightly, but held. I climbed onto it and crouched down outside the window.

The woman was still moaning.

There was no way of making a quiet entrance, I figured. I took out my gun. I shined my flashlight into the room. I saw the woman. It took a moment for me to figure out what she was doing. It took another moment for her to notice the beam of the flashlight and turn toward the window.

It was not the woman I expected.

It was Lisa, Bolton's plump, efficient secretary. She was very naked, and she was straddling an equally naked Governor Bolton.

She screamed, and an instant later the room was flooded with light. I didn't wait to see what happened next. I threw myself back into the branches of the tree and thrashed my way down to the ground. Then I raced for the wall and tried desperately to find a foothold so I could climb it. My flashlight had disappeared in my descent from the tree, however, and I was having trouble in the dark. I finally managed to scramble to the top of the wall, and I was ready to dive back into the alley when I heard a door burst open behind me and I felt myself illuminated by a shaft of bright light.

"Hold it!" someone shouted. "Don't m-m-m—"

I didn't.

"Walter! What are you doing here?"

Danny had come around to the alley while Gus kept a gun trained on me from the back door of the mansion. He looked up at me on the top of the wall with disbelief.

"It's a long story," I replied.

Danny shook his head. "It better be a good one. You are in big fucking trouble, Walter."

I couldn't disagree.

I staggered down from the wall. Danny searched me and took away my gun, then marched me around to the front of the mansion. We went inside, and he deposited me in a dusty wing chair in a downstairs parlor. He kept a gun pointed in my general direction. I heard footsteps. A moment later Bolton came in. He was wearing a bathrobe. His hair was mussed, his scar was throbbing. He saw me and stopped short. "Sands! What is this?"

Good question. I couldn't very well tell Bolton my theory, whether or not it was correct. I had to improvise. "I was staking out the place," I said. "I had this theory, that maybe TSAR might come after you next, so I thought I should hang around in case you needed help."

"Hang around in a tree outside my bedroom window?"

"I, um, thought I heard something. Someone, uh, moaning. I went to investigate."

It didn't sound especially persuasive, but it was the best I could do. Bolton glared at me. "Maybe Cowens is right about you," he said. "Looks like I've been making a big mistake."

Gus appeared in the doorway. Bolton turned to him. "Well?"

"D-d-doesn't seem to be anyone else around," Gus said.

"All right. I called General Cowens, just in case. He should be here any moment." And then he turned back to me. "I trusted you," he said.

"But I told you I was only trying to help."

"You've got a very odd idea of how to help, Sands." He paced for a moment. "The locals have to understand—" He stopped, then began again. "Look, we've exercised the utmost restraint under the circumstances, Sands. That was Cowens's doing as much as my own; frankly, I was dubious. No mass arrests, no torture, no intimidation. We figured that would be what the president wanted—show the people how understanding the government could be. I suppose that was a mistake too, if this is how we're repaid."

I heard cars screeching to a stop on the street outside. The conversation paused until Cowens marched into the mansion, followed by a couple of soldiers. Cowens hadn't shaved and, despite his uniform, he looked old and tired and rather feeble. Not much sleep for him lately, I supposed. He glanced at me, then addressed Bolton. "My troops are surrounding the place," he said. "You'll be all right now. But I wish you'd reconsider moving into the compound."

Bolton waved away the request. "I'll think about it tomorrow. What should we do with this fellow, though?"

Cowens took a moment before replying. He was clearly enjoying his little triumph over the governor. "I think Major Fenneman should continue the chat with him that was interrupted yesterday," he said.

"I was just trying to protect the governor," I said to Cowens. "I'm with you. I thought it was dangerous for him to be living outside the compound too."

"I don't know if he was trying to protect me or not," Bolton responded, "but at the very least we have to keep him off the streets before he does something else crazy."

Cowens nodded. "We'll take care of him." He gestured to his two soldiers. "Take him out to the car," he said.

The two soldiers advanced into the room and hauled me up from the wing chair. One of them snapped handcuffs on me. On the way out of the room we passed Gus, who was looking at me with disbelief and, maybe, disappointment. "Just trying to help," I murmured. Then I was in the dark, high-ceilinged hallway; and then I was back out in the night.

I waited in the car between the two silent soldiers until Cowens returned. A driver sat up front, humming softly. I didn't feel like trying to make any of these guys my buddies; I doubted that I would succeed, in any case. The soldier on my right stank of garlic. The handcuffs were uncomfortable. My ribs hurt.

We'll take care of him. I didn't want to think about how Cowens planned to take care of me. He got into the car after a few minutes and motioned to the driver. "Nashua Street Jail," he ordered.

Oh Lord. I decided to tell Cowens the truth. It couldn't make things any worse for me. And besides, Cowens might agree with my theory. He didn't have much use for Bolton—I was pretty sure of that. And the theory did explain a lot.

Didn't it? I wondered if I believed my theory, now that I had been humiliated for the second time in two nights. After all, it didn't seem particularly likely that the president was being held in the mansion. And if Bolton was in fact guilty, and Danny and Gus were his henchmen, why had he bothered calling Cowens when they caught me snooping? It would have been far less dangerous for them to kill me and not have Cowens and his troops surrounding the place—and talking to me.

Still, Bolton could be holding her somewhere else. And maybe he thought he could brazen it out. It was my word against his, and Cowens was not likely to believe anything I had to say.

But all of that didn't really matter at this point. Right now I simply had to convince Cowens that I wasn't part of TSAR, that I actually was one of the good guys, even if my theories were stupid. "Um, excuse me, General," I said, "but I'd like to tell you the real reason why I was hanging around the governor's place."

Cowens turned slowly in the front seat and looked at me. His watery blue eyes were ready to disbelieve. "Go ahead," he whispered.

I tried. I explained about the TSAR file and the sandals on the thugs at Government Center and the getaway car in the alley off Fairfield Street and everything else that I had tried out on Stretch earlier. As before, it sounded pretty persuasive to me. As before, my audience was not impressed. "You must have a low opinion of Governor Bolton's intelligence, if you believe that," Cowens said when I was through. "Or of mine, if you're making it up and hoping I'll fall for it."

"But don't you agree that he has a motive? And, with a few smart guys working for him, don't you think he could carry out the kidnapping? He's a natural suspect."

"Perhaps he's a natural person to try to make a suspect, if you're trying to divert suspicion from yourself," Cowens replied. "But you're ignoring one thing, Sands. I know Governor Bolton. I've worked with him for years. I may not always agree with him, but I respect him. He wouldn't dream of doing something like this. He wouldn't dream of risking the government and all it's accomplished for his own personal gain."

Something in the way Cowens made this little speech struck me as false. It was like the way Bolton had talked about the referendum: forced, artificial. "Maybe," I suggested, "you've been a soldier too long, General. What if you're too used to carrying out orders from people like

Bolton, and not thinking about the person who's giving the orders?"

His blue eyes appraised me. And then he laughed—a dry, humorless laugh that made me want to curl up and die. "Sands, that just shows how much you misunderstand me as well as everyone else," he whispered. He turned away then, and a few moments later we came to a stop in front of the jail.

The fiendish old jailer with the limp and the incomprehensible mutter took me away from the soldiers. "Hey, what about the handcuffs?" I said, but no one paid any attention.

The jailer carried a torch as he led me through the dark corridors. Our shadows loomed grotesquely on the walls. In the distance someone groaned. I felt as if I had entered hell.

He led me to a cell and locked me inside, then limped away. I sat on the edge of the cot, twisted the handcuffs, and felt fear clutching at me like the hands of the damned.

No one was going to save me from Major Fenneman this time.

I don't know how long I waited in the darkness, but it wasn't long enough. Eventually footsteps echoed in the corridor, and the jailer was standing outside, along with a soldier. The jailer opened the door, and the soldier beckoned. I got up and followed him. No words were spoken.

The soldier took me to the small, windowless room where I had been before. Inside, both Cowens and Fenneman were standing up, waiting for me. If possible, Fenneman looked even angrier than I remembered him. "I wonder if you wouldn't mind seeing about these handcuffs," I said to Cowens. "I don't think they're really necessary now, do you? One of your men has the key."

Cowens gestured to the soldier waiting by the door. "Take care of it," he murmured. The soldier disappeared down the corridor.

Fenneman shut the door. "Sit down," he said.

I obeyed. Fenneman and Cowens remained standing. They stared at me. "Where is TSAR keeping the president?" Fenneman demanded.

"I don't know anything about TSAR," I said. "I had nothing to do with the president's kidnapping. I don't have any idea where she is."

Fenneman leaned over and slapped me in the face. I closed my eyes; he had a powerful slap. When I opened my eyes, the naked light bulb hanging over the table glistened through my tears. Fenneman's face loomed behind it, large and red and angry. "What were you doing sneaking around the governor's house?"

"I told General Cowens what I was doing. I suspected Bolton of being behind all this."

"Weren't you in fact scouting the place out for TSAR? Aren't they in fact preparing to kidnap him too?"

"I don't know anything about their plans. What I told Cowens is the truth."

"But you told Bolton something else—that you were protecting him. So why should we believe you now?"

"Well of course I wasn't going to tell Bolton I suspected him of being a traitor."

"So you admit you're a liar."

"Oh, come on. You're wasting valuable time if you think you can find the president by hitting me and asking tricky questions."

Fenneman hit me again. "Don't tell me how to do my job. Now where's the president?"

"I don't know."

"Who else is a member of TSAR?"

"I don't know."

"How many members does it have?"

"I don't know."

He hit me again. The interrogation settled into a routine of questions and denials and pain. Fenneman was not subtle and not especially clever, I suppose, but at the moment I was not interested in reviewing his performance; I was interested only in the next time he was going to hit me.

Where would he aim? How hard would it be? How much more could I stand? After a while I noticed that Cowens was gone. I wondered vaguely if perhaps he didn't enjoy this sort of thing. Or perhaps he realized they weren't going to get anything out of me. But thoughts of Cowens quickly floated away. They didn't matter. Only the pain mattered.

Eventually I must have passed out, because I don't remember an end to the interrogation. I just came to in my cell; sunlight was streaming in through a tiny window high up in the wall, and it was time to face another day.

I struggled up to a sitting position on my cot. I noticed that there was a tray on the floor with a roll and a cup of milk on it. I wasn't hungry, but after a lifetime of scrounging for food my instinct told me to eat when the opportunity presented itself. I reached down and picked up the tray; wasn't easy. The milk was warm; the roll was hard. My mouth wasn't cooperating. It wasn't one of my better breakfasts. I lay back down on the cot.

Time passed. I drifted along with it, content not to move, not to think. The absence of pain (more or less) is not boring, if the only alternative is more pain. After a while I noticed that my handcuffs were gone. That was an improvement, wasn't it? I stared at a tiny, faded message printed on the wall next to the cot:

I am in heer on a bum rap

The Wiz Kid '97

Staring at the message, I began to feel a kinship with the Wiz Kid, now no longer a kid, now almost certainly dead. And then I began to feel a kinship with all of the oppressed, dead and living. Like them, I didn't belong in jail; I didn't deserve to be tortured. How could someone do this to his fellow man? It was wrong; it had to be stopped.

In the aftermath of pain, this struck me as being quite profound. Henry Fisher would have been proud of me. But the Wiz Kid hadn't stopped it, and Henry hadn't either, and here I was, after all these years, waiting for the steps along the corridor and the rattling of the keys in the cell door and the silent summons. Fenneman is back in the small room.

The pain is about to resume.

I closed my eyes, and I waited.

"Let's go."

I looked over at the soldier standing in the open door. "I am in here on a bum rap," I said to him. It didn't come out very well; my mouth still wasn't cooperating.

"I don't give a fat rat's ass," the soldier said. "Let's go."

I slowly got up from the cot and shuffled out of the cell. The soldier pushed me along the corridor. I stumbled forward, and eventually we reached our destination. Fenneman was waiting for me. As before, Cowens was also there; maybe his presence was required for the beginning of the ritual. He had shaved; he looked somewhat better. He appraised me as I slumped into the wooden chair. "You're not telling us what we need to know," he said softly.

"How can I? I don't know anything."

"And meanwhile your people are still at it," Fenneman said.

"What people?" I asked.

"You know what people." He tossed a piece of paper onto the table.

It was yet another typed message from TSAR. I read it.

You have till sunrise tomorrow to leave Boston.

Then the president dies.

The Second American Revolution

P.S. We now have the meddling reporter Gwendolyn Phillips.

She dies too, as will all who attempt to interfere.

I looked up at Fenneman. His arms were crossed. His florid face was expressionless. Could this be a trick to get me to talk? But what was the point? Maybe the Feds knew about my relationship with Gwen—she was the one, after all, who had written the story about the initial threat from TSAR—but this didn't seem like a good way of making use of that knowledge.

After all, this message was just more proof that I didn't have anything to do with TSAR.

So the message was real. I had gotten Gwen's interview with the president, and she had cracked my case. Sometime or other maybe I should ponder the irony of that, I thought. But not now. Not while Gwen was in danger.

She worried so much about me, about everyone who was close to her. It wasn't fair that she was the one who had ended up in trouble.

I was in trouble too, of course, but all of a sudden my trouble seemed trivial—a minor inconvenience, a misunderstanding, easily cleared up. Fenneman's blows stung, but they weren't going to kill me. I was sure, on the other hand, that TSAR—whoever, whatever they were—would kill Gwen, if it suited their plans.

And that meant I had to do something. Now.

"What do you have to say about this?" Fenneman demanded, gesturing at the paper.

I tried to think. "Look," I said finally. "I don't want to put up with any more of this. I'll tell you what you want to know."

Fenneman and Cowens exchanged a satisfied glance, and then Fenneman looked back at me. "All right," he said. "Start talking."

CHAPTER 16

I shifted in the wooden chair. "Well," I said, "it's like this." I paused. What exactly was it like? "The guy behind TSAR is, well…"

"Yes?" Fenneman demanded. Cowens stared at me icily.

"…well, it's Jim O'Malley."

"O'Malley?" Fenneman repeated. "The Charlestown boss? That's absurd."

"That's just what he wants you to think," I said. I had it now. One more theory, this time with absolutely nothing to back it up. "Everybody's been focusing on political groups, so no one thinks of someone like O'Malley. But imagine what would happen if the Feds just up and left Boston. Could a political group take over? No chance. O'Malley's organization is the second most powerful force in the city now—maybe in New England—and he'd just expand and take over everything if you guys weren't around to restrain him."

"And you're part of O'Malley's organization?" Fenneman asked.

"Sure. I do this private eye stuff on the side, but obviously no one can make a living at it. I used to work for Bobby Gallagher over in Southie, but he's just small potatoes. O'Malley is big-time. You work for O'Malley, you know you're going places. It was just a coincidence that Bolton hired me to find out about TSAR, but it turned out to be a perfect setup, or at least so we thought. I could keep feeding you people cockeyed theories, so you wouldn't see what was really going on."

I paused, waiting for a reaction. "I don't believe a word of it," Fenneman said. Wrong reaction. "O'Malley's not smart enough to pull this off."

"See, you just proved what I've been saying," I pointed out. "You underestimate him because you think he's just a small-time crook. Well, he's smart enough to be more successful than almost anyone else around here—smart enough to have Charlestown under his thumb and a piece of almost every deal in New England. So maybe it's time you reconsidered your opinion."

Fenneman glanced at Cowens, who didn't respond.

"Well," Fenneman said, "I guess it can't hurt to take a look over there."

"Yes it can," I responded quickly. "If you just send a bunch of soldiers to his headquarters, I guarantee you'll have one dead president on your consciences."

"Is that where they're keeping her?"

"Of course not."

"Where, then?"

I took a breath. "Look," I said, "I'm in enough trouble as it is. I don't want this to screw up. You go to Charlestown and get the president killed and you'll take it out on me, no matter how much I helped you. And the thing is, without me you haven't got a chance, even if I told you right now where she is. You're gonna be in enemy territory, and they have sentries all over the place. My idea is that I bring two or three of you over there in an unmarked car and show you the lay of the land. Then we can figure out a plan."

"Sure, and then you have *us* kidnapped, and you escape," Fenneman scoffed. "No deal."

Then Cowens spoke for the first time. "Where is she?" he demanded.

"See, unless you—"

He came over and slapped me. Not as hard as Fenneman, but the surprise counted for something. "Where is she?" he said in a whisper this time. "Nothing more happens until you tell us."

I stared at him. He was smaller and older and frailer than Fenneman, but somehow much more frightening. "Twenty-one Davis Street in Charlestown," I said. "It's an old warehouse."

I held his gaze. Private eyes have to know how to lie, even when they're frightened. I was doing my best. Finally he turned away. "Take a couple of men and go with him," he ordered Fenneman. "Check it out."

"But sir, this seems like a transparent attempt to—"

"Check it out," Cowens repeated. "If you *are* kidnapped, well, that will certainly tell us something, won't it? And if he's lying, we'll just bring him back here and get a little rougher with him. Understood?"

Fenneman did not look happy. "Yes, sir."

"Good." Cowens turned and left the room.

"You better not be lying," Fenneman said to me.

"Why would I lie?" I asked.

"Because if you are…" Fenneman didn't bother to finish the tough-guy thought. "Let's go," he said.

"I don't think it'd be a good idea for you to drive to Charlestown in your uniform," I suggested.

"Yes, yes."

"And I really could use something to eat before we go. The breakfast they gave me wasn't very substantial. I'd hate to faint on you."

"All right, we'll hire a chef and get you a gourmet meal. Satisfied?"

"Only trying to help," I muttered.

Fenneman called in some soldiers, who led me back to my cell. A little while later, the old jailer brought me a tray, this time with a softer roll and colder milk and a hunk of tasty cheese. It wasn't gourmet, but I enjoyed it.

Meanwhile, I did some thinking.

So far so good. The initial goal had simply been to get out of jail, and that was going to happen. I figured it would be easier to escape from the Feds once I was outside. But that had yet to be proved, and I had obviously put myself in more danger by making up the story about O'Malley. The fact was, I had no idea how to pull off the escape, just as I had no idea where 21 Davis Street was—or if Davis Street even existed. It was all too likely that I would end up back in that small, windowless room, with Fenneman furious at me and eager to demonstrate his fury.

Or maybe they would get tired of that game, and I would end up with a bullet in my back, and one more short, undistinguished life would be over.

That was a chance I had to take.

After a while the soldiers came for me once again. They brought me outside, where an ancient gray Subaru station wagon was parked in the courtyard. The sunlight made my eyes water; I felt as if I'd been in prison for years. Fenneman was standing next to the Subaru, wearing jeans and a jersey and looking uncomfortable. A gun was stuck inside the waistband of his jeans. Three other men, dressed in civilian clothes but—like Fenneman—obviously armed and obviously soldiers, stood nearby. "Nice day," I said to Fenneman.

"Get in the car," he replied.

I slid into the back seat, and two of the men joined me, one on either side. Fenneman got into the passenger side of the front seat, and the third man got behind the wheel. Four against one—and they all had guns. I wasn't feeling optimistic. "We're not very inconspicuous," I said. "No one in Charlestown is gonna be fooled for a second. We might just as well be flying an American flag and wearing dress uniforms."

"Shut up and tell us how to get to Davis Street," Fenneman said.

"Head for the Bunker Hill Monument," I said.

The driver started the car, and we pulled out of the courtyard. The car's shock absorbers had apparently been lost to history, and we jounced up and down as the soldier navigated the pot holes and other hazards of our journey. We hadn't gone a hundred yards before I began to feel sick. Maybe you weren't supposed to eat so soon after being tortured: one of those pieces of valuable information that I hadn't picked up in my life. "Is there some way we could keep from bouncing so much?" I asked.

"You wanted an unmarked car, you got it," Fenneman replied helpfully.

We were approaching Leverett Circle, where we would head toward Charlestown and away from downtown Boston. And that's when I had my idea.

I turned to the soldier on my right and raised a hand toward my mouth. "I—I think I'm gonna throw up," I groaned.

We bounced. The soldier looked at me in horror. "The guy's gonna throw up," he reported urgently to Fenneman.

We bounced again. I started making strange noises in my throat; I turned my head this way and that, looking for the best place to do my business.

The soldiers in the back seat squeezed up against the doors, as far away from me as they could get. It wasn't very far. "*Sir?*" they called out in unison to Fenneman.

"Stop the fucking car," he growled.

The car stopped, and the soldiers scrambled out. I scrambled out after them, awful noises issuing from deep inside me. "Watch him," Fenneman shouted.

Too late. I slugged the soldier who got out on my side, and he staggered back against the front door of the Subaru, so that Fenneman couldn't get out. The soldier reached for his gun, but I reached for it first, and I shot him in the shoulder. He screamed with pain.

The driver had gotten out by this time, and he and the other soldier ducked down on the other side of the car. Fenneman was struggling to get his gun out and shoot me through his window. I decided it was time to leave. Walking quickly backwards, I fired a couple of shots at the car, and then I turned and ran, keeping low to the ground. I headed for a building off to my left. I heard the Feds returning my fire, and I prayed that they were as incompetent at shooting as they were at most other things. No such luck. I felt a searing pain in my arm just as I slammed through the front door.

I looked down at my arm; it was bleeding, but the bullet had apparently just grazed me. I tried to think through the pain. I was not so easy a target now, but I was in hardly less danger. I could stay where I was and shoot it out with them, I thought, but I didn't know how many bullets I had left— and besides, Fenneman could just wait me out and bring in reinforcements. No, I had to run.

I took off down the corridor. Through a window I saw the towers of the Federal compound nearby. I couldn't have picked a better spot for them to get reinforcements.

The building was abandoned, as most office buildings still were; the rooms had been trashed, and most of the windows were broken. It smelled of stale urine and mildew. What had it been? A computer company? Insurance? Law offices? It didn't look like a particularly pleasant place to die. I had to get out of it.

Behind me, I could hear Fenneman shouting instructions.

I found a staircase. I tried to go down, figuring there had to be an exit in the basement, but the door was locked or blocked or stuck and I could hear footsteps now, so I had to run upstairs, my arm throbbing, my lungs bursting. Maybe on the *roof*...but I wasn't going to make it to the roof, so I took off down the second-floor corridor.

And that's when I noticed the faded green structure outside. It was the elevated trolley tracks—long unused, of course—coming from Cambridge and heading downtown. I ducked into an office and took a closer look. On either side of the tracks was a rusted railing with wire mesh beneath it. The railing was several feet away from the window. *Must've been noisy here once upon a time,* I thought.

I studied the distance to the railing. *Well...*

The window was broken. I climbed up onto the sill. I heard footsteps in the corridor, doors banging open. I tensed, leaned forward, and jumped.

I managed to catch hold of the railing. I tried to pull myself up, but my arm was on fire. *Can't do it.*

"Goddamn it, where is he?" Fenneman roared from inside the building.

I tried again. I managed to heave myself over the railing and onto the tracks.

I lay there for a moment and then, not surprisingly, I threw up for real.

I looked at my arm. It was still bleeding, and it hurt like hell; every part of me hurt like hell. But I was alive. I could still hear Fenneman shouting in the building, but no one seemed to be coming after me. They'd realize what I'd done soon enough, though; it was time to get out of here.

I took off along the tracks, heading downtown, staying low. Just across the road, it looked like life as usual at the Federal compound. A couple of people were even playing tennis in the sunshine. Ah, leisure! I realized that I had never actually seen anyone playing tennis before; I thought the game had been disinvented. At any rate, the players were too engrossed in their match to notice the bedraggled local skulking along the trolley tracks. The local was grateful.

After a while the tracks dipped down and headed underground. I faced a choice: go underground with them, or take my chances in the streets. Just then a jeep went racing by, not ten feet away from where I skulked, and made up my mind for me. I went into the tunnel.

It got very dark very quickly. I stayed to the right and kept one hand on the cold concrete wall. I moved slowly, in case there was a pit yawning unseen in front of me. I prayed that I wasn't disturbing any mutant creatures that had taken up residence down here. Still, I felt safer with the mutants than I did up above with my fellow humans. I kept walking.

Walking in total darkness is disorienting (as well as frightening). I wished I had my flashlight, but it had disappeared ages ago outside Bolton's house. Soon I didn't know where I was, and a while after that I scarcely knew who I was. All I could feel was pain; all I could think was that I had to get out of here. What if I was heading off into some secondary tunnel that branched endlessly underground without ever reaching a station? What if I was traveling in a circle somehow, and I was doomed to retrace my steps over and over again till I dropped? Logic said these fears were ridiculous. But what if logic stopped working in the dark?

Finally I saw a light in the distance: no, not a light at first, just a change in the quality of the darkness. But eventually it became a light, filtering greyly down from the outside. I was in Haymarket Station, a dilapidated sign informed me. I yearned to leave, but the Haymarket was scarcely any distance at all from where I had entered the tunnel. I kept walking.

I felt a little better now. The darkness was not forever, and I was heading in the right direction. But the next station was not the end of my journey.

Government Center, the sign said.

I figured I'd better avoid Government Center for a while.

I noticed a lot of strange objects on the platform of the station. I hesitated for a moment, then laboriously climbed out of the tunnel to take a closer look.

A bass drum. A chandelier with all its light bulbs broken. A rocking chair. A computer with its monitor smashed. Several cartons of books, their pages charred. Three teddy bears. A juke box (at least, I thought it was a juke box; I was a little unclear on the concept of juke boxes). A motorcycle lying on its side. Empty cans of food: Geisha, Bird's Eye, Del Monte, Spam. The ashes of a fire.

A man pointing at me in the dim light.

I stepped backwards, my heart knocking against my sore ribs. I blinked rapidly and looked again, wondering just how much damage the darkness had done to my senses.

The man still pointed at me, a long gloved finger stretching out in accusation. He was a muffled figure, seated on the platform and leaning back against a pillar.

"Hello?" I whispered, my voice shaking.

He didn't reply.

I noticed that his hand wasn't moving. I approached. A black knit cap was pulled down over the man's head. I reached out and touched the cap. He didn't move. I grabbed the cap and yanked it off.

A skull grinned up at me.

I closed my eyes. I had enough problems. I didn't need this. I opened my eyes. The skull was still there, still grinning, obviously delighted with its joke. I noticed a sheet of paper pinned to the raincoat it was wearing. I hesitated, then picked the paper up. A brief message was scrawled in red crayon on it:

Your gonna die too

I dropped the piece of paper. Well, I knew that. Still, I wasn't happy to be reminded of it. I tried to calm down. I knew what this was all about.

It was a remnant of the Frenzy. Once upon a time people had lived here (if you could call them people; if you could call it living), going out at night to rage and plunder, then returning with their random trophies. A computer, a juke box, a chandelier. What could have been more useless? Perhaps they had chosen the location out of some grim sense of irony—living their savage lives down here beneath the spot where the government had once tried to rule them.

They couldn't have stayed here long—it was not the most comfortable location in the city. But perhaps that didn't matter to them. Comfort was something out of the old days, something that bureaucrats and professors and businessmen cared about. Perhaps they had stayed here until the Feds arrived from Atlanta, smothering the city with their curfews and their laws, and the savages from the subway realized that the times had changed yet again. And so they had disappeared into some other darkness.

But not before they left a message for whoever would come here next.

Too bad for them I had more important things to worry about than my own mortality. I thought for a moment, then left the skeleton where it was; maybe the next passerby would make better use of the *memento mori*. I climbed down from the platform and continued my journey underground.

The next station was Park Street. This one was actually in use on a different track—a solitary train rumbled through it as often as it could, until some precious part gave out and a replacement had to be scrounged up. I decided that this was where I should leave the tunnel; at least I had a chance of being inconspicuous here. The trolley tracks I was following were upstairs from the train tracks. I waited until the train came in, then joined the people as they trudged up the long flight of stairs out of the subway.

Once outside, I blinked against the sun and looked around for soldiers, ready to run once more if challenged. I didn't see any.

"Howdy, Mithter Thandth."

I started, then relaxed. It was only Ground Zero, an old black man who eked out a living by sitting on a milk crate outside the station and singing—badly—while he played the accordion. "Howdy, Ground Zero."

Ground Zero looked up at me from his milk crate. "Been havin' a rough day, Mithter Thandth?"

"Yeah, I guess you could say that, Ground Zero."

"How 'bout a thong to make you feel better?"

"Haven't got any money today."

"That'th okay. For you, I'll thing it for free."

"All right," I said. "Sing something that'll chase away the darkness."

Ground Zero smiled. "I know jutht the tune." The accordion wheezed for a few bars, and then he started in on "The Sunny Side of the Street." The song didn't turn out all that well, actually—the lyrics proved to be rather a chore, given Ground Zero's unfortunate speech defect. But he got through it, and I did feel a little better by the time he had finished. And besides, it gave me a chance to come up with an idea about what to do next. "Thanks, Ground Zero," I said. "I owe you."

"No problem. Jutht leave your troubleth on your door thtep."

I smiled. "I'm sure gonna try." I walked up Tremont Street, keeping my eye out for soldiers, and turned onto School Street, where I found the establishment known as Art's Filthy Bookstore. I went inside, and I put myself in the hands of its estimable proprietor.

CHAPTER 17

M y friend Art is a pleasant-looking little old man with a long white beard. He is also a smut-peddler, but everyone's got to eat. His store is filled with books and magazines that let people fantasize about a world they can never experience. He has his own fantasies, but they aren't sexual: he dreams of literary soirées, of long philosophical discussions over a glass of sherry in faculty lounges, of a world where people can contemplate great ideas and meditate on the mysteries of life instead of brooding about the past (like Henry) or struggling just to stay alive. He feels that I am a kindred spirit, and I think he may be right.

"Walter!" he cried out when I staggered inside. "What happened to you?"

"Long story," I mumbled. The prospect of finally getting some relief made me realize how exhausted I was.

He led me through the bookstore and into the back room where he lived. I lay down on his cot and closed my eyes while he bustled about, trying to find something he could use to bandage my arm. "I should tell you that you might get into trouble if the Feds find out I'm here," I said. "They aren't happy with me at the moment."

I'm sure this didn't please Art, but he was brave about it. "Then we'll just have to keep the Feds from finding out," he replied. He sat down next to the cot and began tending my wounds. "Now tell me everything," he said.

I summarized for him the case so far. He shook his head in wonder as I described what I'd been through. "Why don't you write about these things instead of living them?" he asked.

That had been Henry's advice, too. "Maybe I will, if I ever get the chance. But right now I've got to figure out how to find Gwen before sunrise, or else TSAR says they're gonna kill her."

This was the kind of reality that made Art uncomfortable. It didn't make me feel very good either. "But what can you do, Walter?" he asked. "How can you find her?"

I tried to think. I had no more theories. The only thing I could do was to find out what Gwen's theory had been. How had she managed to find TSAR when no one else could? But to find out Gwen's theory I had to somehow get to the *Globe*. "Have you got a bicycle, Art?"

"Well, yes, but—"

I struggled dizzily to my feet. "I've gotta go to Dorchester and talk to Gwen's editor."

"Don't be a fool, Walter. You've got to rest. You won't help Gwen if you collapse on the way—or if the Feds capture you again."

I supposed he was right. "But I can't just stay here," I said.

"Look," Art said. "Why don't I send someone over to Bobby Gallagher's place? Mickey can come pick you up and drive you to Dorchester."

Bobby and Mickey once again. I decided to buy my own car once this was over and learn how to drive. Couldn't I accomplish *anything* without help? "I dunno," I said. I took a step; it wasn't a very steady one. I sighed. "All right."

"Good. Now rest."

I sank back onto the cot and rested.

Art got a teenage boy who lived next door to make the trip to South Boston for us. His payment was an ancient copy of *Playboy*, which sounded like a pretty good deal to me. While he was gone, Art cooked me some food and tried to keep my spirits up. "Have you thought about a title for your case yet?" he asked.

A title. When I had started on the case, I hadn't thought it deserved one. Now, well—a title couldn't hurt. But I sure was in no mood to come up with one. "Any suggestions?" I asked.

Art brought some scrambled eggs over to me, and I wolfed them down. He sat on a wooden chair next to the cot and considered. This was the sort of thing he enjoyed. "Your case really starts with the president and her dream, right?" he said after a while. "She thinks the referendum is the start of a great new age for America and the world."

"I suppose so."

"Then how about *Locksley Hall* for a title?" He smiled and quoted from the poem. "'For I dipped into the future, far as human eye could see,/Saw the Vision of the world, and all the wonder that would be.'"

"That's some serious irony," I said. I quoted from another part of the poem. "'Heard the heavens fill with shouting, and there rained a ghastly dew,/From the nations' airy navies grappling in the central blue.'"

"Irony is good in titles," Art pointed out, and he topped my quote. " 'Till the war drum throbbed no longer, and the battle flags were furled,/In the Parliament of man, the Federation of the world.'"

The Parliament of man, the Federation of the world. The president was having some difficulty with her vision of the world. All we had gotten so far was the ghastly dew.

"It's a bit obscure, don't you think? We're probably the only two people in Boston who know that poem."

"Why should that matter, Walter? It's not like anyone is going to read the book."

"That's a very good point."

I finished my eggs, and we waited for Mickey.

* * *

Eventually we heard the van pull up in front. Bobby and Doctor J came inside while Mickey stayed behind. I got to my feet and greeted them out in the store. "You didn't all have to come," I said.

"Wally, for Gwen we all come," Bobby replied. "You look like a piece of homemade shit, by the way."

"Thanks very much. Shall we get out of here?"

"Sure. Put that magazine down, Doctor J. Art, it's nice to see you again."

"Please be careful, everyone," Art said.

I shook Art's hand. "Thanks again," I said to him.

"'Not in vain the distance beacons,'" he replied. "'Forward, forward let us range.'"

"'Let the great world spin forever down the ringing grooves of change,'" I replied.

We went outside then, leaving Art behind, and I climbed into the back of the van with Mickey's tools. I waved to Mickey, who waved back. Doctor J and Bobby got in front, and we were off to the *Globe*.

Like everything else, the Boston *Globe* is not what it used to be. Once upon a time, its parking lots were jammed with cars, its rooftop antennae picked up information from around the world, its presses rolled ceaselessly, producing hundreds of thousands of ad-filled papers every day for news-hungry New Englanders. That's what the old-timers tell me, at any rate.

Nowadays, things are much more low-key. They still use the big old brick building on Morrissey Boulevard, but the parking lots are empty, the antennae useless, and the print runs minuscule. They still run some ads, though, including one for a certain private detective agency. And they still have some good reporters, especially Ms. Gwendolyn Phillips.

Mickey parked in the weed-covered lot outside the *Globe* Building. I peeked out the back window, looking for jeeps. If the Feds had any brains, they'd be here too, trying to find out what Gwen knew. There weren't any jeeps. No sense in taking any chances, though. "Go inside, Bobby," I said, "and ask Wolsey to come out here."

"Sure thing." Bobby got out of the van and headed into the building. The rest of us waited impatiently.

Ten minutes later Bobby returned with Gwen's editor, who clambered into the back of the van with me. Wolsey was a tall man with a fringe of black hair going gray. He wore bowties and ancient, frayed dress shirts. He adored Gwen.

"Thanks for coming out here," I said. "I'm kind of in trouble with the Feds, so I have to lie low."

"Walter, everyone's going to be in trouble with the Feds before very long, I'm afraid."

"Have they been here?"

"Cowens came late this morning—before we even knew Gwen had been captured. He asked some questions and poked through her desk."

"Did he find out anything? Do you know anything?"

Wolsey made a despairing gesture. "Walter, I wish I could help. We've got every reporter in the place working on this. But we just haven't come up with anything. Gwen came in early this morning and she was worried about you, because I guess you hadn't come home last night. Apparently you had some damn-fool theory about Bolton, right? Anyway, she wrote up a story about the investigation, and then she said she had a lead she wanted to follow up on, and she left. That's all we know."

"No idea what the lead was?"

Wolsey shook his head.

"And no idea where she was going?"

Wolsey made the same despairing gesture again.

"Did Cowens act like he knew anything?"

"Oh, you know Cowens. He just gives you that icy stare, and you can't figure out what he's thinking. When I thought about it afterwards, though, I was a little surprised that it was just him. I would've expected a bunch of soldiers to come in and turn the place upside down."

"I wonder if they were all out looking for me."

Wolsey shrugged. "I have no idea what the Feds are up to. They're just a lot less pugnacious than I thought they'd be."

"Apparently they're doing what they think Kramer would've wanted. Maybe they figure this'll keep her alive."

"I wouldn't count on their restraint lasting beyond sunrise tomorrow, though. Find Gwen, Walter. And the president. I'm getting scared."

"I'll do my best."

Wolsey shook my hand, then slid out of the van and returned to the *Globe*.

"Now what?" Bobby asked.

"Well," I said, "I guess we could give Louisburg Square a try."

Mickey promptly started up the van and headed back down town.

I was worried about returning home—the Feds certainly knew where I lived—but I was running out of options. Maybe Gwen had gone home after leaving the *Globe*, and maybe she had left behind some clue that the Feds had overlooked. A dim hope, perhaps, but what other hope did I have?

We were silent as Mickey drove. Things were too serious for idle conversation. It was getting late in the day. Another night loomed—and then sunrise. I shivered. "Pull up here," I murmured as Mickey drove along a Beacon Hill street leading into the square. Mickey stopped the van, and I prepared to get out.

"Let me go, Wally," Doctor J offered.

"Thanks, Doctor J, but no. Too dangerous."

"Less dangerous for me than you. I'm just a kid. What are they gonna do to me?"

"He's got a point, Wally," Bobby said.

Everybody wanted to help. The Feds could do plenty to Doctor J. "Look," I said. "Just turn the corner and see if the Feds are watching the place. Don't try and be a hero, okay?"

"You betcha." Doctor J scrambled out of the van and walked around the corner into the square. We waited. "We'll find her, Wally," Bobby said. I didn't reply.

After an eternity Doctor J came back. "Coupla Feds in a jeep outside," he reported. "I said I was lookin' for Stretch. They said nobody's home. They asked if I knew anybody else that lived there. I said nope, I just had a sewer problem needed fixin'. They told me to get lost. I thought about goin' around back and breakin' in, but I figured I should ask you first, Wally."

"Good man, Doctor J. You've done enough." I was disappointed. One more door closed. How many were left open?

We could break in the back, I thought, but it would probably be too risky.

"We should get outa here," Mickey observed, "in case they decide to take a look where Doctor J went."

"All right. Let's go talk to Stretch. Maybe he knows something."

Mickey nodded and started up the van. We drove down the back side of Beacon Hill toward Government Center.

The vigil had grown enormously since yesterday, I noticed as we swung around the plaza, heading toward City Hall. More people were in the plaza now than had been there to hear the president give her speech. Nothing appeared to be happening, though. No speeches, no band playing. Just people, silently waiting. It was impressive.

Our van was the only non-government vehicle in sight. "Kinda conspicuous," Mickey muttered. He parked behind City Hall. Once again, Bobby was commissioned to be the messenger. He returned a few minutes later, alone. "Nobody home in the sewer department," he said. "Sorry."

"Well," I said, "maybe he's—"

A quick gesture from Bobby silenced me. I heard slow footsteps outside the van. The three faces in the front seat turned forward. I slid down out of sight in the back.

The footsteps stopped. "What y'all doin' heah?" a Southern voice asked.

"Just looking for a friend," Bobby said. "Works at City Hall."

"We're kinda suspicious of cars hangin' around these parts, y'know."

"I can well understand. We'll just move along, then."

"Think Ah'll jes' take a look in back first. Open it up."

"Well, of course. Mickey, open it up."

Mickey got out. More footsteps. I took out the gun I had grabbed from the soldier at Leverett Circle. I leaned forward.

Mickey fumbled with the lock, making a lot of noise—as if I didn't already know what was going on. And then the doors were open. I saw the face of a young recruit, his rifle not quite at the ready. I could have shot him then, but I didn't. It occurred to me that the noise would be sure to get us into even more trouble, but that wasn't the real reason I didn't shoot. I didn't shoot because I had a chance to look into the soldier's eyes and see the sudden fear, and that made me feel my visceral revulsion toward death. Too many people have died.

Then Mickey was grabbing the rifle, and the two of them were struggling. It wasn't going to be much of a struggle, I realized, what with Mickey's shriveled arm and all.

I lunged forward and whacked the soldier on the back of the head with the butt end of my gun. He stopped struggling and looked at me, dazed. I hit him again, and he crumpled. I dragged him into the van, and Mickey quickly shut the doors behind us.

I took away his rifle and handed it up front to Bobby.

"Anybody see us?" I asked.

Bobby and Doctor J both shook their heads. "Don't think so," Bobby muttered.

Mickey got back behind the wheel. "Gotta get outa here," he said.

"Is he dead?" Doctor J asked, his eyes wide with fear and maybe a little excitement.

"No, just unconscious."

"Well, uh, what do we do with him?" Bobby murmured.

He wanted someone else to say it: we were a lot better off with the soldier dead than with him unconscious. I wasn't going to be the one to say it, though. "Look," I said, "we'll be okay if we just dump him way out in the suburbs someplace. He won't get back to town before tomorrow, and tomorrow who knows what the world's gonna be like."

"But what about Gwen?" Bobby asked.

"Mickey and Doctor J can take care of dumping the soldier. Bobby, why don't you go back to the vigil and see if Stretch is there? I'll be over on Atlantic Avenue by the Aquarium."

"Why Atlantic Ave.?"

"Because Stretch is a creature of habit, that's why. If he's at the vigil, bring him on over. He'll know where to find me. "

No one else had a better plan, and no one was volunteering to put a bullet into the unconscious soldier, so they obeyed me. I found a coil of rope in with Mickey's tools and tied up the soldier. Bobby got out and walked back to the plaza.

Mickey drove me the few blocks to Atlantic Avenue.

"Thanks for everything, guys," I said.

"Good luck, Wally," Doctor J replied, and he gave me a high five.

"Mickey, drop the soldier way the hell out of town."

"He'll wake up in Rhode Island, Wally." He waved into the rear view mirror. I struggled past the soldier, climbed down from the back of the van, and closed the doors. Mickey pulled away with another wave, leaving me alone in the street.

I walked quickly over to the ruins of the Aquarium. I searched behind a couple of rusted beams and found what I was looking for: Stretch's clothing, hidden while he went jogging. I breathed a sigh of relief and settled down out of sight to wait for him.

The view was as beautiful as ever, and I was as uninterested as ever in looking at it. Storm clouds lurked off to the west, but the harbor to the east in front of me was bright and calm. A few boats bobbed up and down at anchor, gleaming in the twilight sun; gulls dived and soared. But who cared? Gwen had maybe twelve hours to live, I was a tired, hunted man, and the rest of the world was in just as much of a mess as ever, despite President Kramer's dreams. I tried not to think about all of that, but it was hard.

"Get away from my clothes or you're in big trouble," a rather thin voice warned me.

I roused myself. "Who'd want to steal a pair of dwarf pants and a briefcase full of stuff about sewers?" I wondered aloud.

"Oh, Walter, it's you," Stretch said, coming around the fallen beams to where I was sitting. He was sweating, and his face was flushed. "I just saw the top of your head. What are you doing here? What happened last night? We've been so worried." And as he came closer: "Gee, you look terrible. Are you all right?"

"Yeah, I'm okay. Do you know about Gwen?"

Stretch shook his head. I hadn't expected that he would, if he was out jogging. Cowens was certainly flubbing this investigation, I thought; the Feds should have interrogated Stretch as soon as they got the message from TSAR. Well, Cowens was a soldier, not a policeman. "What's the matter?" Stretch demanded. "Is Gwen in trouble too?"

"I'm afraid so, Stretch." And I gave him a quick summary of what had happened since I left him to stake out Bolton's house. Had it really been less than a day?

Stretch was stunned. "You've been tortured? And Gwen's been kidnapped? And I'm out here jogging as if nothing were the matter?"

"Don't worry about that, Stretch. Just tell me if you have any idea what Gwen's lead was, or where she was going today."

Stretch chewed a knuckle. "I can't—I don't—"

"What happened last night? Did she say anything?"

"Well, of course when she got home I told her about you and your crazy theory about Governor Bolton. She wanted to go find you, but I guess she thought you wouldn't appreciate it. We figured you'd spend the night out there, you know, from stubbornness, then come home. We never dreamed—anyway. I went to bed finally, and when I woke up Gwen was gone." Stretch paused for a moment, then continued excitedly. "But wait a minute, Walter, I think she left you a note—you know, on the kitchen table."

"Jesus, Stretch, that's it! That's it!" Then it was my turn to pause. The Feds might have missed Stretch, but they couldn't miss a note sitting on the kitchen table. So they'd have it, and I'd be out of luck. But then I thought: so what? That only meant they'd be the ones to save Gwen, not me. And the important thing was to save Gwen, right? "Stretch, would you go back home and see if you can get that note? You'll have to talk your way past a couple of soldiers. But look: if they won't let you in, tell them about the note, if they don't already know about it. Tell them it might be the key to finding the president, to everything. Let them take it, if they want, just so long as they go looking for Gwen."

Stretch nodded. "I understand, Walter." He started putting on his pants. "Don't worry," he said, "I'll get in there." He fastened his belt with a determined flourish.

I had every confidence in Stretch. When he put his mind to something, he was unstoppable. "I'll wait for you here," I said.

"Right." He finished dressing, then stuck his sweaty running clothes in his briefcase. "Gwen will be fine, Walter," he promised me, "and the president will be fine, and everything will work out for the best. Just wait and see."

"I believe you, Stretch." I didn't believe him. He gave me a reassuring pat and strode off to Louisburg Square.

I was alone again. The storm clouds were closer; the wind was picking up; the boats bobbed a little more actively in the harbor. It wasn't that I disbelieved Stretch, exactly; it was just that I didn't trust his optimism as much as I did his self-confidence. History hadn't lent a lot of support to Stretch's habitual state of mind.

I stared at the ruins of the Aquarium. No, optimism was generally not called for. I caught a quick reflection of myself in a shard of broken glass, and I didn't like what I saw. Wouldn't it have been instructive, I thought, if people in the old days could have had a museum of the future, instead of gawking at turtles and dolphins and whatever else they kept in the Aquarium? Not people's dreams of the future, or politicians' promises, but this thing I was actually living in. Maybe I could be a specimen, to help them temper their optimism with a little reality.

Here, children, is an example of the quite rare oculis privatus postnuclearensis, *or post-nuclear private eve. This creature haunts the subways and ruined buildings of his world, scrounging meals of little nutritional value and rarely, if ever, doing any real work. Note this specimen's bandaged arm and bruised face, indicative of the dangers he encounters in his nomadic-existence. Note also the slightly glazed expression, often associated with the general intellectual deterioration of this era. Don't go too close to the cage, Jennifer! Do you see the gun stuck in the waistband of his patched and faded jeans? Children, you must never provoke an* oculis privatus postnuclearensis.

I grinned a savage grin through the bars of my cage. "C'mere, little Jennifer. I won't hurt you. Everything is fine in the future. *The war drum throbs no longer, and the battle flags are furled.* Haven't they taught you that in class, Jennifer?"

I don't think Jennifer would have believed me. The vision faded.

I started thinking about Gwen instead. Maybe the Feds had already saved her. Not likely, though. If she was saved, the president was saved, and the vigil would be over. But the vigil was still very much in progress. So Gwen would be sitting somewhere, probably not far away from here, and probably alone as well. Perhaps she'd be daydreaming, not of the old days, but of rescue, of a knight in shining armor. I supposed she would settle for a banged-up friend with a gun in his waistband—or even for a few hundred soldiers who couldn't have cared less about her, but were willing to free her while in the neighborhood taking care of more important business.

Maybe, I thought, she wasn't alone. Maybe she was sitting with President Kramer in some grim warehouse room, getting her interview at last. Would the president still be as passionate and convincing as she had been at the Federal compound with me?

Or had a couple of days with TSAR subdued her, shaken her faith in herself and in America? I had a feeling it would take a lot to shake President Kramer's faith.

It was getting dark now, and cold. It would be raining soon. What was the problem? Suppose the Feds hadn't believed Stretch. Suppose they had carted *him* off for torture. The Feds were stupid enough to do something like that. Or maybe they'd all just left without me. Why bother with the Sandman? He'd simply screw it up somehow.

Finally I heard footsteps over the rocks and broken cobblestones, and I saw Stretch's tiny figure approaching. He still clutched his briefcase. I stood up and hurried over to him. "What happened?"

His face was glum; my heart sank. He reached into his pocket and took out a piece of paper. He handed it to me. I read Gwen's familiar handwriting in the fading light.

Walter: Meet me at the Globe before noon.

Please.

Love, G.

"I'm sorry, Walter," Stretch whispered.

CHAPTER 18

I sat down on a rock and stared some more at the useless note.

"People from the government had already searched the place," Stretch said. "Or I guess it was just General Cowens, according to the soldiers I talked to. He saw the note, but apparently he'd already been to the *Globe* so it didn't help him either."

"Did the soldiers give you a hard time?"

"Not really. They were just looking for you. They were the guys who took you to the president that time— remember? The short guy with the bad skin, and the taller guy who stutters?"

I nodded.

"Anyway, I was afraid they might follow me, but I don't think they did. They seemed concerned about you, Walter. They said if I saw you I should tell you to turn yourself in. They said things'll be a lot worse for you if you're caught."

"Okay," I said. "You've told me."

Stretch sat down next to me. "It'll be all right, Walter," he said. "Believe me."

I didn't bother to respond. This time, I don't think he believed himself.

Stretch opened his briefcase. "I brought some other

stuff," he said. "Papers and things that were lying around. I thought—you're the private eye. Maybe you could find something Cowens overlooked."

I reached into the briefcase and grabbed a sheet at random.

Walter: Buy bread!
G.

I closed my eyes. This was not helpful. I remembered reading the note a couple of weeks ago. And I remembered that I had never bought the bread.

Her penmanship was so much like my own, I thought. I had taught her to write, back when we were little more than children, spending an idyllic winter together in an undiscovered fallout shelter. If she were to die...

I tried to stomp out the melodrama. Unprofessional. I reached into the briefcase again and took out a notebook. It was empty. I flung it at the harbor and grabbed again. A reminder to pay the iceman. A draft of a letter to the tax department. A doodle. It was the detritus of our everyday lives, not the fabulous clues I needed to solve this case, to save Gwen.

"I'm sorry, Walter," Stretch said again.

"Not your fault, Stretch."

And then, at the bottom of the briefcase, I found what I needed: a scrap of a yellowed envelope with a single word written on it. I studied the word in the fading light. "Where did you find this?" I asked Stretch.

He looked at the envelope. "Gee, Walter, I'm not sure. Maybe—maybe on that little desk in your bedroom. Is it important?"

I could see Gwen stopping off at home to change her clothes before following up on her lead. Or maybe she returned home to look for me—hoping that I had stubbornly ignored her note and was sitting in my third-floor room and brooding about the case. Perhaps she quickly emptied her pockets before leaving, and this one scrap of paper got left behind as she hurried off to be kidnapped. A scrap of paper that Cowens would have no reason to pay any attention to, because he is an outsider, and therefore can never really understand us. "Yeah. I think it's important, Stretch."

The two of us stared at the word scrawled in pencil on the yellowed paper:

mummy

"I don't get it," Stretch said. "Whose mother? Gwen's an *orphan.*"

"We're all orphans," I murmured. I stood up. "I've gotta get going."

Stretch scrambled to his feet. "Wait a minute, Walter. You have to tell me what you're up to."

Did I? "If I told you," I said, "you'd just want to bring in the Feds."

"Well, what of it? You were willing to bring in the Feds when I went home to get Gwen's note."

"Only if there was no other way to get it. Look, if the Feds are involved, they have only one priority: saving the president. If Gwen happens to get saved too, well, that's okay, but no big deal. Also, what if I'm right about Bolton? I haven't entirely given up on that theory, you know. It'd be just what he wanted, to have us go tell him we know where he's keeping the president."

"And you won't even take me along?"

I shook my head. "This is a job for a professional, Stretch. You'd only get in the way."

Stretch glared at me. "I don't believe any of your reasons," he said. "You're just trying to be a hero. You've botched everything in this case and now you want to make up for your mistakes."

"That's not true." At least, not exactly. "Would I risk Gwen's life just so I can be a hero? I haven't got time to argue with you, Stretch. Just go back home and try to relax. Everything will be fine. Trust me."

Stretch continued to glare. He didn't exude trust. Where was his optimism when I needed it? He didn't say anything; he knew he wasn't going to get anywhere with me. I could be as stubborn as he was. I turned and walked away from him finally, and he didn't complain, and he didn't follow.

I had a long walk ahead of me, I realized as I started down Atlantic Avenue. I was not in the best of shape, and it was starting to rain. My arm throbbed; my head hurt; I was hungry. But there was no one to help me, even if I wanted help. Bobby was still at the vigil, presumably, waiting for Stretch to show up; Mickey and Doctor J were off somewhere dumping the unconscious soldier. And I had dismissed Stretch as unworthy of being my sidekick.

Well, I honestly did think he'd get in the way. And I *was* worried about the Feds. And I did believe I could save Gwen by myself.

But I had to admit I was glad things had turned out this way. I was in control now, with no friends to lend a hand, nothing to rely on in solving the case but my own ingenuity and courage. What more could a private eye ask for?

A bicycle. It would take forever to get where I was going without one. So what was I supposed to do? I sighed. It was time to be a bad guy. I took out my gun.

The street was deserted, but I figured it wouldn't stay deserted for long. I stopped by the bridge that goes over the Fort Point Channel into South Boston. There was a bad section of pavement at the end. I stood in the shadows just past the bad part, and I waited.

Eventually I saw a lone, hooded figure pedaling across the bridge. I watched the figure reach the broken pavement and slow down, then finally dismount and start to walk the bike across. And that's when I came out of the shadows. "Listen," I said. "I'm really sorry to do this, but I need your bike."

"Oh, shit," the figure said. It was a woman's voice. She took off the hood of her sweatshirt. She was pretty but tired-looking. She had the defeated expression of someone who has struggled for too long with too little to show for it. She stared unhappily at the gun. "But I need the bike," she said. "I'm a messenger. The bike is how I make my living."

I sighed. Gwen had been a messenger before she had become a reporter. "I'm sorry," I said. "This is an emergency. I'd pay you, but I don't have any money right at the moment." I had an idea. "Tell me where you live, and I'll bring the bike back to you afterwards."

The woman didn't seem to think this was such a great idea. Then she had one of her own. "Look," she said, her voice shaking. "I'll let you have sex with me if I can keep the bike."

She knew that this wasn't such a great idea either. If I wanted to rape her and still take her bike, I could do it. But she was desperate. Well, I was desperate too. This is a desperate world. Why couldn't I have run into a thug instead of her? "How about this," I suggested. "If you don't want me to find out where you live, I'll bring the bike to Art's Filthy Bookstore, over on School Street. You can pick it up there tomorrow."

I thought this was pretty reasonable, but the woman started crying instead of carrying on with the negotiations. The rain was coming down harder now, and her face looked as if it was going to dissolve in all the moisture. "Why does everything have to happen to *me*?" she sobbed. "I didn't ask to be born. Why is life so *hard*?"

I had no answers. And I had no time to listen to her life story, which she seemed about ready to tell me. All I had was a gun and a need. I gently disengaged her hand from the bike. She let it go and sat down in the middle of the street, wailing. "Art's Filthy Bookstore," I repeated. "Everything will be all right."

"Why me?" she asked the darkness. "Why always me?"

I got on the bike and pedaled away, and soon the woman's wailing became just part of the distant wind.

I went as fast as I could through the dark streets. On Essex Street I hit a pothole that sent me flying. What were a few more bruises at this point? On Columbus Avenue a couple of soldiers on patrol decided I looked suspicious, and I had to zigzag through a few side streets before they gave up the chase. But finally, wet and weary, I ended up where I wanted to be: on Huntington Avenue, facing one of those massive reminders of the grandeur of the past and the degeneracy of the present.

It was the Museum of Fine Arts. Here, I was certain, I would find Gwen and the president.

The Frenzy was irrational, to be sure, but not totally mindless. People made decisions about what to deface, what to destroy. And what they chose were generally the most precious things from the old days—not just the weapons and the computers and all the now-useless high-tech apparatus of the old civilization, but its books and paintings and beautiful buildings as well. These objects were as useful (or useless) as they had ever been, but the people in the Frenzy hated them just the same. They were reminders, I suppose, of an era that was now irrevocably over, of wealth and leisure and joy that we in the new era would never know—of a smug, self-satisfied world that could create this wretched new world we had to live in, out of ignorance or arrogance or simple, inexplicable evil.

The Museum of Fine Arts was therefore one of the main targets of the Frenzy. I don't know how much of its contents have been destroyed, but it was enough, I know, to destroy some people too.

I had a friend once named Martha Comstock. She was an old lady—well, perhaps not so old; I find it difficult often to tell what in a person's appearance is due to age and what is due to suffering. At any rate, she had been in high society in the old days, serving on committees and giving teas and generally leading a life that is scarcely comprehensible to us recent arrivals. After the War, her son disappeared and her husband died and she had to struggle like the rest of us. But she did all right. She managed to hold onto her home on Beacon Hill—not far from the residence we had commandeered in Louisburg Square—and she survived by selling her precious possessions to the likes of Bobby Gallagher.

She took an interest in Gwen and Stretch and Linc and me. We were the harbingers of a future that held promise of being somewhat better than the past decade or two. We in turn kept an eye on her, and tried to shield her from the harsher aspects of her new life. She was a tough woman, though, and didn't need much shielding—at least, not of the sort we could offer.

I brought her a bag of apples one September afternoon.

I found her staring out the window with that glazed-eyed look I recognized as that of an old-timer remembering the old times. This wasn't like Martha; she never mentioned her family or her friends or her lost pleasures. So I was worried. "Martha?" I said. "What's the matter?"

She turned away from the window and stared at me. "The past is gone," she said in her patrician accent.

"Uh-huh," I replied. This was not news.

"I went to the Museum of Fine Arts today," she continued.

Her tone was neutral, as if mentioning a trip to the corner store.

"You did what?" People did not go to the museum, for a reason I will soon get to.

She waved her hand, dismissing the unspoken reason. "I kept myself from going all these years," she said. "It just seemed too hard. But today I woke up and I saw the leaves turning brown, and I started wondering how much time I had left, and I decided I had better do it before it's too late." She looked away. "I should not have gone," she whispered.

"Why, Martha?"

She got up from her chair and went into the next room. She returned a moment later with a painting.

A painting of a cathedral, shimmering in blue against a blue sky, and fading to darkness at the bottom.

Done in little dabs of color, so that the cathedral seemed real and yet not real, so that it seemed as if you were seeing cathedrals—seeing the sky—in a whole new way.

"Monet," Martha said. "My parents used to take me to the museum as a child, and this was my favorite painting. I don't know why, exactly. Perhaps because the world just seemed so beautiful when seen through Monet's eyes. I wanted to look at the world that way myself, but I suppose I lacked the imagination, so Monet had to do it for me. I never grew out of my love for this painting. You would think—well, I became a grownup, a mother, too old for such feelings. But they didn't change. They have never changed. Even the War...the War simply made Monet more important than ever, because it made the beauty so much harder for us to see. And now..."

Her voice trailed off as she stared at the masterpiece.

It was a painting of a cathedral, shimmering in blue against a blue sky, and fading to darkness at the bottom.

Ripped almost in half, and across it was scrawled in black ink: "Fuck Art." The ink dribbled down from the words and over the cathedral, like poison dropping from the sky.

I had never seen Martha cry. But she was crying now. "And we did it to ourselves," she sobbed. "We did it to ourselves."

I tried to think of something comforting. "You know," I said, "working for Bobby, I've noticed that a lot of art has been saved. He's always coming across people with impressive paintings and sculptures and what-not for sale."

Martha shrugged as she tried to compose herself. "But what's gone is gone forever," she pointed out. "The books that you read—there may always be another copy somewhere, if yours is destroyed. Not my Monet."

I didn't have much of an argument to counter that. I just had the one all-purpose cliché everyone used to lift each other's spirits. "At least you're still alive," I offered. "Life is worth something, isn't it?"

Martha shrugged again.

She died that winter.

So. Another cheery story from my vast repertoire. The obvious point is that the Museum of Fine Arts no longer contained much in the way of fine art—at least so far as anyone knew. And this brings up the less obvious point—

and the one that was especially relevant to my case. Martha is the only person I know who has been in the museum since the Frenzy.

The reason is not very reasonable, but these are not particularly reasonable times. Among the treasures of the museum had been a few mummies. In a world that has been filled with corpses, it is somehow strange to think that these particular corpses were once considered to be worth displaying (like the future *oculis privatus*) for public edification; such were the inscrutable ways of people in the old days. At any rate, the mummies had also been destroyed during the Frenzy. And that, you see, had caused the Mummy's Curse to fall on the museum.

I have never heard a precise explanation of just what the Mummy's Curse entails. But certainly people believe that the ghosts of the destroyed mummies haunt the museum (looking, presumably, for those who disturbed their peace), and that anyone who dares enter the museum had better not expect to come out. Even people who don't believe this (or profess not to believe it) stay away from the museum as well, out of cultural solidarity, perhaps, or simple prudence. Oh, I suppose some Northeastern students from across Huntington Avenue sneak in as a rite of passage—but maybe not. I imagine they could find easier ways to prove their courage than risking the wrath of these dead Egyptians. I certainly had never ventured into the place. And that's why I had been so surprised at Martha's trip there.

And that's why the museum was the perfect place to hold a kidnapped president and a nosy reporter.

The museum was completely dark. But the place was huge, and there was no telling from the outside what was going on in its bowels. I pedaled up the circular drive and dismounted by the large statue out front. The statue was of an Indian on horseback, looking up at the sky with his hands outstretched. He seemed to be saying, "Why me? Why always me?" like the poor girl whose bike I had stolen. I left the bike there and walked toward the building. Was I scared? Oh, maybe a little. Did I think about the curse? Oh, maybe once or twice. Actually, I was looking forward to meeting a bunch of cold-blooded thugs inside, because if they had survived a couple of days in the museum then there would be less of a chance I would run into any of those dead Egyptians.

Who would those thugs be? Bolton's people? Members of the Church of the New Beginning? Henry Fisher and some angry friends? More likely, it was someone I had never heard of, and all my efforts to figure out the case had brought me nowhere near its solution.

I walked slowly up the long steps to the carved wooden doors. I tried the handle. It wouldn't budge. I groped along the front of the building, looking for a window. A flashlight sure would have been nice. Finally I found a window with its bars bent back and the glass broken, and I squeezed my way inside.

I brought my right foot slowly down onto the floor, and then my left. My left foot landed on something round—a vase?—which promptly rolled away. I lost my balance and fell on my wounded arm. The noise echoed through the building. I stifled a groan and waited. I didn't hear anything else. I was sweating. The room had the familiar abandoned-building smell of dampness and rot. The darkness was deeper here than it had been outside.

I closed my eyes and rested for a moment as the pain in my arm subsided. It seemed as if I had been spending a lot of time in the dark lately. I thought of the darkness on the way to the Church of the New Beginning, rural and frightening, like my childhood; and the darkness outside Bolton's mansion—the lonely darkness of the cruel city; and finally the subterranean darkness of my journey underground—the darkness that always lurked beneath the surface of our lives, no matter how sunny the world appeared to us dwellers in the light. *Your gonna die too.*

So what kind had I come upon now?

This is real life, Gwen had told me. And Gwen, as always, was right. What I had here was simply one more obstacle to be overcome, something that stood between me and Gwen—and Gwen was all that mattered. I opened my eyes and got to my feet. Time to press on.

But where? It took me several minutes just to grope my way out of the room I was in. And then what? I picked a direction at random and set out. Every step was an adventure, every movement was dangerous. I began to feel the way I had in the subway. If I didn't find some thugs or some mummies, I was going to be stuck wandering in the dark here forever. Or at least until dawn. And dawn, I realized, would be too late.

I wondered if the mummies felt this way.

My arm throbbed. My stomach started to growl.

And then I saw a light. At first I thought it was a match appearing out of the darkness right in front of me, and I tensed for battle. Then I realized that I had lost all my perspective, and the light was really some distance away down a long corridor.

Thank God. I moved my hands carefully along the wall till I found a room off the corridor, and I slipped into it. I waited there as the light approached.

Now, I thought, it will begin.

CHAPTER 19

With the light came voices, murmuring. Mummies don't talk, I figured. I strained to make out what was being said. It was difficult; my pounding heart seemed to be louder than the voices. Eventually the light reached the room in which I was cowering, and there it stopped. I ordered my stomach not to growl. I saw the flickering shadows of two men against the far wall. Between the shadows was a painting of Boston Common at twilight back in the old days. It is winter. A mother watches her child feeding pigeons. There are trolleys and gas lamps. I suddenly ached with memories I had never actually experienced. And then I noticed with horror that my own shadow was part of the tableau. Too late to do anything about it, though. I pressed back against the wall and listened.

"I bet it was rats," a man's voice said.

"Yeah, rats," another male voice agreed.

Neither voice sounded sure of itself. Both voices sounded familiar.

"Can't search the whole fucking building," the first voice said.

"Just draw attention to us," the second voice pointed out, "if it's only a couple of kids screwing around."

"Who'd want to screw around in this place?" the first voice whined. "I wish we could get the hell out of here."

"Won't be long now."

"We shoulda left as soon as that other broad showed up."

"More dangerous movin' than stayin'."

"The whole thing's too fuckin' dangerous."

"Too late to back out now," the second voice said glumly. "Christ." There was a pause as the two men contemplated their situation. I prayed they didn't contemplate their shadows at the same time.

"I suppose we should go downstairs and check on Freddy and the other broad," the first voice said.

"Can't hurt," the second voice agreed. And then the light started to fade.

I carefully stuck my head out into the corridor and watched as the torch returned the way it came. My eyes were used to the dim light now, and it was easy enough to make out the retreating forms of my old Charlestown bike-stealing buddies Pete Santoro and Eddie Grimes.

I didn't have time to figure out what the hell they were doing here. Right now I had to figure out where they were going, because "that other broad," clearly, was Gwen.

I followed them along the corridor. It wasn't easy, since I had to go faster now to keep up, and their torch wasn't much help to me. If I tripped again, I was doomed. Eventually the torch turned left and headed down, leaving me in darkness. I decided not to risk following them downstairs. I retreated into a room off the corridor, and I waited for the torch to reappear.

Santoro and Grimes. Damn them, it didn't make sense. But then again, I supposed it did. Damn them.

There were footsteps on the stairs, and the torch came into view once again. "—much more of this," Grimes was saying.

"Just till morning," Santoro replied. "He promised. We just gotta stick it out till morning."

"I'll believe it when it happens," Grimes said.

The torch continued up the next flight of stairs. I waited until its light had disappeared once again and the sound of their footsteps had faded. Then I crept forward to the staircase.

My hand grasped the smooth banister, and I started down, pausing on each stair to minimize the noise. When the staircase made a turn, I saw a light, and I saw the guy they had called Freddy. He was closing a door across the corridor at the foot of the stairs. I waited as he set down the smoky lantern he was carrying and settled into a chair outside the door. Then he picked up a magazine. From where I was lurking, it looked like he had bought it at Art's Filthy Bookstore.

The chair was angled half toward me and half toward the door he was guarding. Freddy didn't look like a very formidable adversary—he was short and scrawny, and the top of his head was bald. Had he been one of the thugs on O'Malley's porch? It didn't really matter who he was or how strong he was; I had to get past him.

I didn't want to shoot him, although I felt capable of it to save Gwen. Santoro and Grimes were at least smart enough to figure out that rats don't make *that* much noise. But doing anything else meant I had to get closer.

I moved down a stair. It creaked. I froze. I hoped Freddy's magazine was interesting. He shifted and kept reading.

I tried another stair, then another. *Creak.* The magazine dropped into Freddy's lap. I got out my gun, ready to shoot. Freddy's head fell to one side, and he started to snore. The poor guy was making it easy on me. I descended the final few stairs, then crossed the remainder of the distance that separated us. I turned the gun around and whacked him on top of his bald head. He twitched a bit, and I cursed silently. I had simply roused him instead of knocking him out. But then he slumped still farther down into his chair, and I took a deep breath. I had won the first round.

He was wearing a shoulder holster; I lifted his arm and took the gun out of it. Then I picked up his lantern and hurried over to the door he had been guarding. The key was in the lock. I turned the key and opened the door.

It looked like a workshop of some kind. There were long tables surrounded by stools, and lots of cupboards and shelves.

But where was—?

In a corner of the room, I made out a human shape on the floor, covered by a sheet. "Gwen!" I whispered.

She didn't respond, and my heart stopped. Was she—I couldn't bring myself to think it. Besides, why would they be guarding her if she was—

She turned over on the floor and started to snore. Softer than Freddy, but audible nevertheless.

I went across the room and shook her. "Hey, Gwen!" I whispered. "Wake up! I've rescued you, goddamit!"

She opened her eyes and gazed up at me groggily. "Walter?"

"Yes, it's me. You're not dreaming. Are you okay?"

She thought for a moment. "I guess so. They put me in here, I dunno, a long time ago, and after a while I figured they weren't going to kill me or anything, and there was nothing else to do, so—" Her gaze got a little less groggy. "You look terrible, Walter," she said.

"Yeah, well." I wanted to mention how I'd been tortured and shot and chased and all of that while she was having a nap, but I decided to let it pass for the moment.

Meanwhile Gwen was becoming more and more alert. "The guard," she said.

"I knocked him out. We've gotta tie him up and gag him before he comes to. You suppose there's any rope in here?"

Gwen got up, and we searched through the workshop. We found some cord wrapped around a canvas, and we ripped up Gwen's sheet for a gag. Within a few minutes, Freddy was bound and gagged in the room where Gwen had been relaxing all afternoon.

We stayed with him for the moment; we had some talking to do, and we didn't want to make any noise. But there was one more thing to be done before talking: a long hug was required under the circumstances. We did what was required.

"I knew you'd rescue me," Gwen whispered finally.

"Then you knew a lot more than I did."

"You're the best private eye I've ever met."

"And you're the best reporter. How'd you find out about the museum, anyway?"

She shrugged. "A guy was walking along Huntington Avenue last night, and he saw a light, and he thought for sure it was the mummies' ghosts. So he came to the *Globe*, and I was the one who talked to him. I wasn't really sure it had anything to do with the president, but I figured it was worth checking out."

"Good thinking."

"I wish you'd been with me, though. I'm no private eye. I barely got inside before they captured me."

"Well, I was busy, I guess. Did you see the president?"

Gwen shook her head. "What exactly is going on? I don't even know what time it is. Are you alone?"

"Yup." Now was the time to rehash my exciting day for her. I did so briefly.

Gwen was appropriately impressed and distressed. "Oh, I'm so sorry, Walter. But you know, that Bolton idea was completely—"

"Yeah, yeah. You're right. Stretch was right. It was stupid. But I didn't hear anyone coming up with the real perpetrators." And I recounted my discovery, moments before, of who the real perpetrators were. "How do you like that?" I said. "All my clever theories turn out to be hogwash, and this other theory about O'Malley, the one I make up on the spur of the moment to escape from jail— that turns out to be the right one. How do you figure it?"

"Maybe your made-up theory was more, I don't know, instinctive."

"But my instincts still tell me it's wrong. Or I just want it to be wrong. It's so damn banal. O'Malley wants to take over Boston, so he kidnaps the president to get rid of the Feds. He keeps her here because he's afraid the Feds will suspect him and start searching in Charlestown. So O'Malley's thugs were the ones who beat me up outside our house. Big deal."

"But how did they know you were on the case?" Gwen wondered. "And what about the sandals? What about the empty file?"

I threw up my hands. "I dunno. This is real life, I guess. It's messy. Or I'm just stupid, and I can't tie up all the loose ends."

"Anyway," she said, "we should figure out what to do."

"Why don't we just leave? You're safe, and that's all that matters. Let some other folks risk their lives saving the president."

"But that won't exactly improve your position with the Feds, will it?" Gwen pointed out. "There's no way you can clear yourself now unless you hand over the president. That lucky guess or whatever it was about O'Malley clinches the case against you, if they ever do figure this out."

"Shoot," I said. I had forgotten about that.

"Besides," she said, "I still want my scoop."

"You already have a scoop."

"I want a bigger one."

I sighed. She'd had a nap. That obviously could do wonders for your ambition. "I'm tired," I said. "I'm hungry. I hurt all over. And what's more, I'm in a bad mood. Can't we just go home?"

Gwen stared at me for a moment, and then smiled. "All right," she said. "Give me those two guns you've got. And wish me luck."

I stared back at her. "You'd never do it on your own," I said. "You're incompetent. You said so yourself."

"Sure. But this is important. Let me have the guns."

She held her hands out to me.

Well, I thought, private eyes finish their cases, even if they're in a bad mood. And sometimes private eyes do have sidekicks. I gave Gwen one of the guns. I kept the other. "Now what?" I asked her.

"I don't know," she replied. "You're the private eye."

CHAPTER 20

I tried to think. The first thing to do, I supposed, was to figure out our odds. "How many people did you see when you were captured?" I asked Gwen.

"Just one—no, two. That guy who was guarding me, and someone else. I don't remember what he looked like."

No help. O'Malley could have had an army here—although the fewer who were involved the better, from O'Malley's point of view. Less chance of someone becoming an informer. And Santoro and Grimes hadn't sounded as if they had a lot of company. Was O'Malley himself here? Could be. But he was probably back in Charlestown, monitoring the situation. He had to have some way of finding out if the Feds were meeting his demands, and it wouldn't be a good idea to have too much traffic going in and out of the museum.

So, there were at least two people left to deal with—but probably not many more. I supposed we could handle that. Of course, if they were willing to shoot the president as soon as they found out they were being attacked, we'd be out of luck. But I doubted they'd do that. O'Malley was a businessman, and President Kramer was his merchandise. He would make sure his employees didn't destroy the merchandise.

"All right," I said. "I think they're upstairs. Let's stay together and go slow. And we get rid of the light when we think we're getting close."

Gwen nodded her understanding.

I picked up the lantern and took one last look at Freddy. He was still unconscious. We left the room, locking it behind us, and headed off.

I noticed as we went upstairs that we were in a newer part of the museum: glass-roofed, and decorated in whites and grays. I could hear the rain tapping on the roof, and the distant howl of the wind. It was turning into a good night for ghosts. We reached the first floor, then took the staircase up another flight. We paused at the top. We couldn't see any lights, but we could make out the murmuring of voices, in spite of the wind and rain. It was impossible to tell where the voices were corning from, however. I picked a direction, and we continued.

Eventually we saw a glow off to our right. I immediately doused the lantern and set it down on the floor. It would just get in the way now. I grabbed Gwen's hand and, with guns drawn, we walked toward the glow.

Our hands were slippery with sweat before long. I strained to hear, to see, to be ready for the battle that might start at any moment. There were no voices anymore (suddenly I wondered if I had ever heard them) and the glow was no brighter. I was so tired of darkness. I was so tired. Gwen bumped into something, and I could hear the sharp intake of her breath as she stifled the urge to cry out. I squeezed her hand. She squeezed back.

The glow seemed to get brighter finally, and we groped our way toward it along the wall of a long gallery. We came to the end of the gallery, and I signaled Gwen to stop. The light was clearly stronger. I saw a rotunda with a high painted ceiling, a small circular wall in the center, and other galleries branching off from it. The light was strongest to our left now. So we turned left, following the light—

—and I almost fell over Pete Santoro.

He was sitting in a metal folding chair and leaning back against the outer wall of the rotunda. He seemed to be half-asleep. His half-closed eyes gazed at me, but I don't think he saw me. I think he saw the bandages on my arm—a mummy, for sure. I think he saw his worst nightmare coming after him in the flesh.

He screamed. The noise echoed in the rotunda, making it sound twice as loud. Santoro scrambled off in the direction of the light. I caught a glimpse of some Egyptian-looking statues. I dived after him. Gwen had a better idea. She shot him in the back.

The noise was deafening. I looked back at her, my heart pounding. She had come damn close to hitting me. Her eyes were wide, and fixed on the man she had just shot. He crawled a foot or two, and then stopped. Blood started leaking out from beneath him. Gwen stood motionless, her gun still aimed at Santoro. "Get down, Gwen," I said. "They're gonna be—"

There was a gunshot from behind the statues. Gwen flopped onto the floor. I couldn't tell whether or not she had been hit, because then the light disappeared, and we were in darkness yet again.

"Gwen!" I whispered urgently, but another shot let me know it wasn't a good idea to talk. I crawled to the inner wall of the rotunda, and followed it around until I was out of the line of fire.

I lay there as my eyes became accustomed once again to the darkness. I was a wreck. Had I screamed when Santoro screamed? Private eyes don't scream. They do what Gwen had done. They shoot the bastard.

Didn't matter. I had more pressing issues to consider. Like Gwen's safety. And how to fight a gun battle in the pitch black.

Something wet plopped on my head, and I started. There were two more plops before I figured it out. The roof was leaking. I heard a plop down below me, and I realized that the rotunda was open to the first floor, and the wall I was leaning against kept your casual museum-goer from plunging to his death.

I heard movement in the rotunda. Was it Gwen—or Eddie Grimes? There was another gunshot. What was going on? I risked peering over the edge of the wall, but I couldn't make out anything. Grimes could have been inches away from me, for all I knew.

There was a thud and a muffled curse. It sounded like a man—Eddie Grimes, then. Maybe he had stumbled over Santoro's body. So he was coming this way. I picked up a chunk of plaster from the floor next to me, and I flung it into the darkness. It hit against a wall, and immediately there were two answering shots—aimed, I assumed, at the wall. That was encouraging. I couldn't make out anything in the brief flashes, but one of the shots could have come from Gwen.

And Eddie Grimes was probably one confused thug. I tensed myself and inched forward. If he was still coming this way, he wouldn't be expecting anyone crouched to his left, ready to spring.

Another step, and I could see his outline in the darkness. I raised my gun—and decided not to shoot. I couldn't be absolutely sure of who it was, and I didn't want to make a mistake. I paused for a moment to summon up my energy. Water plopped onto my head. The figure in the darkness breathed quick, frightened breaths.

I leaped forward.

I came in low to keep him from having a chance to use his gun on me. My head hit him on the knee and knocked him backwards. He fired wildly into the air. I felt his leg to make sure it *was* a he and not Gwen. The leg was definitely male, so I tried to shoot him, but he lashed out with his arm and knocked the gun from my hand as I fired. That meant I had to jump across his body and pin his right arm to the floor to keep him from shooting *me*.

Grimes pulled at my hair with his left hand as he tried to loosen my grip on his arm. I howled with pain but didn't budge. Instead I banged his arm on the floor until he too let go of his gun.

And then we were just two bodies rolling around in the dark, like energetic lovers. I didn't feel like a lover, though. Grimes was hurting me in the few remaining spots on my body that hadn't already been hurt. *Help me, Gwen!* my mind screamed. But how could Gwen figure out who to help?

Grimes broke away from me finally. I caught up with him by the inner wall. We were standing now, each trying to push the other over the edge. I didn't have any strength left, and soon my head was dangling out over the emptiness, and it seemed like just a matter of time before Grimes sent me tumbling down into the puddle on the first floor.

Your gonna die too.

Not yet, not yet. I found a reserve of energy somewhere, out of my anger or fear or will to live, and I decided I very much did not want to take that tumble.

So I maneuvered my leg between his legs, and I kneed Grimes where he very much did not want to be kneed.

He let out a low "Oof" and his grip on me loosened for just a moment. But that was time enough for me to switch positions with him and give a shove, and suddenly he wasn't next to me anymore. There was a scream and a thud and a little splash, and then there was just the plop, plop, plop of the water dripping from the roof.

I collapsed against the wall and stared down into the darkness. I felt dizzy, nauseated. For a moment I thought I might lose my balance and follow Grimes. For half a moment I thought maybe I *should* follow Grimes: who was I to take someone's life? He was a jerk and a bicycle thief, but he was human. I hated death. To be on the safe side, I stepped away from the wall.

And I felt a gun pressing into my back.

"Don't move," Gwen said. Her voice was trembling.

I breathed a sigh of relief. "I wouldn't dream of moving," I replied.

"Oh Walter, thank God."

I turned, and we embraced. Her whole body was trembling. "It's all right," I said. But there was no time to comfort each other. "I think we'd better go find the—"

I didn't have a chance to finish the sentence. My words disappeared in a beam of light that was suddenly aimed at us. I raised an arm to shield myself, but the light was too strong after so much darkness, and I had to shut my eyes against it.

"Move apart," a voice said from beyond the light. "Drop your weapons."

I knew that voice, but it was not at all the one I expected.

CHAPTER 21

We obeyed. Gwen's weapon fell with a clunk near Santoro's body. I didn't have a weapon to drop, so I just raised my hands. Meanwhile my eyes started adjusting to the light, and behind it I could make out the figure that went with the voice. The fringe of white hair. The icy blue eyes. The gray-green uniform.

How had General Cowens managed to get here? He really had found something when he searched through Gwen's things, I decided. But where were his troops? And why hadn't he stopped the gun battle? I was puzzled. And, of course, frightened.

Cowens was holding a large flashlight in one hand, a gun in the other.

"I just came to rescue my friend here," I explained. "You know—the meddling reporter Gwendolyn Phillips? Those two that we killed—they're the ones who did the kidnapping. There's another one downstairs. We locked him up. Interrogate him if you want. You can get the truth out of him."

Cowens didn't respond at first. Finally he said, "I've been too lenient with you all along, haven't I, Sands?"

And I thought: Why is he alone? And why had he come out of the same statue-filled room from which Grimes had appeared?

And why had he resisted my participation in the case every step of the way? Why had he tried to pin the blame on me, even when it didn't make the slightest bit of sense to do so? Why had he agreed so easily to let me take Fenneman on that wild-goose chase to Charlestown?

"You're the one behind this," I whispered.

"Don't be ridiculous, Sands," Cowens said. "*You're* the guilty one."

"*You* wrote the threats from TSAR," I went on, as things clicked into place. "You started the file on TSAR to distract Bolton, not the other way around. And you had the kidnappers wear sandals to distract me. We played into your hands all along."

"Every soldier in New England is looking for you, Sands. You proved your guilt by escaping from us. It's a pity such a talented young man turned out so badly."

"So arrest me."

"I'm afraid you may be much too dangerous to arrest."

Then why didn't he shoot me? I realized that he wasn't quite sure what to do. Had I told anyone I was coming here? If he didn't kill us, could he manage to bluff his way out? I didn't seem impossible. "Why am I dangerous?" I asked. "Who' going to believe what I say about any of this? Even if people didn't think I was guilty, I'm the guy with the theory du jour after all."

"People believe the strangest things," Cowens observed.

I decided this had gone far enough. Time to act like a private eye. But how did private eyes act in situations like this? I decided that I needed a trick, but the only one I could come up with was the old "Look out, the president is behind you" trick. It would have to do. "Listen," I said. "Before you do anything you might regret—maybe Gwen and I can help you. You're short a couple of people right now, so maybe you ought to consider—" My eyes slid to his right. "No, Ann, don't do it!" I shouted.

Cowens didn't flinch. "Oh, come on, Sands," he murmured. Then he raised his gun—

And Gwen whipped a gun out of her back pocket and shot him.

The beam of the flashlight veered away from us, up toward the ceiling of the rotunda. Cowens fired, and we both dived for cover, back around the corner in the long gallery from which we had come. I cautiously peered out to see what Cowens was up to. He was lying on the floor; he still held the gun, and it was still pointed in our direction. The flashlight was on the floor next to him, and its beam shone on his face like a spotlight. The front of his uniform was bloody. "Damn you," I heard him mutter when he saw me. "Damn her." Then he kicked the light away and fired in my direction. I pulled back.

"Where'd you get the gun?" I whispered to Gwen. I was slightly in awe of her.

"From the guy I killed," she explained. "I picked it up while I was waiting for you to beat the other one."

"Oh." She was certainly making progress as a private eye. I thought about the failure of my "Look out, the president is behind you" trick. Gwen would be too polite to mention that. I hoped.

I had more important things to worry about, however. I couldn't tell how badly Cowens was hurt, but I figured it was time to try and get some information out of him.

"I was right, wasn't I?" I said, keeping my head back out of the range of his gun. "It was you."

We waited a long time for a response. The water plopped. The wind howled. I could make out the sound of the general's shallow, ragged breathing.

"It…was…me." The words sounded as if they had been pulled out of him by an iron claw. "She had…to be stopped."

"But why?" I asked. "You've followed orders all your life. Why change now?"

"Yes, yes, I've followed orders," he agreed, with more energy. "I've been a good soldier. No one can deny that."

"Why then? Because her referendum was jeopardizing America?"

There was another pause. "That's right," he said finally. He sounded resigned now. The confession had begun. Why not complete it? "Everything I've worked for. At risk. For what?"

I tried to think through the case. The letters, the file, the sandals. But what about—"What about O'Malley's men? How did you get them to work for you?"

"We have our spies in Charlestown," he muttered.

I thought about it. Well then, the spies could tell Cowens who was happy working for O'Malley and who wasn't. Men like Santoro and Grimes—they realized they were lackeys, no matter how much they swaggered in front of someone like me. O'Malley was never going to promote them. So they might agree to come to work for the Feds. It was dangerous, but Cowens could offer them what even O'Malley couldn't. "You promised them an exit visa if they did the job?"

"Yes, of course. Florida."

I supposed most people wouldn't mind being a lackey, if they could do it in Florida. I took a quick look at Santoro's corpse, lying a few feet away from Cowens. The poor guy was never going to see Fort Lauderdale now. And it must have seemed so easy at the time. After all, he would be working for the top soldier in New England.

"You controlled everything," I said. "The security at the speech, the investigation afterwards. I bet you even encouraged the president to take her walk through the crowd. You controlled everything except Bolton and Gwen—and me."

"And you," Cowens agreed weakly. He seemed to be running out of energy.

"But even Bolton hiring me turned out well for you, because I messed things up so badly that you had a perfect suspect for people like Fenneman to focus on."

"Not quite bad enough, I guess," he managed to say.

I looked at Gwen, huddled close to me in the corner of the gallery. She gave me an encouraging smile. Yes, well, I hadn't messed up totally. I leaned out into the rotunda.

"Look," I said to Cowens, "why don't you drop your gun and we'll get you some medical attention."

Cowens raised the gun instead and fired at me. I quickly drew my head back. "Damn you," he said.

"It's over," I called out to him, keeping myself out of sight. "There isn't anything you can do now. You've served your country well. I'm sure the president will take that into consideration. There's no sense in dragging this out and maybe making things worse for yourself."

"You understand no one! You understand nothing!" Cowens said, his voice suddenly stronger. "I'm an old man," he said, but he sounded young. "I remember movie theaters and—and ATMs and the Super Bowl and Sunday drives. I remember fireworks on the Fourth of July when I was a boy, sitting on my mother's lap in a meadow and waiting for darkness to fall so that—that—" The burst of energy disappeared as abruptly as it had arrived, and his voice became barely audible. "All I've ever wanted was to be a good soldier. To do my duty. To serve my country. And that has become so hard. What duty? What country? Everything is changed now. Not just the Super Bowls but—but the way we see ourselves. The way we see America. I have tried to be faithful, but it has been so…hard."

I could hear him start to sob. "Good soldiers obey their commander-in-chief, General," I said. "President Kramer is your commander-in-chief. So why don't you just drop your gun and do what she wants you to do?"

"You understand nothing," he sobbed. There was a pause, and then he fired his gun again.

And then there was silence.

Gwen and I looked at each other. I peered cautiously into the rotunda. In the dim light, I could see General Cowens lying on the floor. The gun was by his side; blood was oozing from his mouth. His eyes stared sightlessly up at the leaking roof. If he was looking for his duty, he was never going to find it now.

CHAPTER 22

"He's dead," I whispered to Gwen.

"Are you sure?"

I crawled out into the rotunda and took the gun from Cowens's hand. I felt for a pulse. "Yeah," I said. "I'm sure."

Gwen followed. She picked up the flashlight and aimed it at the dead soldier. Water dripped onto his face and made him appear to be sweating, as if death were as much of an effort as life. "Poor man," she murmured.

I stared at him.

"Quite a scoop, huh?" she said.

I stared at him some more. "The big scoop is when we find the president," I replied finally, breaking my gaze away from the corpse. "Let's go."

We headed in the direction from which Grimes and Cowens had both appeared—into the room filled with statues. There seemed to be a light further on, but we walked slowly among the ancient gods and kings, in case there were more surprises lurking there for us.

The Frenzy had been able to do nothing more than topple most of these statues, and they stared at us from strange and unpleasant angles; many looked like corpses themselves. "Spooky," Gwen murmured.

I didn't disagree. There was another roomful of statues off to the right; that's where the light was coming from. We walked into the new room. The light, it turned out, was from a torch stuck in a bracket on the faded yellow wall. I gazed around the room. I was getting nervous—not because I anticipated any more trouble, exactly, but because I sensed that the end of the case was approaching. And endings are always the hardest part.

We heard a whimper. I glanced at Gwen, and we hurried toward the sound.

We found the president of the United States shivering in the corner, her face to the wall, sitting next to the shattered statue of a pharaoh. Her dyed hair was streaked with plaster dust; her elegant clothes were filthy.

I thought of Ozymandias. *Look on my works, ye Mighty, and despair!*

I thought of Richard the Second. *For God's sake, let us sit upon the ground/And tell sad stories of the deaths of kings.*

I thought of General Cowens, water dripping onto his lifeless features, blood oozing from his mouth down toward the uniform he had worn so proudly.

"Madam President?" I said.

She turned her face from the wall and looked at us. Without her makeup, she appeared older, more vulnerable. *Was this the face/That like the sun did make beholders wink?* "Walter?" she whispered hoarsely.

I nodded.

She got slowly to her feet, then stumbled through the debris and into my arms. "Oh, thank God," she said. "Thank God. You've saved me."

I looked at Gwen over the president's shoulder. She stared impassively at me. I fingered the gun I still held in my hand. The president's back was heaving with her sobs. I could smell the faint remains of her perfume. Outside, the wind howled.

I shook my head. "It won't work," I said.

President Kramer moved her head from my shoulder and looked up at me. "What do you mean?"

I stepped back, out of her embrace. "General Cowens just committed suicide out there," I said.

"Oh my God," she replied.

But she didn't say it quite right. Things were getting too complicated, I figured, and she couldn't think it through on the spur of the moment.

"Before he died," I went on, "he confessed that he kidnapped you to stop the referendum. And he said that all he ever wanted to be was a good soldier. But see, that's kind of a contradiction, as I pointed out to him. Good soldiers obey their leader, and you're his leader. He never responded to my point. Or rather, his response was to shoot himself."

"Well, he must've shot himself because of the contradiction," President Kramer said. "He couldn't live with the situation he had put himself in. Don't you think?"

"Maybe. But it seems to me that there are only two ways his story makes sense. First, if he had killed you. That removes the threat you pose to America's future, and your successors would certainly cancel the referendum. Second, if he kidnapped you, but made sure you believed a radical group like TSAR was responsible. That way, when you were finally released, you might cancel the referendum yourself and become a lot tougher on the locals.

"But you're very much alive, Madam President. And if he was keeping you in the dark about who your real kidnappers were, he was doing a pretty sloppy job. Gwen here was locked up from the moment she was captured. But you're out in the open, and this was where Grimes and Cowens both came from when they went out to the rotunda to try and kill the intruders. How could you not have known Cowens was involved? You certainly didn't sound particularly surprised when I told you he was dead."

President Kramer stared at me in disbelief. "Look at me," she commanded, gesturing at her dirty clothes and haggard appearance. "I have *suffered* here. Can't you see that?"

"Maybe I see a very good actress playing a part for all it's worth. Maybe you were preparing for your role after you sent Cowens to stop us. Maybe you said to him, 'Go out there and try to kill them, but at least give me some time to dirty myself up in case you can't. And be prepared to take the rap if you get into trouble. Do whatever you have to do to protect me. You're expendable. I'm not.'" Maybe that's a better explanation of what's been going on here."

The president made an imperious gesture, as if to end the discussion. "But this is ridiculous," she said. "You're implying that I kidnapped myself. Why in the world would I do that?"

Good question. I took a deep breath. This was my final theory about the damn case; I wanted to make sure I got it right. "'You can accomplish anything you want, if you're willing to risk everything you have,'" I quoted. "Remember? It sounded like your personal philosophy when you said it to me the night before you were kidnapped. And what is it that you want, President Kramer?"

"I just want to be a good president, to help America."

"You want a lot more than that, if you were telling the truth back then. You want to be the Lincoln of the new age. You want to establish a world government with America—and you—at its center. I don't know that you could set your sights any higher. But let's face it: as of that night, you didn't have a prayer of accomplishing any of your goals. Because the very first goal you had set for yourself was to win the referendum—and you didn't have a prayer of doing that. And if you couldn't do that, all the go-slowers back in Atlanta would've kept you from accomplishing anything. Maybe someday America would be what you wanted it to be. But not while you were president."

"I have ambitions," President Kramer said. "I want to accomplish wonderful things that will help the entire world. Is there anything wrong with that?"

"I guess not. Depends on what you do to achieve your goals. You decided you had to speed the process up, to make sure you were successful. You decided to give people a demonstration of what the alternative was to your government, to your vision. Make them think about the dangers waiting for them beyond the boundaries of law and order. Remind them that the Frenzy may not have been a temporary aberration—it may always lurk below the surface, and government may be the only force that can keep it from bursting out into the daylight once again.

"So you told your trusted general, your long-time friend, to set up a kidnapping. Maybe he thought it was a great idea. I bet he thought the opposite, but that didn't matter, because he was a good soldier, and you knew he'd obey. And then you carried out your part while he carried out his. You made it clear to everyone that you wanted security to be minimal, and that made it more credible when the kidnappers struck. You went out into the crowd to shake hands after the speech, so you'd be in exactly the right position for them. And then all you had to do was wait here for the people to respond.

"And they have responded, of course. Cowens ordered the troops to go easy, and that made everyone surprised and grateful. And I'm sure Cowens told you about the vigil in Government Center, about all the people who hadn't cared before who were now suddenly sympathetic to you and your cause. It was working, no doubt about it. And tomorrow morning, I suppose, General Cowens would have rescued you—just in the nick of time. The kidnappers would unfortunately escape—or maybe they'd be killed by the brave Federal soldiers. In any case, you'd be a heroine and the Feds would be heroes, and the referendum would pass. Your gamble would have paid off, and your dream would begin to come true. It was a risky plan, but it was clever, and it almost worked."

I stopped. The speech had exhausted me. I stared at the president; she stared back at me. And I had that awful moment of uncertainty that private eyes never have in the books I read—the feeling that it was all a dim-witted fantasy, that I had overlooked some obvious but compelling piece of evidence or logic that would invalidate my whole theory and make me look like a fool. I couldn't prove any of it, after all. And Lord knows I had been wrong before.

"You can't prove any of it," President Kramer said, repeating my thought.

I tried not to look relieved. That was tantamount to a confession, as far as I was concerned. My theory was right. Finally.

Gwen came to the same conclusion—or maybe she had believed me from the beginning (although I kind of doubted that). At any rate, she spoke now for the first time since we had found the president. "We don't have to prove it," she pointed out. "I just have to write a story for the *Globe*. Not everyone might be convinced, but people would have doubts—enough people to make your referendum go down the drain."

President Kramer turned and looked at Gwen—also for the first time, I think. She seemed unimpressed. This did not endear her to me. "But how will you write the story," she asked, "if you're in jail?" And then she smiled. "You two were clearly the masterminds of this whole plot. Your own kidnapping, Ms. Phillips, was just a ruse to divert suspicion. And of course people already know that you're guilty, Walter. The two of you killed Cowens when he tried to rescue me. Why should people believe anything else?"

The president sat down on the trunk of a statue and ran a hand through her hair, shaking out some of the dust. She seemed in command of the situation now, no longer required to act the role of the terrified victim. "You know, Walter, in a way it's all your fault," she said. "We had worked up the plan, Cowens and I, but I was undecided about actually going through with it. As you say, it was awfully risky. Even after Cowens had posted the first threat from TSAR on the governor's door, even after I arrived in Boston, I still wasn't sure. Maybe I didn't need to go to such lengths. Maybe my speech would do the trick, and I wouldn't have to resort to the kidnapping. I decided to put it to a test. You were the test. I wanted to talk to the kind of person I needed to convert. You seemed to be just right, so I summoned you the night before the speech. I felt confident I would succeed."

I thought back to that night, the intensity of her belief, the power of her words and her physical presence. "You almost did," I said.

"But in fact I failed. And if I couldn't convert you, alone, just the two of us, how was I going to accomplish what I wanted with the rest of New England? So I had to go ahead with the plan. Don't you see? The alternative was more of the same—the country, the world limping along without purpose, without hope, lurching toward more wars and more deaths and more despair. And I would know that I hadn't done all I could to prevent it. I couldn't simply let it happen, couldn't let my opportunity slip away. I had to take charge of events. And that's what I did."

She fell silent. I listened to the staccato rhythm of the rain, the hissing of the torch. I felt a twinge of what I had felt before when she had spoken to me, when she had shown me her dream. Here we were, standing in the rubble of the old civilization, with only a leaky roof between us and an uncaring universe. We weren't very much, and we weren't going very far. Didn't we need someone to take charge of events? Didn't we need someone who had a dream?

But the twinge went away, and as before I remained stubbornly unconvinced. "Arresting us might not prevent us from getting the story out," I said.

"Maybe not," the president agreed. "But consider this option. I can let you move down south—with enough money to start a new life and forget about everything that's happened here."

"That's the deal Cowens offered his thugs."

She nodded. "And it's a pretty good deal, if you ask me."

"How do we know we can trust you?" I asked.

She shrugged. "I don't think you have a choice."

I looked at Gwen. There is always a choice. It wasn't up to me to speak for both of us, though. I had been given my chance to leave Boston once before, but this was a first for Gwen. And it wasn't such an easy or obvious decision, after all. You struggle and suffer all your life, and suddenly you are offered a way out. And it's not as if you're doing something so terribly wrong by accepting the offer. On the contrary, many people would call it patriotism. If you turned it down, they would despise you for disobeying your leader.

Gwen glanced at me, but didn't seem to need any soulful exchange of telepathic insights. She turned to the president. "Do you really think a government based on deceit is worth having?" she asked.

President Kramer sighed. These stubborn New Englanders. "Would you really prefer anarchy based on the truth?" she responded.

I was pleased that Gwen hadn't been tempted by the president's offer; I hadn't expected she would be. But oddly, what bothered her didn't particularly bother me. A private eye can live with deceit, even if a reporter can't. What bothered me was death. "Those corpses out there are your fault, not ours," I said to the president. "When is the killing going to stop?"

"There wouldn't have been any corpses if you hadn't interfered," she pointed out. "No one had to be killed for my plan to work. But if the plan did require some deaths— so what? What makes you think that the killing can stop? Nothing I've ever read or experienced suggests that it can. You just have to kill for the right reason. Lincoln killed to keep America united, and I would do the same. Maybe you wouldn't. But if you could prevent another nuclear war by shooting a few people, wouldn't you pull the trigger? Shouldn't you?"

She stared at me, waiting for an answer. And it suddenly occurred to me that I had the future of America in my hands. Literally. The guns that Gwen and I were holding seemed to have been forgotten in the course of our conversation with the president. President Kramer had said we had no choice but to accept her offer, but here was an obvious alternative. Shoot her, and walk away from it all. Who would know? Freddy, locked up downstairs? Shoot him too.

Was that killing for the right reason? Why not? We were in danger. Her offer of a new life down south was probably a sham; she was much better off with us dead. If I killed her, I would still be in trouble, but I would be master of my own fate, instead of dependent on Kramer's good will.

If she were dead, the result might be repression, or anarchy, or some awful combination of the two. But, like the corpses, that would be her fault, not ours. It had been her plan; she would have to take the consequences.

I looked at the gun. As usual, the future was contained in a weapon. I thought of Santoro, and Grimes, and Cowens. Of the general's memories. Of the terror in the thug's eyes. Of water plopping down onto motionless bodies. I thought too damn much. I had to make a decision.

But there was someone else making a decision, too. Gwen suddenly dropped her gun and turned away from the president. "I'm leaving," she said. "I'm going to write my story. Arrest me if you like, but the truth will be told." And she started to walk out of the room.

Well, I couldn't disagree with that. Maybe, I thought, I could keep the president here until—

But I didn't have time to finish my thought. Before I could, four men stepped out of the shadows of the next room and confronted us.

CHAPTER 23

There were three regular-sized fellows, and one dwarf.
Two of the regular-sized fellows wore uniforms and
carried guns.

"Hi, Stretch," I said to the dwarf. "How'd you know
where we were?"

"I've heard of mummies too," Stretch replied. "I'm just
not a private eye. It takes me a little longer to put things
together."

"How long have you been out there?"

"Long enough."

Governor Bolton stood next to Stretch. He was staring
past Gwen at President Kramer, who had risen from the
statue. Just behind the governor were my buddies Danny
and Gus, looking perplexed.

"So you heard?" President Kramer said to Bolton.

He nodded.

"Then you understand that this is a very serious
situation."

He nodded again.

"I know you haven't approved of the referendum," she
went on. "But you've got to put that behind you now. If
you let these people go, you're jeopardizing America's
future. They'll destroy the years of work we've put into

rebuilding our country. You can blame me for everything if you like, but you can't let that happen."

"What do you want me to do?" he asked.

The president paused. "Order your soldiers to kill them, Governor Bolton," she said.

Bolton's gaze shifted from the president to me. I studied him. Standing next to Stretch almost made him look tall; the scar by his right eye almost made him look tough. I had been wrong about him before; I had no idea what he was going to do now.

I tried to think about practicalities. I was still holding my gun. I could take out Danny or Gus, but not both. Gwen had dropped her gun, so she couldn't help. We were dead if Bolton gave the word.

Bolton's expression changed as he stared at me. The almost-toughness seemed to melt away, and what replaced it was a mixture of fear and weariness I had seen too often before. It is the expression of people facing a universe too cruel and complicated for humans to live in—but they must live. A universe where every choice is a bad one—but choices must be made. The Feds had sheltered Bolton for a long time from the complications and the choices; but now the shelter was gone. "This isn't right," he whispered.

"It doesn't matter if it's right," the president said. Her voice was soft, persuasive. "This is your country. This is America."

Bolton looked at her for a long time, and then turned silently away.

President Kramer grimaced, then shrugged. She didn't need Bolton. She turned to the soldiers. "I'm your commander-in-chief," she said. "I order you to kill these people."

Danny and Gus looked at each other. Their eyes were wide with fear. *A soldier is supposed to obey the president,* I recalled Danny saying a long time ago. "Couldn't we just arrest them?" Danny asked, his voice trembling.

The president shook her head. "That's not good enough, boys. You must protect your country. I know it's hard for you, but I will take the responsibility. You must obey orders. Kill them."

"B-b-but they didn't do anything," Gus protested.

The president didn't bother to respond. She simply stared at the two frightened young men with eyes that were used to having their way.

Danny and Gus raised their weapons like good soldiers.

And slowly aimed them at their leader.

"Walter," Danny said, "I guess your friend should go write her story now."

It was decided that Gus would drive us to the *Globe* and then get reinforcements to clean things up; the museum would never be the same again. Bolton walked with us out to the rotunda while Danny remained behind to guard the president. "I don't know what will happen," the governor said. "We'll keep her here until you write your story, Ms. Phillips, but after that? I'll have to talk to Atlanta. There'll be an impeachment or something, I suppose—unless she can talk her way out of it. This is a terrible situation."

"Just don't take it out on the locals," I said.

"I just hope the locals don't take it out on the Feds," he murmured.

Still caught between the two worlds. I didn't envy Bolton. His universe had just become a lot more complicated.

We stood for a moment in the rotunda and surveyed the carnage. Bolton shook his head. "All this to pass a referendum," he said. "What a waste."

"Can I quote you?" Gwen asked.

He sighed. "You can quote me," he said. And then he returned to the president.

We noticed Stretch standing by the staircase on the far side of the rotunda. Not surprisingly, he looked unhappy. Gwen went over and put her arm around him. "It's okay, Stretch," she said. "Things will get better."

This was Stretch's most deeply held belief, but it didn't seem to comfort him now. Maybe he needed something besides comfort. "How come you didn't do what I told you to do back at the waterfront?" I demanded. "I said to go home and relax. You could've got Gwen and me killed, coming here."

Stretch glared at me. "I did go home," he said. "And Gus and Danny were there, guarding the place. We got to talking. About Bolton, and how bad your theory was. And about mummies. And we decided we'd better do something about all of it. So we came here and saved your life. So how about a little gratitude?"

He was right. I supposed I wasn't cut out to be a loner. I supposed my friends were just going to help me, whether I wanted them to or not. And I supposed that was okay. But I didn't feel like saying all that, so I simply grinned at him.

Pretty soon he grinned back. "Why do I put up with you, Walter?" he asked.

"I dunno. Because you don't have anyone else to put up with?"

This seemed to make sense to him.

"We'd b-b-better go," Gus said.

We all headed down the staircase to the first floor. Gwen shined the general's flashlight (which she seemed to have inherited) ahead of us to light the way. We opened the front door of the ancient building and stepped outside.

I immediately began to feel better. I didn't know if there were ghosts in the building; if there hadn't been, perhaps we had created some. At any rate, my spirit felt lighter leaving the place behind. The rain had stopped. The night was cool, the wind refreshing. Every part of my body hurt, but the pain would disappear, and the memory of this moment would remain.

Gus's jeep was parked by the statue of the Indian. We piled in. Then I noticed the bicycle leaning against the statue. I piled out and strapped it to the back of the jeep. After driving to the *Globe*, Gus wouldn't mind making an extra stop at Art's Filthy Bookstore. It would make a local happy.

"I should've asked Bolton about the referendum," Gwen remarked as I got back in.

"Why bother?" Stretch asked. "If they hold it, probably only one person will vote yes. Me."

I coughed from the back seat. "Make that two people," I said.

Stretch and Gwen turned to look at me.

"Well," I said, "private eyes are fond of lost causes. Besides, I want to keep Danny and Gus in town."

Gus grinned. "Shall we g-g-g—?"

Yes, I felt pretty good, all things considered. This case was solved, and there was always the next one, lying in wait for me in the unimaginable future. I thought of Art once again, and *Locksley Hall.* "'Not in vain the distance beacons,'" I said. "'Forward, forward let us range.'" Gus took that for a yes and started the jeep. My companions smiled at me tolerantly, then turned and faced forward as we headed off in the darkness to the *Globe*.

Turn the page for an excerpt from

WHERE ALL THE LADDERS START

The Last P.I. Series

Book Three

———◆———

Richard Bowker

I got off my bike and stared at the guy in the brown robe. The guy in the brown robe stared at me. He was sitting at the front of a cart piled high with apples, pumpkins, squash, and other fall produce; half a dozen dead turkeys hung from hooks at the back of the cart. He was big and broad and scary, with small black eyes, long stringy hair, and a scraggly beard that was interrupted by a deep scar on his left cheek.

"Hiya," I said, trying to break the ice.

He stared at me for a second, and then his eyes moved to the horse, who ignored him.

"Looking for me?" I asked. "Walter Sands? Got a bit of a late start today. Sorry if I kept you waiting."

The guy didn't respond. I hadn't really expected him to be looking for me. But Lower Washington Street was an odd place to park a cart filled with food.

"The Food Market is a few blocks over," I tried. "They'll love your stuff."

Nothing.

"Well, have a nice day."

He didn't look like he was interested in nice days. Fine. The world is filled with strange people, and he was just one more of them. I walked around the cart and entered the building that housed my spacious, well-appointed office.

Okay, those adjectives aren't entirely accurate, but the place fits my needs, which mainly consist of a stove to keep me warm and shelves to hold the books I read to pass the time while I wait for clients to show up. Also, a desk and a couple of chairs in case a client actually does show up. Not that this had been happening much lately. Or, well, ever.

I carried my bike inside and walked upstairs.

From the hallway, I noticed that the door to my office was open. I always close the door when I leave at night. Of course, the door doesn't lock, but that doesn't really matter. Nothing worth stealing in my office.

I took out my gun. I wasn't especially worried, but it pays to be careful. "Please don't do anything stupid," I announced, and then I went inside.

And there, sitting by my desk, was the most beautiful woman in the world. She was wearing a powder-blue robe, and she was staring at me.

"Mr. Sands," she said calmly, ignoring the gun. "Do you remember me?"

It was impossible to forget her. "Of course," I said. "Sister Marva. How are you? And please, call me Walter." We had met during one of the many disastrous episodes in my previous case. She was a disciple in the Church of the New Beginning up in Concord. Long black hair, creamy white skin, deep blue eyes. I found it hard to break my gaze away from those eyes.

I sat down behind my desk, and that's when I noticed that she was pregnant. Well, that was interesting. Beautiful pregnant woman shows up in the private eye's office, needing his help. That's the way it's supposed to happen.

"So, um, what can I do for you, Sister? The last time we met—"

"You almost killed Brother Flynn," she reminded me.

"Yes. I'm very sorry about that." Flynn Dobler was the leader of Sister Marva's Church. A very smart, charismatic fellow. I snuck into the Church in the middle of the night and pointed a gun at him while he lay in bed. I remembered Marva coming in and leaping on top of him, desperate to protect her master from the intruder. All because of a really stupid theory I'd come up with about a kidnapping I was investigating. This had not been my finest moment as a private eye.

"It's all right," she said with a sympathetic smile. "Everyone makes mistakes. But now we need your help."

"We? The Church?"

She nodded.

"Why?"

"Brother Flynn has disappeared," she said, and the smile faded, and her beautiful blue eyes filled with tears.

"Disappeared?" I repeated. "How? When?"

"A week ago. He was there one night in his room, and then—in the morning—he was gone." The tears started falling down her cheeks.

Again, this was the way it happened in the novels I'd read. And now it was happening to me. But this didn't feel like a novel—this was a real human being, shedding real tears. I wanted to comfort her, but I also needed to do my job.

"I'm sorry to hear that," I said. "Was there a note? Were there witnesses?"

She shook her head. She wiped her cheeks with the sleeve of her robe. I wished I had a handkerchief to offer her. In my novels, the private eye always had a handkerchief.

"You've checked around the Church's farm, I suppose? There are plenty of wild animals up there, I'm sure. Wolves. Wildcats. Feral dogs. Probably some crazies, too."

"Yes, of course. We've looked everywhere."

"Well, um, any theories? Do you suspect foul play?"

Sister Marva lowered her eyes. "Brother Joseph does," she murmured.

"Who's he?"

"He's the disciple who, who runs things. Brother Flynn's second-in-command, I guess you'd say."

"Who does he suspect?"

"You should ask Brother Joseph, I think. He asked me to come here and talk to you. Because I go to the Food Market every day, with Brother Reggie. He'd like you to come up to Concord and investigate."

Brother Reggie was presumably the giant in the cart. "You said Brother Joseph suspects foul play," I said. "What do *you* suspect, Sister Marva?"

She blushed. "I think that perhaps God took him from us."

I struggled to figure out what she meant. "You mean, like, he died of natural causes?"

She shook her head. "I mean—God brought him up to heaven. While he was still alive. Because He loved Brother Flynn so much."

"Why do you think that?"

"Because Sister Lucy saw it happen."

"Sister Lucy saw God take Brother Flynn up to heaven," I said, making sure I had this straight.

"Yes. You should talk to her too, I think."

"I think you're right." Maybe a more experienced private eye would have decided right there that this case wasn't going to be worth the trouble. But I'm not very experienced. And, frankly, I had nothing better to do. I decided to change the subject. "By the way, congratulations on your pregnancy, Sister Marva."

She smiled and inclined her head. "It's a blessing." Her smile made you happy to be alive.

"Do you mind my asking: is Brother Flynn the father?"

Her face clouded and she looked down at her belly. "I don't think—I don't think that has anything to do with Brother Flynn's disappearance, Walter," she replied. And then she fell silent.

OK, one more mystery. I considered. My friend and occasional employer Bobby Gallagher had a van, but it was out of commission while his driver/mechanic Mickey tried to scrounge or repair or manufacture a gasket or a flange or a defibrillator or some-such item; I don't know much about vans. "I'll take the case," I said. "But if you want me to go up there today, I'm afraid I don't have—"

"You can ride with us in our cart," Marva suggested. "We return to the Church after we finish selling our food. We should be at the Market now, actually. I'm sure Brother Reggie is tired of waiting."

I considered some more. "That means I'd have to stay the night at the Church," I pointed out. "I need to be back in Boston tomorrow."

"We come to the Food Market every day. You can come back with us in the morning."

That was that, then. I had a case. "All right," I said. "I get two new dollars a day. Ten dollars in advance."

Sister Marva gave me another smile. She looked relieved and grateful. "That's wonderful. But would you prefer to be paid in food instead?"

That wasn't a bad idea. Inflation was getting to be a problem. Who knew what the Church's money would buy when I got around to spending it? "Food would be fine," I replied.

We went back down to the street, where Brother Reggie did not in fact seem to be tired of waiting. It wasn't clear that he had even moved since the last time I set eyes on him. But his face lit up when he saw Sister Marva, like a dog recognizing his master. Marva and I agreed to meet at the Food Market later. I filled a bag with produce from the cart and grabbed one of the turkeys. Looked like ten dollars' worth to me, and Marva didn't haggle. Then Brother Reggie helped her up onto the cart, and they headed off.

I watched them go. The Church of the New Beginning. *Leave the past behind*, it preached. Start fresh—no technology, no government, none of the baggage that still weighed so many of us down. Look at where all that stuff had led us—to the War, and the violence and chaos and despair that followed in its wake. Reasonable enough, I supposed.

But now, strangely, the Church had a missing-person case on its hands, and it had decided to call on that useless relic of the past, a private eye. Well, I had already seen some strange things in my brief career; no reason for this case to be any different.

I brought my bike out of the building and arranged the sack of food over the handlebars; I held onto the turkey. Then I pedaled home to the townhouse in Louisburg Square where I lived with Gwen, the most wonderful woman in this godforsaken world, and Stretch, the most wonderful dwarf in the world. Both of them were at work—Gwen at the Boston *Globe* and Stretch in the governor's office. I put the turkey in the icebox and the produce on the kitchen table, and I wrote them a brief note:

Off on a case! Won't be back today, but I will *be back tomorrow. Enjoy the food.*

—Walter

There, that would intrigue them. I left the note beside the produce, and I headed off to the Food Market, munching one of Marva's apples.

Where All the Ladders Start

available in print and ebook

Richard Bowker is the author of *Replica*, *Senator*, and other novels. He lives near Boston with his wife and two sons.

You can contact Richard through his website: www.richardbowker.com